MW00760357

DEAD RINGER

THE PARITY OF LIVES ABRAHAM AND JOHN

R O B E R T   R A S C H

authorHOUSE®

AuthorHouse™
1663 Liberty Drive
Bloomington, IN 47403
www.authorhouse.com
Phone: 1 (800) 839-8640

Published by AuthorHouse 10/24/2018

ISBN: 978-1-5462-6455-2 (sc)
ISBN: 978-1-5462-6456-9 (e)

Library of Congress Control Number: 2018912331

Print information available on the last page.

This book is printed on acid-free paper.

The quotes from this book have been taken from many different sources
and are not meant to offend any beliefs that are core to the reader, even
though the author says it's based upon certain truths. This book, which
will soon be a movie, is for entertainment purposes only. The publisher
cannot guarantee the accuracy of content and the collaboration of facts.

CONNECTED IN TIME

ULTERIOR MOTIVES/PLOTS THAT WILL CHANGE OUR HISTORY!

To my family, for giving me the support and confidence.

A special thanks to all involved in
sharing their books and research,
I am truly appreciative.

❀ ❀ ❀

ABOUT THE BOOK

The book's genre is Historical Science Fiction, yet it also leans into other varieties of classic literature, including: Adventure, Mystery, Fantasy, Romance, Drama, Tragedy, Comedy (Satire), Mathematical, Religious, Political, Time-Travel and Self Help.

QUERY LETTER
Title: "Dead-Ringer" "The Parity of Lives - Abraham and John"
Based on a Historic Science Fiction Novel by Robert Rasch

Logline: A Non-Fiction story written/narrated by the "Original Abraham Lincoln," who was replicated by the "Watchers" (Guardians of the Earth). The new genetic copy of Abraham Lincoln is inserted into the timeline in order to change history and correct a 100 year skewed timeline, which is coincidentally connected to John F. Kennedy. The original Lincoln sacrifices his life and is voluntarily inserted in a new preselected time period, so as not to risk contaminating the timeline continuum.

Conceived in 1998.

Book trailer: Sneak peek in the Epilog: *The survived Lincoln appears that he is living in the 1800's when he finishes writing his novel, but as the book closes slowly, the title on the cover reads, "The Parity of Lives-Abraham and John." Lincoln then exits in this old fashion room while his children are calling him from outside, followed by a dog bark. Next, Lincoln subsequently walks through a room with a modern kitchen, looking outside at his wife and children where they wait alongside a 1973 Chevy station-wagon.*

CONTENTS

F O R E W O R D

The story is set in motion when a younger Abraham Lincoln encounters an advanced race called, "The Watchers." The Watchers begin to reason with the younger Abraham Lincoln and explain about Earth's erratic original timeline, which occurs every one hundred years (earth-cycle). They explain how they have repaired certain timelines for a more positive outcome and have done so for thousands of years.

The Watchers had sought-out Abraham Lincoln and John F. Kennedy and chose them to be the best probable result in order to repair a corrupted temporal timeline. Regrettably, Lincoln learns that the original timeline he is in... will in the future; have President James Buchanan serving an eight year term, which is a different outcome to our historic reality.

In our history, President James Buchanan only serves one "four year term," as the 15th President of the United States. During these original timelines, Lincoln is not there to stop the "South" from seceding from the "Union" (North) and if Lincoln's timeline is repaired, as a result, one hundred years later, Kennedy is absent from being president. Therefore, a would-be President Hubert Humphrey enters the United States of America into a nuclear holocaust, stemmed from the Cuban missile crisis and creates havoc upon the world.

Lincoln and Kennedy both agree to help the Watchers in order to change their connective timelines, but are unaware that Andrew Johnson (Lincoln's Vice President), the chosen mentor for both Lincoln and Kennedy, would abuse his power in an unprecedented way.

In order not to contaminate the timelines, duplicates (doppelgangers) were created by the Watchers and because of these results, the original Lincoln and Kennedy could <u>not</u> remain in their current timelines.

Andrew Johnson was the exception to this rule and at the time was considered to have only himself and his counterpart Lyndon Johnson, when indeed there were actually two additional extra versions created, unbeknownst to Lincoln and Kennedy (Hence, a younger Lee Harvey Oswald and John Wilkes Booth).

A previous warning the Watchers did make clear and stated, "If an individual creates more than one person (being) of themselves, the result would have adverse effects with all other versions of their own counterparts (becoming corrupt and evil). This also included their original self as well.

Johnson's unsuspecting involvement while the Vice President of the United States, in regards to the assassinations of both Lincoln and Kennedy, depicts the original Lincoln finding out a smidgeon too late. Though, after the original Lincoln does find out about his counterpart's death (President Lincoln) and thereafter, President Kennedy, he immediately travels through a time portal (star-gate) in order to prevent each of their deaths.

Additional subplots and classic storybook varieties that are within the book

- The romantic side of the original Lincoln is in full mode, as he tells the story about his first and only love, Anne Rutledge. Does Lincoln lose the love of his life or does he save her?
- From time to time Lincoln attempts, in some cases, dry humor but yet becomes very entertaining at times. Also, he tends to explain some mathematical quandaries corresponding to the Watchers, which reveals the attorney side of Lincoln.

- In some cases Lincoln is highly opinionated while referencing, religion and politics. He also offers the reader with inspirational wisdom that leaves you thinking after the read.
- After the book has ended, Lincoln leaves snippets of information about quantum dynamics hidden in plain view towards the back of the book. He explains about the secrets of the universe, which he acquired from the Watchers while existing, both in the future and from the past and so he figured, *what the heck!*

The harmonic coincidences between the two presidents were necessary, because the thicker the time-thread, the more unraveling that is needed, in order to change time. When time is altered, the universe automatically "condenses" that particular timeline, thus crafting difficulty within time-overlaps, which in essence renders additional coincidences.

The importance of trust within a group (esoteric) connection is intertwined in a time loop of hundred years. This nail biting murder mystery gives way to historic conspiracy and spreads over the top with historic fact, leaving the individual in a wondrous state of imagination. To figure out how, when and why is truly the challenge in this great adventure.

INTRODUCTION

It all begins in a small town in the state of Illinois. Lincoln is about to attempt another business venture before he encounters an alarming presence and is swayed to make a decision that would change the world. This determination would lead, in part of who he is; to strive and become the President of the United States of America. The problem was he had to lend himself, to assist in a new identity and leave his new self to be the most significant figure to alter the political frontier.

James Buchanan Jr., the 15th President of the United States, was a stark character who was soft natured and quite flamboyant. In accordance with history, he was the only president not to have a wife or a female companion during his tenure. His personality type was to avoid conflict at all cost. This set the stage for the secession of the United States' southern region in order to avoid a civil war in his second term. This is what would have happened in the previous history, if left unchecked and if Lincoln was not to become president. This bleak history of the original timeline, (not the familiar timeline) emerged stemming from Buchanan's second term in office and was disastrous for the future of the United States, whereas, millions would have perished.

President James Buchanan only served one four year term as president in our historic reality. However, in this original (before) timeline version (soon to be corrected), he serves "two" four year terms and creates a negative temporal time-tangent in need of adjustment. Thus the Ancient Guardians of our Earth, *The Watchers,* were dissatisfied with the results and therefore, needed to intervene and correct this lineage in time.

If President Lincoln is successful in becoming the 16th President of the United States, then simultaneously, there is an unfortunate immediate time rift 100 years later, because the 35th President of the United States will be Hubert Humphrey, instead of John F. Kennedy. Kennedy never desired the office of president and therefore, was not a political figure in the original timeline. As a result of Kennedy's absence, a nuclear holocaust disaster erupts during the Cuban Missile Crises, because of Humphrey's inability to act.

This disaster was the reason to insert Kennedy by the Watchers, into the new timeline and to make sure that Humphrey is defeated in the 1960's democratic primary. Kennedy then must defeat Richard Nixon in the 1960's presidential election, rather than Humphrey. This change in the timeline will avoid nuclear fallout and save millions of lives.

❈ ❈ ❈

Through the influence of apparitions and with the assistance of ancient time portals, the Guardians, also known as the Watchers, have helped steer certain key historic figures throughout history. Their interventions go as far back to the times of Julius Caesar, during the Roman Empire.

These time adjustments are necessary in order to benefit the human race towards a more favorable (time-continuum) outcome. The adjustments that occur in time are approximately one hundred years apart from each other and must be executed at the same moment in time (past and future). The Watchers have been altering time throughout history for thousands of years, yet their prime directive is to never prohibit freewill. Nonetheless, the Guardians and Lincoln did not account for the misuse of the mechanical apparatus that produces a duplicate of one's self, the Doppelganger.

President Lincoln's Vice President, Andrew Johnson was thought to have only himself and his counterpart, Lyndon B. Johnson, who would become the Vice President for John F. Kennedy. When indeed there were actually other additional versions of himself reproduced. This was forbidden by the Guardians.

The unsuspecting Andrew Johnson while vice president, is scheming a plot against both presidents. The creation of the third and fourth younger (adversarial) versions of Andrew Johnson, will give rise to the infamous John Wilkes Booth and Lee Harvey Oswald. Johnson's reasoning or assumptions for making the younger copies of himself, were to avoid the mental contamination of himself and the rest of his entourage. These actions were pre-warned by the Watchers.

✾ ✾ ✾ ✾

Lincoln is no stranger to pain and suffering. Throughout his childhood and as an adult, he had more than his fair share of misery. President Lincoln experienced the loss of his two sons, but still manages to move on without any subtraction of sincerity towards his fellow man. His wife, Mary Todd Lincoln has to bury their third son, leaving one son left to carry on the Lincoln heritage. His name was Robert Todd Lincoln.

As a younger adult, Lincoln's ability to give himself, mind, body and soul to another woman was brought to an end when the love his life, Anne Mays Rutledge "passed on" because of the tyranny of typhoid fever. This was the dreadful disease that plagued many of Lincoln's family and friends during his lifetime.

Abraham Lincoln, the 16th President of the United States, becomes one of the most profound and important presidents as well as a significant historical figure of the 19th century. Throughout this parallel shuttling of time is the alternating spiritual tradeoff between sacrifice and perseverance and it will eventually leave our present day time period in a much better reality. Though the original Lincoln might seem more influential in the underlined story, he too did not escape the tragedy that he wished to avoid. He would have to live with great remorse, if he was unsuccessful with any of his attempts to alter time.

Because of certain tragedies that occur during the story, Lincoln feels motivated and partially responsible to use the Watchers' facility, in order to change these hideous historic outcomes. Amongst his time-travels, he encounters good cheer but also some disappointments, namely the assassinations.

There are blatant coincidences between Abraham Lincoln and John F. Kennedy. We are all too familiar with the history we have all come to learn. This new, never told version will fill your thoughts and bring out what you already might have wanted or hoped within the connection of this profound historic happening. Let us begin this action drama and witness how this new time sequence came to be, thereby providing the "New Historic Reality."

Enjoy the excitement of this historical adventure,
highlighted by multiple time exchanges.
Pay close attention and follow the plot to the end!

P.S. *Lincoln is telling the story in the first person from the future and had the luxury of using the Watchers' advanced technologies in order to increase his intellect and physical abilities. Dead Ringer lends a unique and entertaining value when reading Lincoln's 1800's style of writing. The story begins in an historic fashion but then immediately within the first chapter accelerates to the art of imagination. Please don't read the end of the book first, for all of you, end of the book readers! Reason being: because there is a certain level of irony towards the end, which the entire book is built-up to.*

Best to you,
Robert Rasch

CHAPTER ONE

HISTORIC ARCHIVES

Viewpoint:

The blade of an axe is close-up, in motion as it comes down swiftly upon a thin metal chain used for measuring property lines. The axe thumps into the Earth and remains jammed within the dirt. Lincoln is alone, miles from town, at work as a surveyor. He is wearing a white loose fit shirt and black trousers. The view from above is a vast area of flat land that surrounds him.

Lincoln is in his mid twenties and begins to write his personal memoirs, from this day forth. He explains about the fantastical adventures he encountered and the alternate events in time, which ultimately splits his world into two.

"The Original Abraham Lincoln"

It was springtime 1834, Illinois. For a few months I have been working as an assistant surveyor, appointed by John Calhoun, who at the time was overwhelmed with boundary line cuts in the Sangamon County region. I appreciate the opportunity that was suggested by Pollard Simmons, a Democratic politician and farmer, who forwarded a positive reference for this surveyor job.

I was quite satisfied with the practical challenges contained within the art of surveying. Additionally, this employment would further my ability to pay back a debt I incurred from my last failed business venture. The job paid as much as $2.50 for establishing boundaries on a quarter section of land and $2.00 for a half quarter lot (equivalent to a day's work). These potential earnings were a fair amount, but most of all I was very appreciative to further my ability, to acquire new benefits towards this type of "work trade."

Remaining focused and steady are two important virtues I had to learn. Too many times I have been distracted by my passion for politics. Less than two years ago I had lost an election; a run for a seat in the Illinois General Assembly in 1832. I had lost sight of my work responsibilities because of this political run for office and thus during, I failed within the business I was acquainted.

At the time, a Henry Clay, who jockeyed his way to be the leader of Congress, once said to me, "You're missing that little something to make you great, I should know, because I'm missing it too." Later on, Henry Clay would seek a total of five attempts to run for President of the United States and lose in all efforts. This motivated me to move forward, not rapidly but with a steady pace, helping me to make precise decisions.

Traveling east from New Salem, unknowingly at the time, I passed through a village that would one day be named after me. Fully attached and labeled, also to "my name," will be other historic varieties of lakes, parks and roadways as well.

History has taken great favor upon me and for that I am appreciative and thankful; humbled to say the least. But be reassured and trust that my contributions were few and halted from this day forth. For my counterpart; he is the one who deserves to be held in the highest regard, along with sincere appreciation of all he had accomplished. It would be altogether fitting to clarify or make plain to this co-equal arrangement, but nor can I put it into print, but I also cannot tell or confide in my closest acquaintances.

For the sake of dedication and protection to all who were involved, this collection of information and writings would have to be stowed away until an acceptable time period in the future. Until that time, when the people can absorb and believe, because then and only then, can they verify and confirm these outcomes.

Never could I or anybody imagine, what would transpire on this most peculiar day. The truth, hmm; it is amusing that the word "peculiar" has "liar" within the context of the word, because what happens to me, if told, would unanimously be considered an "untruth." Therefore, with mixed feelings I carefully expose certain key people contained within our history and also part of the reason to safeguard these writing-logs and journals on this unique matter.

To bring forth a summary of what is to come: I will use the analogy of riding into an intersection, but without a choice of what direction to follow. So, I answered "yes" to the question posed to me in the immediate future and thereby, with strong conviction I say, "It should not be a choice for any man of noble and moral stature." This stands to reason and with this honored decision that points to the needs of the many.

The answer to me was the obvious, an obligation to the Almighty. I will try to resolve the confusion (quandary) to simple parts, taken from my daybook and journal. This will translate to a hopeful understanding, in connection to the parity of lives between Abraham and John.

"Overshadowed by this life changing event."

****

"From the future comes a different me"
"And so I carry on"

Far from town, out across the Sangamon River in the northern region of Monticello, I am alone marking out a point of reference amongst a vast area of treeless grounds. I feel the freshness of spring blooming. Silent and still, I hear only an occasional rustle of the marking chains or the ruckus of my compass following in and out of my pocket…When suddenly; I feel my skin surrounded by static energy and simultaneously, I think I hear something? Studying my arm after rolling up my sleeves, I notice the hairs on my forearm lifted. The scalp of my head tingles, but before I reach to touch that part of my body, I am distracted and look up puzzled.

I see a spherical globe of some sort, positioned weightless in the sky, while a circle of darkness surrounds the outer bright reflective area of this vision. I think I see stars through a dark ring around this lighted globe? Is it appearing in space or part of the sky? To this I am unsure.

Silent and motionless it lies undisturbed, yet with sharp contours within the center of the sphere and outwardly, it has a bright radiance that gleams around its exterior. Along with its luminescence, there seems to be a low continuous blend of natural sound, resonating similar to the motion of an insect emitting a bristle hum. To approach or to be drawn toward its star spiked white glare, suggests a powerful production of much physical strength.

The harmonic tones become pronounced with a wave of magnetic pressure increasing on my body. Frightened, I begin to feel paralyzed and thus lifted apart from my being. I cannot speak, while fear overwhelms me as I get closer to the spherical bright light.

The intensity is sudden, as I am about to collide with this blinding ball of light. Alone asking myself, "Am I going to burn, am I going to shatter violently?" I twist and turn my head forcefully to look away, while I close my eyes and clench every muscle in my body to prepare for impact!

"Wait, wait!"

I am inside. I exhale, while I have just passed through smoothly and unharmed. Am I dreaming? This is not heaven. The vibrating noise is gone, but I am now hearing a vague shuffle of high pitched (rhythmic) tones. The features within this vehicle facility are eerie. I'm feeling strange and seeing gases floating in a blurry and slick auditorium.

I am unable to move from a standing and resting position, but yet I am able look at my arm, so I wave with my hand and fingers, to create motion. This is fundamentally strange. I try to reason with myself but I am unable because my heart feels strangled by my throat, so I anxiously pray. Whoa to be becalmed, but still nervous and shifting my attention sporadically all around the area. Hoping, the visual mystery of this room will entertain my thoughts and keep my intellect intact.

Above is a domed ceiling adorned with lines of soft lights, captured by curved walls that cascade down to a circular transparent floor. The walls flow further in either direction and seated below are rooms with a hollowed out center. Beneath the center of the clear floor, appears to be a light, regenerating blue hues flailing from its central position location.

I am in some kind of holding facility, for what possible purpose; maybe it is something to do with a higher source. There are glass windows, but without frames, systematically positioned throughout the room with lighted symbols that look like Egyptian hieroglyphs. The language or code is racing vertically, up and down. It is hard to see through the gaseous mist, but I see the windows of symbols connected and communicating with one another, through some order of lighted beat tones.

Since childhood, I have always thought there was more to our plain simple existence, because I truly believe that God's life spirit is everywhere. Engrossed, I continue to pray with eyes wide open, searching and looking for answers. At the center of the floor, there seems to be an Abacus counter (colored beads along rods for counting) for controlling the complex, along with windows that appear to be observing something.

Mt breath is not settled, as I continue to observe. I see an odd instrument attached to the center floor with a silvery base neck, supported by a lit globe with miniature dials that looks similar to a timepiece or then again, maybe shiny coins arranged evenly all around its surface.

Startled, I see an image of figures lurking about. Not sure if they are shadows from the modern lantern lights or just a ghostly figures in my imagination. Unsettled, my heart begins to race again! There is someone nearby and approaching. I look to follow the image to my right. "What?" My voice distorts and rides high trying to exclaim words!

Frightened, I see a man sleeping in an upright stance, in a cylindered shell with a force of light captivating his being. His clothes are unique and he has strange hair. I wonder why I can see him, is there some purpose to this? I attempt to announce a greeting but with no response. While bending my head I ask a question, "Has someone made a mistake with me being here? Hello!" I remain and wait for a reply.

I stand tilted in the same holding apparatus with the gentleman across from me, thinking of a possible escape. All of a sudden, without my control, my head turns straight ahead. Am I being punished for my negative thought? Clearly, whoever is here is free from ignorance and able to read my thoughts. I suddenly flinch as a thought in my mind answers me with a resounding, "No, you're not being punished at all." I speak out in a confusing manner and say, "Oh?"

Unsure of myself, describing what are lighted and partially transparent angels or entities coasting around me. Are they? Maybe I should not assume or have thoughts? One thing is sure, they are communicating to me. The moving symbols inside the translucent glass surprisingly halt in their vertical motion and I sense the task of its purpose is complete. I sense that whatever is supposed to happen to me is going to occur now.

A flurry of information is being directed and collected about to my thoughts. An astounding feeling is brought forth while the information fills my mind. I have been assured that I will have free will, and the choice is mine to decide.

I am perplexed that they are not using any sound for language in order to conduct an open dialog with me. Ultimately, they share and convey to me, a reflection of a whole entire emotional feeling (whole sentences) and not as individual words. My comprehension through this unusual portal of messaging, has granted me extra abilities, for a more keen perception of linguistics and communication.

I began to receive their introduction to whom they are and why they are here. They proclaimed, "We are called the "Watchers" and are a collective of "referential entities" (Between God) that exists, not in your third dimension, but in an energetic realm of a dissimilar harmonic orchestration.

Yes, you are safe. We have overseen your planet since its inception, along with the protection of its natural development, physically and socially. There are other factions of entities that struggle to influence the human race and create some conflict among their own species. We limit their interventions and keep balance within the universe by monitoring and making sense of temporal outcomes (timekeepers)."

Before I can ask anything, they would answer me anticipating my every thought. They further explained, "We as a species were once in a similar type of existence to earthborn people. Millions of years in the remote past, our beings went through an evolutionary transformation. Our body's subatomic molecular structure metamorphosed (changed), by an implosion fusion process.

Further, to answer your thoughts. Reason being, is the cause and effect of external pressure compressed within the cells. This caused a vacuum to absorb certain tissue fluids, assisted by a subatomic vibratory frequency signal activation that caused an implosion within every cell of our being. Simultaneously on a subatomic level, the (subatomic) particles began to weave and spiral within the inter-dimensional spatial fabric, traversing at light-speed (suchlike a micro-solar system). Gravity is then formed and thus grasps onto a higher dimension, leaving the effect of adapted radiation that spews and morphs into our (pellucid) translucent species. We call this result, "Astral-Meiosis.""

In my mind I wished for an easier explanation, but then they quickly responded, "That was the simplest explanation." I was amused by this and drew a smile. Still, I wondered about the gentleman across the room, as to myself. Who is he and what is the rationale behind his presence? One of the Watchers responds and says, "This information will be disclosed to you once the basis of knowledge is presented to you."

As I acknowledged what was presented to me, I then realized that I was contained in this small housed unit for life support, because the conditions in this facility were not compatible for humans. In looking about, I presume that there is an important process or function to why I am here? I cannot stop thinking, that at anytime I could possibly lose my ability to breathe. Yet, by building my trust towards the Watchers I seem to be more and more at ease.

The time awaited was short but it did indeed feel like an eternity and finally, my purpose to why I am here. The Watchers begin to illustrate and show reason for the cause and share their knowledge of the current problematic circumstances. The future of the United States of America is presented to me with two tangible outcomes through a prism, separated by approximately one hundred years. The first timeline's tangent, stated as the "Original Timeline," which is during the middle of the 1800's, is offered by the Watchers by the use of a "performance learning tool." The learning tool seems entertaining and uses visual and an acoustic sound sense, by means of advanced equipment. This extreme teaching is so that I may acquire knowledge of what could occur in the immediate future.

My journal notes about this learned knowledge, stemming from the 1800's "original" future historic timeline:

They hereby present a gentleman by the name of James Buchanan, Jr., born April 23, 1791. Earlier in his career, he represented Pennsylvania in the United States House of Representatives, Senate, and then Minister to Russia. Later on, he was named Secretary of State. Yet through numerous appointments, Buchanan steadily pursued an outside occupation with the Court of St. James in England.

My unwavering attention continued at full gaze, while images and portraits move on a display glass, representing the times of future events. This learning technique is much more effective than a book, I might add. More effective than a book, well, that is a notion I thought I would never say.

It seems Buchanan will be nominated by the Democratic Party in the future, before the 1856 Presidential election, but yet still continued to work in London as a minister to the Court of St. James before his nomination. While he was in England, he developed very close relationships with his constituents, siding with Europe on many political issues.

Buchanan's presidential election slipped into triumph, because of a three man race, which includes John C. Frémont and Millard Fillmore. While between each other, they offset and absorbed the competitive vote, leaving the inevitable victor to be James Buchanan. The Watchers explain why Buchanan cannot win a second four year term, eventhough he had done so in the original timeline. As president, he lived in the North, but his policies leaned towards the Southern States.

Buchanan's do nothing policies was the reverse to maintain peace between the North and the South. Furthermore, President Buchanan alienated both sides, causing the Southern States to seek more power and eventually declared their secession to be completed in 1863. The United States will now become divided into different countries, never to be what it was intended for; hence, the reason why Lincoln needs to be inserted into the timeline, because the result of this original timeline would be deemed unacceptable.

The Watchers embrace the results of these actions and present scenes of real life representations and portraits, which are on display in every decade for a hundred years thereafter. The results of these futures lacked growth and principles to say the least.

When I was taught and became privy to this information, I felt my body tinge and my emotions slump, becoming more uncomfortable with each bit of information. Buchanan's view of the secession (separation) was or will be lackadaisical. He was highly against going to war, on the basis that it would have an effect between his constituents and acquaintances.

He represented and sided with England and the Southern States. Buchanan's famous saying was, "I acknowledge no master but the law." This phrase alone kept the public pressures away, so that he could fulfill his agenda. Buchanan was a leader whose sole purpose was to control the people and not be for the people. To serve the people is what are founders intended for the Presidency of the United States.

His executive decisions, cemented the fate and failure for the Northern United States of America. He forced and restricted banks in lending monies, creating bills to lower the credit levels of $3 to $1 of specie; specie is money in the form of coins. He also limited the use of federal or state issued bonds as security for bank notes. The economy never recovers and is a recipe that is tried again and again without success over the next one hundred and fifty years. The South, because of its agricultural production, was less affected than the Northern manufacturers, which were permanently damaged.

In the original timeline, Buchanan will have left office

in 1868 and would accumulate a federal deficit of $51 million plus and more than tripled the debt of the Northern portion of the United States, crippling the economy and their citizens. Panic ensued, while monies and the value of currency were of little or no value. This halted all expansion projects and left the people to rely on England for their survival, ending any hope of prosperity in the United States of America permanently.

Most of all, Buchanan's legacy will be remembered for how one person was able to break up, what was supposed to be the greatest nation on Earth. Sadly, the people of the South revered Buchanan following the separation, but soon turned their allegiance towards him after the meltdown of the entire financial system. The now Confederate States of America, would crumble and ironically be split into smaller individual countries. Some Southern States even elected to join, once again to the Northern States in a desperate measure in order to survive.

Interesting enough, the Watchers are about to ask for my participation to alter these occurrences, but the thought this decision weighed heavily, in the understanding to be "permanent" and to bear a major change in the direction of my life. Nevertheless, it does remedy this would be tragedy. For the point of no return; "yes," to a decision I was already on board with. I could never forget the tragedies hereunto. To further, the notes I am about to write are from my possible future, if I "*do*" lend my hand and therefore, to what is written, would be noted to have already happened.

Further historical notes: Where would I be inserted into the new timeline? Thereafter Buchanan's first four years and restricted to only one term as President of the United States, I will reassure that he does not serve a second term as President of the United States.

With just the one term as president, Buchanan was or will be the sole President to remain a lifelong bachelor. My belief in regards to this, "If you cannot or do not want to be in a relationship, then you don't deserve to have a position to where from, a marriage is made to the American people; or to be their President of these United States!

When saying this, I noticed that my hand was very hostile toward the lapel of my favorite jacket; I guess because I become intense when I know that someone's intentions are purposely designed to undermine others.

To further continue, he was or will be the last president to be born in the 18th century and the only president from Pennsylvania. Also, he will be the last former Secretary of State to serve as President of the United States.

When he left office, in either timeline, the Democratic Party was divided, adding to the great disappointment toward that of his own party. He, who was supposed to become one of the most revered presidents in history, failed immensely because of his inability to identify with the people, along with his neglect about the gross principals towards each side of the slavery dilemma and ignoring the better good for all.

By using the United States to enhance England's strong hold on the world, he was and will be able to carry out what the British failed to do in the past and without war. In so, to destroy the fabric of the United States of America, while increasing the wealth and world domination for England. This furthers his legacy to be viewed by public opinion and historians, as one of the worst presidents to take the stage.

This damage was and will be in just one term as President. The thought does arise as to why the Watchers do not start four years earlier, before this occurrence. There is probably a solid reason, but I do leave this thought with a stale smirk.

While the first four years of his administration was or will be dreadful, the second four years would be disastrous beyond repair. This reinforces why the original timeline of Buchanan receiving a second term as president must be stopped and for the Watchers to alter or rework "time" for a more constructive result.

Holding my breath and then releasing it slowly, I try to regain my composure. Every part of my being is extremely unnerved, by the intellectual trail of deceit. The staggering numbers of people to be killed, (if time-measures are not in place) are in the millions and numerous more that will become poverty stricken and maligned with diseases. This is by far, a dreadful and unacceptable existence.

The Watchers are in motion on their task at hand, because I have elected to join the cause. They have started the process and left their first mark. According to the Watchers, a sudden timeline change occurs and it is in the future, during Buchanan's 1857 inaugural address, he declares not to run for a second term as president. At this point, the issues are only half resolved, because the Watchers are now focused on how to set the standards to restore the United States of America and for Lincoln to become victorious in order for the United States to remain as it was intended. The immediate issue, when it arises, is the turmoil towards a possible civil war that is left behind by Buchanan, but since this happens many years in the future, it will be addressed when the time comes. The reason for this is because of the many probable outcomes that will occur between now and then, on the basis of free will.

At this moment I become captured by the prism of information, thus identifying with a different time period. This is what I copied to my daybook: The Watchers look as if to be illustrating a scientific anomaly, signifying an alignment phenomenon that takes place every hundred years, due to orbital and planetary positioning abnormalities. Please, do not think I am a teacher of science; I am merely taking what information the Watchers have taught me and with great effort, try to put into plain words.

These happenings cause a disruptive magnetic draw on a

very basic brain function of man. The results dither (disrupt) a natural biological signal, which becomes distorted within the signature of certain inhabitants of the Earth. These disruptions of basic thought seemingly skip to different locations around the Earth and occur on what is called, "Ley-lines." These are the invisible magnetic alignment waves throughout the Earth and increase one's spiritual abilities. If you are good person, they will make you better, but if you are not of noble stature, they will make you worse.

Even though this phenomenon only exists for a short period of time, the ramifications or consequence of these decisions made by the governing leaders, have a devastating effect on societies. As a result, certain civilizations are left flat and in disarray, which leads to their ultimate demised or an abandonment of their homeland.

The Watchers explained to me, that these periods are what they call, a "Cyclical Non-Enlightenment Periods," (Dark Ages) and occur approximately every one hundred years. The corrective process for these malignant temporal tragedies is to daisy-chain two definitive time periods together forming from a hundred years apart.

In order to permanently change time, the chain reaction must be completed and inserted within a forty-eight hour period. In each time zone, although a hundred years apart, the participators will have to alter time and complete the favorable outcome inside the forty-eight hour threshold.

"Oh dear, I am going to need more ink and or wits about me; a light hearted comment to say the least. To disclose: during my stay with the Watchers and with my consent, they enabled my ability to set in motion, parts of my thinking that laid dormant. This was part of the requirements, if when I said yes."

In this case, the time (continuum) break point needs to peak and transpire on October 25th of both 1860 (Lincoln) and 1960 (?). I tip my hat, to the thought, towards a lifetime of work devoted to their one pinnacle point in time.

God must have a foolproof system built in, because according to the Watchers, once a timeline is changed or fails, the ability to change that time period again becomes more difficult, since the thread of time thickens automatically.

To conclude, the Watchers have calculated and processed many of these time tangent changes in the past (5000 years worth) and will do so again in the future. They have never failed in any attempts because of strict regiments during planning and assistance when needed (interaction). Once the timelines are sewn, there is to be no further contact directly with the Watchers.

My decision and duties seem to be rather simple, but of course with hard work. Plainly put; it was to stop James Buchanan from being re-elected, which has already been done, according to the Watchers' temporal machines and restore our country, so the "Southern" United States does not separate from the "North." I assure you this will be done, by carrying myself up and not by any means of bringing any individual down.

The Watchers feel my decision, as decided, to be quick and haste. They required a full disclosure of the complete history and its effects up to the current time point. The Watchers were earnest and presented any or all of their findings before any actions would occur or to be engaged.

They explained that certain outcomes cannot be predicted and are under the umbrella of "free will." This is understandable, because every day is a chance and to feel free to choose is our God given right, if of course your choice is dignified…

As my curiosity settled, as though it seemed, new data instantly unfolded, detailing the second time period (100 year alternate) that required attention. The new historical data, paints a stained vision of the president elected in 1960, whose decisions cost the lives of millions, because of failure to communicate. A nuclear fallout and devastation occurred with several countries (United States, Russia and Cuba were the root causes).

To subscribe to an "open mind" is now an understatement for the rest of my life. My decision to immediately help the cause and keep the United States from the hardship of splitting into two and save the self-worth of a nation, would surprisingly cause a worse ripple effect in time (future). Reason being, is the new timeline of one hundred years would simultaneously cause a multitude of devastation that is brought forth in 1962.

I feel extremely guilty because of my young quick decision, even though it is for something that hasn't happened yet. But it still lingers, quite like the bitter taste of humble regret. I pledge to this new 1960 tangent in time and the reason for the man idled across from me.

He is held in a sleeplike state. For my answer, if to be a "yes," would predicate onto the matter of understanding both timelines. Then so would the gentleman across from me; he must agree and choose to join the cause for the betterment of many. Willingly, my commitment is a steady "yes" and to be based on a decision ascribed to an absolute.

At first, the word "nuclear" appeared to me as just a future scientific term, but to my enormous disappointment, I learned fast by watching hours of moving portraits, displaying the horrors and tragedies of these explosive mistakes. After viewing this, I am bullied into emotional distraught. I attempt to collect myself after the sight of all that has or will perish.

I am grateful, because of the Watchers' polite release of this information and was done so, at a tolerable rate. Even though I have a slight increase of aptitude, yet still, due to my human emotional capability to contend with, they would only present drips of information until I was comfortably ready to address these violent future historic findings.

This additional original timeline is also about to be changed, which is a different timeline than mine and will be one hundred years in the future, led by someone other than me. The person across from me is that man and will have his turn to be briefed by the Watchers. I am sure he is a skilled choice by the Watchers to take on the 1960's timeline.

Journal notes stemming from the 1960 "original" future historic timeline:

If my 1800's timeline is corrected but the 1960's timeline is not, then the saga that falls through onto the "original" 1960's timeline appears instantly, unfortunately. This can be further explained by beginning with the 1960 victory of the 35th President of the United States, here within Hubert Humphrey Junior and not John F. Kennedy who did not dive into the wave of politics but became a writer and a professor at Harvard University.

He was born 1911 in Wallace, South Dakota and worked as a pharmacist at his father's store from 1931 to 1937, until he became a professor of political science. Hereafter, in Minnesota, he forged ahead into various political work standings.

After Humphrey's failed attempt in his run for the presidency in 1952, he decides once again to run for the United States presidency in 1960 and succeeds in the new original timeline. He barely defeats his opponent Richard Nixon, because of information released right before the election, accusing Humphrey of possibly avoiding the draft to the Air Force in WWII and or any other divisions of dangerous active duty, simply by a claim of having disabilities.

Additionally, Humphrey's huge lead in the campaign was also in reverse because of Nixon's last ditch effort to lay claim that Hubert Humphrey's "tolerance for the people" slogan was a ruse (misleading). Nixon cited that Humphrey and the democrat party were characterized by having "intolerance," because during this time period, a large majority of the Democratic Party wanted black people to be segregated (discriminated) in certain Southern States because of skin color.

This was done not to lose the southern vote. This pressure added to a close battle during the election and for what was a secured, soon to be victory by Humphrey because of his outstanding performance at the debates. If the race for the presidency was slightly longer, Nixon would have won.

Unfortunately, Humphrey "did" display characteristics of "intolerance" once he became president, as Nixon stated and at the worst time possible.

Intolerance is defined as the unwillingness to accept views or behavior that differs from their own, such as religious, cultural and or political beliefs. This simple personality trait spewed over to stubbornness, which caused an excessive delay with a commander-in-chief decision. Urged to make a simple compromise by members of his cabinet, he refused. Leading up to, what would be called, "The Mistake for All Ages."

Nuclear catastrophes struck on November 28th, 1962, after a 44 day political and military standoff, between the countries of Cuba, Russia and the United States. The time period during the 44 day standoff, was called, Castro's Cuban Crisis Protest (CCCP). Fidel Castro was the young dictator in charge of Cuba, whose values did not match the United States' (Humphrey's) administration at the time. The acronym CCCP was used purposely to describe this "crisis" because it also represented the symbols of the Soviet Union's

(Russia) translated name and who coincided as partners with Cuba against the United States in this political tug of war.

This triangulated conflict of intense strategic military maneuvering, created a lot of nuclear missile position changes and maintenance for both sides of the military. An unnamed soldier from the United States was on a routine mission to make sure the entire mechanical nuclear launch systems were geared to be just one step away for an immediate launch, considering the high alert levels ordered because of tensions between the U.S. and their adversaries.

The soldier accidentally engaged a full launch release sequence because of his unfamiliarity with a new launch design. This result caused a single nuclear missile to strike Russia's homeland, invoking a spontaneous (knee-jerk) reaction from Cuba and Russia, to retaliate with a response, which escalated to a global World War III. To make matters worse, the devastation spread to other countries that were not involved in this conflict among the three nations.

I elect to keep brief, this portion of what I learned from the visual and sound moving portraits. All things considered, this 1962 nuclear catastrophe would happen instantly, unless the man across from me agrees to join in this 5 score (100 year) timeline adjustment and succeed.

Once I change "my" current timeline with a "yes" decision, I will be a part of what is to come, involving the 16th President of the United States in 1860 (thus preventing the South from separating from the North). Then so, simultaneously, would a hopeful "yes" decision be formed, by the gentleman across from me. I will be heartened and inspired by his willingness to be vested and become the 35th President of the United States in 1960 and thereby preventing this alternate time tangent of nuclear catastrophe (100 years later).

CHAPTER TWO

THE AWAKENING

My answer to the Watchers was a resounding "yes" in its entirety. As for the outcome to what transpires from this decision is by far going to be special unto itself, whether good or bad I am dedicated to the needs of the many.

As for a question that was asked to me in the future, I answered, "Of course I cannot assume to be overzealous with my need to help, because the Watchers will not move forward without my full understanding and for both parties to be united; a positive unison decision in order to start."

It chiefly depends on which timeline you are reading this, because the people in my era would consider, what I am about to say, "The farthest reach from the truth." My responsibilities in this overall matter were to oversee and manage the connection of lives between the two timelines, but with a greater emphasis on my counterpart's life and of course, at an arm's length (doing what was expected of me). Nevertheless, an explanation or an excuse for my lack of devotion at this point can be better clarified by taking you back again to this day in 1834.

❖ ❖ ❖

Weary and exhausted because of the long time spent absorbing a tremendous amount of information; I remain, still onboard the Watchers' vehicle and thinking of food.

Instantly appearing in front of me is a light green oval shape of moving gas or liquid. It is suspended near my mouth. In my mind it is confirmed that this is food and to trust its origin. I hesitate to ingest it because of its unusual form. Then again, I am starving; this helps sway my decision to indulge.

As I open my mouth, I have full control of the pace to which I consume the gaseous nutrients. Slowly, I finish this mixed taste of odorless grub and soon after, a scan of light passes from above my head to toe upon my body. Feeling vibrant and sensational I suddenly notice a moving portrait display now positioned in front of the man awakening across from me. His eyes begin to fully open while my eyes become laden, and so I sleep.

Determined that I am sleeping, yet information is still being received clearly and defined to my thoughts. I start to awake slowly, as it appears the gentleman I am with is being briefed. At this moment, it seems that an hourglass of time has passed. Afterwards, it appears as if his choice is an honorable "yes" at this present stage.

Both of us are given the last leg of information before a final verdict is made by the Watchers. Now that we are both awake, we acknowledge one another with an already known respect. In cooperation, together we nod to each other with a friendly gesture because of the familiarity of shared knowledge between one another.

Shocked to receive this foremost information from the Watchers; the two of us answer separately. We reply with the same question; how is that possible, "a counterpart?" The Watchers announce to us, "The life that you surrender to this "cause" will not be your own, but your extended spirit. For you must lead a different life outside your previous one. Your most important requirement will be to lend your experiences and qualifications when all of your instructions are completed.

Once you have been prepared and when you choose to do so, a counterpart will be created from each of you, in your exact image and likeness; a duplicate if you will, of all that you are and have accumulated to that point in each of your individual lives. This again, is necessary because of the sensitive nature of time. One cannot change time if they occupy a different space from what was supposed to be.

You will have many years available to live the same life you are familiar with, up until the specific turning point in time that needs to be changed. At that moment, a duplicate is then created and unfortunately, you will each have to abandon your current lives.

In the past we have observed, that many elected persons that undergo this change, are mixed in their choices. Some choose to separate right away and some wait till the last moment. The sacrifice will be to exit your current core life and to be an observer from afar. This necessary choice keeps the timelines secure and possible. There are no alternates to these givens."

Once we received this information and was informed about the process, it seemed to be straightforward, along with very little effort or time. Well, accept for starting a new life. There are hundreds of foreigners that start "anew" every day in the United States. The positive outlook for both of us is that we have many years available, if when we choose to decide. The Watchers mention as a given, that they do not know who would be alive or where family members will go in the future.

Unable to talk or communicate properly in this gaseous facility, we look at each other with a confused look for support. The Watchers give us time before we render a final decision. Our minds are in deep thought amongst the silence.

We both know this is so much bigger than our individual selves. The feeling right now is like looking into a stagnant mirrored lake of cold water and working-up the courage, to get excited enough to plunge in. We both nod to each other and nervously approve to move forward.

Our conclusions, not known at the time, were similar and were as follows: Our lives would have been good and yet very ordinary but it seemed this was an ambitious journey to have something great or a once in a lifetime opportunity. So to our answer once again, we elected to come aboard or should I say, "Jump ship right now to get back to our lives." I mean this as a jest, I smile.

I stand eager for an explanation, on how the Watchers are able to transform our individual bodies into separate counterparts of identical characteristics, physical and mental. I will try to highlight the points of interest and not layout the full working details, for the sake of properly understanding the full task.

The use of the Watchers' machine, called the "Doppelganger" (duplication device), transforms a person into a perfect match by scanning their body, which is done within one second. Thereafter, mixtures of subatomic particles are adopted and customized towards the build. The particles consist of matter, liquids, gases and something called "plasma." The materials are selected and perfectly disbursed, according to who is being duplicated. All seven days are needed within the process because every step has to blend, settle and fuse in order to transform into a particular purpose or function. In regards to the scanning device, it is so ironic that "one second" of time can create what would take thousands of years to develop here on Earth.

The Watchers clarify this riddle of duplication with a crafty circle of procedure, to and from different time periods. They present locations of two caves with flowing water beneath both. The Watchers indicate this special component of flowing water to be necessary. One cave is located in New Salem, Illinois and the second would be in Brookline, Massachusetts just outside the city of Boston. Each cave is equipped with a built-in Gateway, which connects these two locations.

The Gateways, according to the Watchers, have been here for thousands of years and others that exist, appear to be scattered all around the Earth. In case of emergencies, the Watchers disclosed to us, all of the Gateway locations, so to be transparent with their purpose. The main function of our two Gateways are preset (roughly one hundred years apart) and used to pass through and connect the locations of New Salem, Illinois (1800's) and Brookline, Massachusetts (1900's).

To operate the Gateway is just a matter of passing through a doorway, but with a cautionary measure at the center of the passage. This indicated area is marked with a four foot band of white quartz stone and is essentially cloaked (hidden from view). Smooth in its appearance and its purpose is most important for time sequential travels.

There are two very small protruding pyramid stones on the sides of the cave wall, inches from the ground and are set diagonally across from each other. This is to indicate the location of the Gateway. This area looks to be natural to the onlooker, but when a "coin" is within this four foot band of the cave, so does the control panel mysteriously appear.

There is a preset timetable (default) tied into the travel time periods. If traveling through the Gateway from Illinois to Massachusetts, the user or traveler will automatically arrive in 1934, April 5th, if they pass right through the quartz band mark. The same is the reverse if travel is made to Illinois from Massachusetts, it would then be 1834, April 5th, one hundred years connected.

In order to control the date, hour and minute, the user or traveler stays and waits without passing through, within the marked quartz band area and for every second that ticks on their second hand watch, a year, day, hour or minute is added depending on the settings within the timetable's (defaulted) original, April 5th settings. This is one of two ways to control the Gateway, which is important if something were to go wrong.

Since April 5th 1834 was the original first contact, the Watchers do not allow us to go back beyond this time and the same for the April 5th, 1934 timeline. Meaning, the 1934 limited timeline is restricted only to the Massachusetts' cave, which also was the exact date of contact for my new acquaintance.

Insofar as to pick the day and hour is an easy learned process by touching an individual four inch crystal square, within a smooth quartz calendar. This second method to control the Gateway is quite sophisticated in the manner it is built. The center of the square indicates the day and the outer portion of the square, represents the hour and minute for a desired preference. This is quite similar to a pocket watch, where you can choose a precise time of the day.

A simple touch on your selection and then wait while inside the band and thereafter, release when you are ready to exit (pass through is only allowed in one direction). In order to safeguard the Gateway from any person accidentally using it, the Watchers have supplied me with three coins. I was instructed to keep the coins safe in separate locations, because of their extreme importance.

I am smiling, because of how interesting things are developing. The coins are devices disguised as thick pennies or coins and it appears to have my bust inscribed to its surface. Perhaps the reason for my profile to be on the coin is so I know it is mine, because my new acquaintance was also given three coins with his face on the surface. The reason for three coins is because the Watchers tell us that we will need a chosen team leader a trusted colleague to help us succeed in our efforts to the mission.

My coins are dated 1963 and have some sort of monument building on the tail back of the coins. The Watchers explain that the significance of the coins is twofold. Reason one, gives a person the ability to pass through the Gateway to their destination and time choice. Without this special coin being in your possession, the Gateway will not work.

The second important significance occurs when the same single coin is placed heads-up on the floor of the Quartz band threshold opening and in addition, make certain to put your feet in the right place and stand firm. Because within seconds you are transported to the unmanned facility designed by the Watchers, which is located many stories under the Earth. This is the forbidden area of Antarctica, beneath the Hercules Dome. Yet, not in a particular time period, but a location for transformation, knowledge and training. A coin is needed in order to enter and exit this advanced facility in order to prevent any misuse.

There, in this unmanned facility is the instruction, tutoring and transformation device, called the "Doppelganger," as I mentioned before. It is a machine designed by the Watchers to duplicate oneself in order not to skew or disrupt the timeline (continuum) in regards to the original self. The "original self," is supposed to carry on their life without interacting with their other self or counterpart. This is hopefully done while correcting both ends of the 100 year negative rift in time.

Most importantly, the Watchers were very insistent and made aware (caveats), that the original person is the only one to hold and control the three coins and the new self is not allowed to possess or use any of the coins. Secondly, the highest priority to follow is to only use the Doppelganger to make one of your-selves to complete the mission.

In regards to time correction, once the point of duplication is reached, the original self is generally (chiefly) released from the task and can go about their life to enjoy and observe from afar, as mentioned before. But be forewarned, if an additional self is made other than the original two persons, there are repercussions. Regrettably, once the third person is duplicated, each person from that group, including the original person who was processed, will become self fulfilling by any means possible (wicked). This natural distortion is created and protected by nature in order to keep things in check, and is called "inhertablemuttism."

The Watchers have concluded their discussions and are confident in both of us. They ask if we are satisfied with our task at hand and to be of mutual understanding in all that will apply. We reply with a positive confirmation of agreement.

Suddenly, we are being prepared to exit the foreign facility. In an instant we are placed besides the foot of the cave in New Salem, Illinois (1834). The both of us are nervous, right after a short burst of light and a hum noise, finding ourselves safe and standing next to each other. I was unable to talk to my new acquaintance because of the lack of air and the stifling position in the holding facility, until now.

We look at each other with a friendly glance and smile, along with a mutual handshake. I say, "Glad to meet your acquaintance." He responds, "Hello, my name is John or you can call me Jack, that's what my family calls me." So I respond, "Jack, my name is Abraham, Abraham Lincoln."

Thinking in my mind, "How young he is and also the vernacular (speech) of his time period, how quite interesting it is. It is oddly enough, how words in his dialect seem to say a sentence that slurs into one word, without hesitation; most fascinating."

John says, "Can you believe what just happened to us?" As the two of us stared up into the sky and all around, wondering if the Watchers or their vehicle was in sight. After the paranoid jitters and feelings settled, we both look about. The grounds around the area seem clear of anybody or anything, I respond. "Well," I hesitate thinking, is he thinking it was a dream or maybe the gases about the facility distracted his reality. So I reply with a direct answer, "Well, to never forget this happening would be an understatement to say the least." When I said this, John hesitated but quickly drew a smile from ear to ear, joined by a timed laugh between both of us.

We look into the cave opening. Slow to act; rather we take our coins and compare the inscriptions on the surface of our three coins. While I look down at his coin, I make an observation and say, "Interesting, your coin is made of silver and is a fifty cent piece, whereas mine is made of copper and labeled as one cent." John says, "Hmm, yeah." I continue, "I don't think the numeric value has any bearing for personal use, but I am puzzled about the significance of the monument on the back of my coins." John suggests, "Maybe the money value for the given time period equals the purchase price for food, because in just the last ten years in my time, the cost of some goods have doubled in price. Or maybe perhaps it could be just a symbol of historic meaning, like the eagle on the back of my coins?" I respond, "Yes, the United States National Emblem and I might add, two very reasonable suggestions.

I can see now, why they favored in choosing you." John smirks then cackles while he looks down and says, "Ah shucks, to tell you the truth Abraham, I think the both of us have a lot work in front of us. I'm just happy to still be alive after all of that, my goodness!" While John reads and stares at his coins, he looks at me and says, "After looking at the dates of my coins; it reminded me that I am a hundred years in the past."

Surprised and distracted in our talks, I realize now that for John, it is not such a light matter, seemingly, to be so far from home for a younger man. I know I shouldn't worry because the Watchers proved to be extremely advanced and promised to keep a close eye on us, but I'm still a bit uneasy.

I tapped John's left shoulder twice and said, "Not to worry Jack, let us test the Gateway immediately and proceed to your time period, then I will travel back alone to where we are now. This will remove any doubt to where we stand with this functional (Gateway) part of the task.

A slight sigh of relief came over the two of us but still nervous nonetheless. The anticipation of using the Gateway is an uncertain feeling similar to letting go of your grip from a high branch up in a tree; afraid for the long drop down.

I feel comfortable with my new acquaintance and refer to him as John respectfully, when not in direct contact. Yet by calling him Jack in our venture is a sought of warm fellowship that I know one day will grow to a noble bond.

We are about to enter the cave. I mention to John, "Wait," while I kneel on one knee at the entrance. I grab some of the ground soil with my hand while scouting the area saying, "I am surprised not to have noticed this cave entrance before, being that I have passed by this section of land many times. John steps back while he looks at the entrance and says, "It seems the only way to see the entrance is to be in the water on the edge of the river." So I nod my head in agreement and reply, "Yes, in addition, the onlooker would have to be much higher than the water level during any part of the day. Jack, this soil type that surrounds the cave is sandy-loam," as the granules are released from my hand I stand back up and mention, "This cave has been here for millions of years." John responds, "I didn't do too well in geology class, you seem to have a liking to it?" As he lets out a quick laugh I explain, "Actually, I am an assistant surveyor and was in the processes of marking out boundaries lines today, until my encounter with the Watchers. For part of my work logs involve soil type registrations in regards to land analysis.

If you don't mind me asking, how old are you currently?" John replies, "I will be seventeen on May the 29th and you? "I just turned twenty five in the month of February, oh; I didn't receive your surname before." John apologizes if he was rude for not mentioning his surname, so I respond quickly with, "That is quite alright good sir." He explains his full name to be, "John Fitzgerald Kennedy is my birth name and Fitzgerald is my mother's last name. Here is a photograph I carry in my wallet." He hands me a shiny portrait with eight children upon it, five sisters and the three brothers. He points to the picture and says, "That's me, I am the second oldest child in the family."

While I look at the photo I glance back up at John and hand him back the picture, to say, "God bless your mother. All we are and hope to be; we owe to our angelic mothers." John gives a swift glance at the photo before he returns it to his folding case (wallet) and responds sensitively, "Yes indeed, sadly, I feel mothers are not appreciated enough from where I come from Abraham." I agree with John, then add a heavy look and utter, "Hmm, the same is true in my era but it is up to the "individual" to show by example, to what is acceptable behavior and to transcend beyond this ill-mannered challenge. For I remember my mother's prayers and they have clung to me, all my life." John is captivated in the moment, so I change my composure to mimic what was his excitement.

I say to John, "Are you ready?" I pierce a stare into the entrance of the cave, while my hand rests against the lentil above the opening; of course to mind my head. I said to John, "You go in first and I will keep "an eye on you," I'll be here." Using a cliché that John had spoken earlier, to joke with a laugh, knowing he was nervous. He responds, "Age before beauty Mr. Lincoln sir," while his posture straightens with his arm and hand politely gesturing to go. Thinking, there must be buckets of books filled with clichés over the last hundred years.

Without further ado, we enter the inside portion of the cave, placing our hands aside the wall for balance, touching the cool rough surface of the stone walls. I am wearing my old Sunday best, which-what use to be and now a worn-out cotton work shirt, but I might say, my black vest is rather dapper with its gold and silver threaded embroidery.

We both meander through the cave. The floor is not exactly smooth, while we stumble along and carefully navigate to an open section. Right before the neck of the open area, John shouts my name, "Abraham!" I look over to see John point towards the bottom of the wall, where there are two small protruding pyramid stones set in a diagonal formation. Both of us get excited about locating the possible Gateway but still nervous, like something is going to attack us. We both look over our shoulders to see that nothing is lurking about.

John asks, "So what do think?" I feel for my coins in my pants pocket and say, "Well, we have our coins." John taps his suit against his chest to feel for the coins, where an inside pocket is located and replies, "Yes, got-em!"

I make a suggestion for both of us to proceed towards the area of the Gateway together. John agrees with an ambitious expression on his face. At the moment, the walls appear to be made of old natural stone.

We stall and wait, side by side and then John suggests, "On the count of three, we can step with our right foot forward together." As John counts, "One, Two, Three," our smiles unlock to an alarm of fright, while both of us say the number three. Instantly, an amazing glass calendar appears in a lighted glow. The both of us are mesmerized and basking in the appreciation of the advanced device.

The Watchers said there is an automatic preset on the Gateway to the same day of April 5th, 1834 and April 5th, 1934, which is the earliest in time we can travel. In this case, we don't have to set or pick anything at the present moment. This made it easy in regards to the calendar for this test trip. It is just a matter of walking through the Gateway and so I hope.

We back up two steps before the Gateway and watch the calendar controls disappear. We do this several times for entertainment, in and out, while spewing off a few ah's and wows. We finally rest and John says, "Well, the good thing is, I don't have to be worried about being late for dinner with this mechanical gismo." I laugh while I speak the word "yes" and say, "Yes, I suppose so."

My laughter settles and I mention, "I guess all we have to do is walk through then." I seek confirmation from John. John spurts out, "Wait, what if the Gateway makes a mistake and we get stuck in-with the dinosaur age or worse yet, are clothes are removed and we are then naked running from the dinosaurs." John rattles off his nervous concern with a funny laugh and undertone, while the pitch of his voice rises. I respond with a confused question, still laughing nonetheless and ask, "What are dinosaurs?"

While still in a nervous pitch, he states, "They are giant reptile mahnstirs (monsters) who lived millions of years ago, right where we are standing. But trust me, if we go there, it will only be a few seconds to realize what they are." His smile spreads as I think impart of what he is saying is another joke. So I reply, "You mean giant "monsters?" He looks back to me and says, "Yes, giant reptile Mahnstirs, like the size of a house. I answer John with my eyes wide open and say, "Really? I was entertained by this notion and will explore further into this subject, as it does have a remarkable flight of the imagination.

After the friendly banter, I suggest, "Jack, we have to get you home before your seventeenth birthday lad," laughing out loud. Once we go through the Gateway, we are supposed to stay in our current time period for more than a few weeks, so that we both can settle down and digest this experience."

Once John agrees I ask, "How do you think you can keep this secret from your family?" John quickly says with confidence, "That's easy, since I do have a big family; we tend to always share most of our things. This will be my own thing and I will own it and not like an imaginary friend, like when we were younger, either!" John smirks and taps my arm to draw more excitement from me and so I further indulge hereto his humor. It was out of the ordinary and amusing, so I hesitated, then laughed and was very entertained by his unique wit. We both settle down and adjust our postures while we stand to stretch. Getting ready for our departure, insofar as to the return home is concerned.

"Honored to know you Jack, let me know when you're

ready?" Heightened anticipation awaits going through the Gateway, so I reassure John and say. "I am sure all will be fine and may God bless you with a safe passage." John lets out a sneeze and tries to say, "Ah gee Abraham, it sounded like you just read me my last rights." I smile, laugh and quickly say "Good luck then for your trip and God bless you for your sneeze" I continued to say. "Sorry for the sobering farewell my friend, but it has been a pleasure," as my chuckle settles. John looks confused and says, "The pleasure is all mine, Mr. Lincoln, but aren't we going through together to test the Gateway?" I smile and reply, "Oh yes, indeed," as I laugh once again.

John reaches over and shakes my hand, then makes a suggestion that both of us wrap his tie around our hands. He said this, in order for us to be connected as we travel in-through time, while passing through the Gateway. A safety precaution we agreed upon and mind you, the countdowns were no longer one, two, three, but "ready, set, go."

Both of us are at attention, upright and galvanized. John is on my right with the tie strapped to his left hand and my portion of the tie is connected to my right hand. Our faces cringe as we speak, ready, set, go! Right leg forward, here we go across the threshold of the Gateway. Within three steps, we are absorbed by a wand of electro-static power and instantly rematerialize with a sound similar to a long piece of glass crackling but never breaking.

We stand firm after exiting the Gateway, faced in the opposite direction. Seeing the entrance of the cave in Brookline, Massachusetts or so we hope. Our feet are in the right place, as we look back to see the usual markers on the wall, where it lies secretly hidden. We are both sure footed but light headed and slightly dizzy. This doesn't stop us from hustling to the exit of the cave, where we see sunlight bathing about the opening, and a reflective tint up from the earthly soil.

We both make a right hand turn coming out of the cave

and find an area on the outside of the cavern to lean against. Squinting and trying to explore the area for anybody. Safe and sure, John notices in the distance and declares, "I see the top of the steeple on the church, so we are good!"

Then without hesitation he blurts out, "It's got to be 1934 because I remember this broken branch in the exact spot, over there," while he points with brewing excitement because of the sense that he is going home.

John walks towards the town looking back as I wave goodbye. I yell out, "Jack," whereas he turns completely around and I shout, "Keep an eye on those coins!" He smiles, then waves and I think he said, "I will," but the distance was too far at this point. I watch and wait till he is out of sight. I am eager to get back to my own time period and so I do.

Time travel is easier than chopping wood, that I can assure you. My curiosity lingers thinking about the future of 1934. "How do the people live and what changes have mounted?" Nevertheless, in accordance to the Watchers request, John and I are supposed to meet at the cave in New Salem, on May 30th, 1834. Since there is the ascribed 100 year connection, it will be the same date in John's time but a hundred years later. This will be the day after his seventeenth birthday.

The Watchers told us to tread lightly on the matter, in regards to our future transformation. They asserted that when the time is right, each of you will know. John discussed this subject in a confused way but we agreed to brush the notion aside till we attain the knowledge and training by means of the Watchers' facility.

Seems fanciful (imaginary), but it is a staunch reality of not being able to see a "second" me and is suchlike, being kept away from your own twin brother. I sought to avert this thought with a reasonable understanding because of the logical clarification from the Watchers, on this issue. They explain the importance of the "substitute self" (counterpart) towards the mission and the devotion to their new respected timeline and the fact that it is of major importance.

Adding and presenting the notion, that I would have taken a completely different path to my life. I agree that I had no intention to achieve what the Watchers have set forth for my counterpart, yet the Watchers showed many mathematical explanations of time, equating that I should fill my personal void within the temporal (time) continuum and strive to attain happiness.

Once John and I meet again, we will learn more, in order to make a decision, of what date we need to undergo the conversion. To then release ourselves and our lives. Do I question the ethical issue that might be at hand? Yes, and I have taken the matter very seriously, but each time I lay down the possible consequence of what could happen, I feel only a positive reaction from the result of what didn't happen.

I lend and offer my sincere spirit to God and beg Him to borrow my heart and replenish it with His Will. I am not pushing a change to a definitive religion, nor should you be told what to believe in. But I hope I can change my fellow man for the better, not with just words but most of all, with my actions. My closest friend, she says on occasion, "A better you is a better me!"

Plainly put: A simple understanding I have is, "When I do well, I feel good. When I do badly, I feel bad. That is my religion! I hope you are smiling. Actually, my family's religion was Baptists and they were avid church going people.

I, on the other hand, was an occasional attendee but I do thoroughly enjoy the readings within the Bible. I do believe the Bible is an historic account with lessons to grow from a spiritual point of view and to resolve contrast between plants and animals and or from water or rocks. A vital commitment I work towards is "honesty." I aim towards this virtue because I think, "One of the very best works of God is an honest man."

I think the Watchers in some regard gave me a systemic and overall view of religion as a seeding necessary amongst the variance cultures throughout the Earth. This left me to internalize my spirituality, promising myself to insure growth and gratitude in my life.

I am alone, lodging in my temporary ten dollar a month room in the main heart of the town, New Salem, Illinois. One step away from being a loafer, I laugh out loud, whilst I am whittling a piece of wood, into an idea I had for assisting grounded boats. Maybe something could come from this idea; I continue to laugh but the happiness from this laughter is a bit unsure.

So I think back to a time when I had a friendly quarrel. It happened seven years ago, with Otto the German Baker, in regards to using the word "loaf." Without thinking I used the word "loaf" to describe a lazy moment on this particular day and because of this, it has taken a toehold to become a word in the dictionary.

The story was I wanted two loafs of bread and he had only one left and mind you, this was not the first time that Otto has a minimum inventory. He was notorious for this in our town. So while holding the last loaf of bread in my hand I complained to him and pointed the loaf, directly towards him and in jest I said, "Please, don't be a loaf tomorrow." The people in the store began to laugh for a long-while.

That was a fond memory. We both laughed because we had just spoken about his property issues from land he still owned in Germany and the word land-loafer was discussed about his land. I did not understand most of the conversation at any rate because of his accent.

The many people in the store that overheard our friendly banter, spread the use of this word and so years later I would hear the term being used on many occasions to describe a lazy person in a family household or sometimes at a work place.

As for my idea for assisting ground boats, I think one day I should patent it. Of course my carving is a miniature scaled down version of the idea, made possible for a usable model just for the sake of illustration.

My thoughts drift, thinking about the population within the New Salem area. It has me worried because many people from the New England territory are settling out west, here in town. In my opinion, the population of eighty people is currently a bit over crowded. Nevertheless, I guess it will keep my survey work going at a strong and steady pace, but more letters to deliver in my Postmaster position, hmm.

I have a cozy room in the back of what I call, "An Everything Store." It sells a variety of things for the home, old and new. I am fond of the easy access that I currently have from behind the store. It gives a private exit and entrance atmosphere, good to be focused, no distractions.

Trying to settle down from a bizarre couple of days, I look at my fireplace, which is more like a hearth with a metal box container with a pipe leading outside. Tomorrow, I have to get an early start to my part time Postmaster job (in the wee hours of the morning) and I am beginning to have a harder time in order to complete my work because of the ever increasing population within the town. Afterwards, I have to rush out to finish my current survey job, which I did not finalize yesterday.

I wake up to a knock, on the inside door, between my room and the store. It is Charles S. Taft who runs the store, asking if he can temporarily keep some antique furniture within the confines of my room. I said, "Sure, as you see fit, because the only thing I have to keep myself company here is this old school desk and my bed. Would I be able to rest some of my belongings on top of the table?" A frown drawn upon Charles' face and so he says, "By all means, it's just remnants from an old barn cleanout from last week; I've been bumping into it, inside the store. Oh and I don't know how long it will be there, but thanks again Abraham." While I brush the tips of my fingers on the surfaces of the tables in appreciation, I respond while covering up my yawn, "Of course and thanks, see you soon."

The next morning arrives without delay. After I am set to go to work, I look in a blurred mirror with one of the corners missing and notice my clothes are a little worn, "Hmm." No worries, I know what to do, but before going, I take a moment and jot down more tidings (information) in my daybook, "so I do not forget." Inside the daybook I also have my logs for the two jobs I am acquainted with. Well, on the wings of "maybe," probably three jobs. Now and then, I transfer the outlines I have conjured from the daybook and post it to my journal.

Any happenings stemming from the Watchers I will record, because it is so intense. I am hopeful in the future, I can publish a complete tome (book), having all the necessary ingredients. For what comes from this historic time change, will have a far-reach of consequences into the future.

The journal I keep under my pillow and the coins for now I hide inside my pillow, between the feathers. I am not afraid that anyone would steal the pillow because it looks squally and ragged, but very comfortable I might add. I will soon separate the coins into various hidden areas within my room, once I rearrange my new furniture this weekend.

The daybook though is the size of my hand and is a rectangular blank book with a black spine with faded red covers. I always leave the daybook tucked in my trousers that I will wear in preparation for the next day, in order not to forget it. Let the day begin.

CHAPTER THREE

THE MEETINGS

Every morning I would exit left out of my room. Onwards to work I would pass an open porch, which was connected to the back of a tavern. This warm wooded portico (porch), attached next-door is one of my favorite places to relax and is just a few paces away from my living quarters. In fact, it is amongst a full row of dwellings, consisting of stores and homes.

Above the tavern is an inn, both owned by a Mr. James Rutledge, who is one the original founders of New Salem. He is married to Mary Rutledge and on occasion I will call her, "Aunt Polly," because of the warm care that she casts towards me and others.

I would sometimes treat myself to a stay at the inn, if when I had a good week or two. I would put certain monies aside, hid beneath my mother's large serving plate. Close at hand, the plate lies, while never used, with four painted stemmed roses atop. God rest her angelic soul. She died when I was nine years old, by ingesting toxic milk from cows that were eating the poisonous plant called "white snake root."

Unfortunately, at the time, Midwestern settlers were unfamiliar with the effects of the plant. I care for this plate and a portrait of my mother, to be dear to my heart and when so, I have enough money to receive a taste of lodging in comfort, I feel faithful that I do so with my mother's blessing. So from time to time, I collect happiness and anticipate a short walk over to the Rutledge Inn, to receive my reduction in price for my usual stay.

I have a certain fondness towards the Rutledge family and with one member in particular; for she brightens my life and there can be no substitute. My life came to a blissful blessed halt a little over a year ago; it was the day between my birthday and Valentines Day. The day my heart became filled and hereafter, resides endlessly with the beatified spirit of Anne Mayes Rutledge.

The first time I had met her; she had just finished knitting and thereafter, was in the midst of draping and tying a curtain to one side of the window. The rocking chair was still in motion with her yarn and needles presiding towards the back of the chair, and I assumed she had just left the chair or used it as her work station. Her voice heard, was as sweet as can be and her presence held to be very handsome.

Many minutes passed, not realizing I was firm in my stance, looking at Anne as if I were watching a theatrical performance. Her arms flowed as if they were lighter than air, aloft beneath her peacock feathered shoulder pads, with every movement she made. The lace at the bottom of her hoop skirt seemed to be dancing with each stride. While her fingers hold the curtain to secure the drape, she promptly wraps the strap to one side; the long pleats become perfectly arranged, after one enchanted swipe of her fingers.

I immediately wakeup from my trance dazed and turn to the mirror that was behind the stacked whiskey bottles and quickly straightened my attire. After I collect myself, I approach Anne Rutledge slowly, not noticing anything or anyone around me. My spirit is uplifted twofold in my move to become oh so near. Afraid, I am looking spookish in my stiff route to her, so I quickly loosen up and replace my tenseness with becoming light-minded and sure-footed.

Meet-Cute: February 13th 1833.

"Greetings, I am admiring your wonderful dressing work for the window." I smile with confidence, thinking; I cannot *misstep*. She smiles back and says, "Oh? Yes, I have just two more left to finish and thank you. My name is Miss Anne Mayes Rutledge, glad to meet you." Her eyes open wide, while she slurs and extends the end of her sentence, along with a motion of an upward look, to "press" for the receipt of my name. I quickly reply, "Abraham." I hesitate briefly, taken by her stunning blue eyes and with a shy delay I release my last name, "Lincoln."

She wittedly responds, "Mr. Lincoln, if you had to choose to describe yourself, what'll it be: Tall, Dark or Handsome?" My mouth moves but no words are spoken; caught by surprise. Quickly thereafter, I give my answer, "Well Miss Rutledge, I choose Tall." Without hesitation she says, "Oh why would that be?" So I slide my heels together with a gentleman's extended posture and answer, "I choose 'Tall' of course good lady, so that my tallness may assist you in your efforts towards the final two window treatments." I hereby draw a smile. She laughs and rewards me with a smile in return.

I would be a very rich man to accumulate more of these expressions of happiness from her and on a daily basis. That would be altogether delightful. "Oh Mr. Lincoln," she responds as her face fills with blush. So I quickly say, "Please, call me Abraham." She turns to grab the handle to her sewing bag and asks, "No middle name Abraham?" I look down sadly at my shoes and shuffle them slowly while my hands become tucked in my pockets and reply softly, "My family could not afford to give me a middle name, too costly at the time." I look up and sneak a funny grin in order to see her reaction. She looks poised and serious for a second and then we both immediately laughed together. After the laughs settle, she states, "Even if you were threadbare and poor, like most people, you are not without wit."

We worked together on the rest of the drapes as if we were a good team for years. I marveled at her fine features and her fair blond curled hair, held within a flowered cloth. Two hours must have past. All the time I restrain myself from complimenting her and asking if she was an angel.

Grateful goodness, she asks another delicate question towards the completion of our work. While in line with previous discussions, she exerts, "Abraham, people define things differently, even though they hear the same word, do you agree? While sweeping the floor below the windows I respond, "Hmm that chiefly depends on the word at hand, but agreed, that most of the time, there would be a difference of interpretation between two people concerning the same word.

Miss Anne that is a very interesting insight in order to deal with people, thank you. If I might add, there are some words chosen that are better than others as well." I smile as I set aside the broom and she says unexpectedly, "Well then, how about the word 'Love' Mr. Abraham Lincoln? How do you interpret or define love?" I gulp but without water and nervously walk four steps slowly towards Anne. With the full pan of material in hand that I had picked up from the floor and while in her full attention I respond, "Love, whether you are threadbare, poor or rich, the defining moment of love is to share one's time with one another and expecting nothing in return, except love." I slowly look at the window we had just finished together, but try hard not to lose eye contact with her, while discarding the trash from the dustpan into the can.

With love in my heart, I look back into her glazed sapphire eyes and bow to her ever so slightly. She looks at the windows and readily glances back to me with nothing to say.

She sighs, and a relaxed smile stayed with her long enough to stretch-out my hand to hers and depart with a gentle goodbye.

I have painted a portrait in my mind of this exact moment and highly anticipate our next meeting, come-what-may. I had made mention of my living quarters being within a stone's throw away, so if there would be a need for any assistance, I'd be much obliged.

Over the next year our relationship was dear and growing with every wakened day. Familiar in our partnership to know we were meant to be together. We agreed that in respect to her previous engagement with a John MacNamar, we would wait for him to release her from any obligation. John MacNamar left for New York, promising to return. His letters to her were becoming shorter and pale, to the point of ceasing completely. He was a dubious character so I hear. Nevertheless, my increased devotion to Anne, dedicates to the confidence for our eventual marrying. In secret we are engaged, for that one night beneath that full lit moon we became forever loyal to our love.

Soon as Anne is respectfully released from her commitment to John MacNamar, I will divulge thy attained facts and missions thereof about the Watchers. In the between time, I have made it a note to arrange some of the conversations amid Anne and me, to be science informative, along with hints of the related topics circling the Watchers.

* * * *

The summer of 1834 is almost here. It is the day after Mr. Kennedy's seventeenth birthday, which indicates the day of our awaited meeting that is to take place. I arrive early to the New Salem cave, which is our stated location to meet. I am with anxiety because of the time settled away from this extraordinary high emotional state. I am anticipating the unknown, even though I was briefed entirely by the Watchers.

It still presents discomfort to plunge into a completely different world of humanity. The harsh reality discovered at this intersection is the furthest notion of any untamed dream that I ever possessed or could imagine.

A sudden wand-whip noise is apparent from within the cave, followed by some scuffling. Appearing into the sunlight is a greeting from John and held in his right-hand is a bag. "How do you do Abraham?" I replied, "Great, and your birthday was?" "It was the best birthday ever Abraham!" I surprisingly said, "Oh?" John is excited and starts to explain but says, "First, I have brought you a surprise; this is a 'hot dog' with a drink beverage called 'cola.' I figured you might be hungry and just to let you know, these are the two most popular foods stuff in America's future." As I receive John's thoughtful gesture of food I say, "Thank you Jack."

We both begin to drink the colas and eat the hot dogs. I announce, "Hot dog is a very funny name for food, yet very good to say the least, mmm tasty and the cola taste sweet, like candy. Thank you kindly for the food Jack." While John is eating he stops and says, "You're welcome," but then he quickly adds, "Oh darn, I forgot the mustard. It is a condiment that we put on the hot dog to give more spice." I mention, "Well, I am feeling a little peppy from the cola, so no worries about that." I toss him a satisfied smile and ask, "Is that a bag made out of paper?" John replies, "Yes, and sometimes we write things on it so we know what's in it." I laugh and say, "That is very smart, I like that."

From the future comes a strange occurrence about this moment with John. My fascination with the paper bag had been passed on to my counterpart in the transfer. In so far as, my other self was campaigning in Pennsylvania and there, he made an acquaintance with an American priest of the Moravian Church. His name was Francis Wolle and he had a slight dilemma. During discussions with my counterpart, Francis Wolle explained, how he wanted to give his parishioners items that could not fit in an envelope. My counterpart quickly made a suggestion about using a paper bag and tried to explain its construction.

So from then on, into the future, Francis Wolle in 1852 invents the paper bag making machine and later on, he and his brother started company called, "Union Paper Bag Machine Company." Soon after, the company generated millions of dollars and was bought and still owned to this day, by a company called, "International Paper." This happening was the only known mishap that occurred within the timeline. Thankfully, it did not bridge time or have any adverse effects on future outcomes. Nonetheless, while getting back to John and my conversation. After the paper bag discussion, his face had a sudden drawn look to it.

John changes the subject while he chews and says, "Abraham, when I went home, when I went home..." I show concern and say, "Yes," expressing for him to continue. John again says, "When I went home my entire house was better and bigger. In fact, the whole neighborhood was improved. I had been living in a town where everyone would survive on the bare minimums, but when I had left you last month and came back home, things have changed dramatically. The people still, were working hard but the despair was lacking thereof."

In deep thought for what I just heard. It has me concerned and so I respond, "The Watchers did mention there would be three major changes as both of our timelines unfold, that's why it is ever so important to follow their instructions, so that we can build on this positive status quo, nor should we veer otherwise." John whispers a "Yes," while nodding in agreement.

I continue to say, "It seems that our decisions to become a part of the missions are predicated on changes within the immediate timeline, hence the differences in your hometown."

"I totally agree" John says. Looking puzzled John states, "It was so strange that nobody knew about the changes accept for me. My sisters were playing in the front yard as if they lived in this house forever.

I didn't question anything and knew, what the Watchers said, was coming true. It was amazing; I went along with it and enjoyed it thoroughly. Thank God it didn't go the opposite way, I'd be living in a log cabin and oh I mean a hut." John stutters while saying, "Oh, oh no, definitely a hut, I meant no offense Abraham." I laugh and pat him on the shoulder and say, "Please, no worries I can vouch for the close quarters and confinement within a log cabin and I am in agreement with you." John then scuffs the ground with the sole of his shoe and explains, "Just a tidbit I notice in my current time, that we sometimes deal with uncomfortable issues or happenings from the past history, by making light of it, with the use of humor. I guess, once mankind overcomes certain obstacles and evolves, it is easy to make fun, out of what use to be a struggle. John bears a serious face and so I mention, "That is very true. I guess throughout time mankind favors more pleasures than pain in order to move forward as a group." My face wears a straight grin because I lost my train of thought and John says, "Can't disagree with you there Abraham." He nods in agreement. So I guess, whatever I said to him made sense.

I move up from my leaned position on the wall and bring John within the opening of the cave into the shade and say with great interest, "Jack, the Watchers suggested strongly to limit our extent of knowledge about future events, because it might detract from the new "you or me." Their ability to choose correctly is paramount when it comes to making important decisions. Meaning, until we are both ready for the identical process separation (in order to create our own counterpart), suggesting, until such time, we should restrict any information regarding the future.

We both concurred and realized, that whatever we know up until the point of separation, we will be passing along to our counterpart. So I concluded, "To keep things safe and moving forward, let us quicken our task and secure the chances of a positive permanent change, but not until we finish our hot dogs."

I smile and hold up the last bite of my hot dog with a spout of honor and say, "My first hot dog," and awkwardly whip the last bite into my mouth. John laughs and says, "I agree, but how can you not be nervous?" I reply solemnly, "I have been nervous for almost two months. I sometimes feel by taking action, the nervousness seems to shed away, but then again, it would be nice to get our lives back to ordinary or an attempt of normal." I mutter a nervous short laugh and John does the same.

We set forth towards the Gateway machine and place our coins face up between the floor markers, knowing we are about to transport to the "Knowledge Study Center" inside the Watchers' facility. Within three seconds, we are absorbed by the Gateway. The sound was unlike when we traveled through time, it was a short, whipping pop noise. I gather because it is merely a location transfer without the use of time.

In the center of the facility is where we land, without any adverse reactions. We both gasp while we bend down to pickup our coins but without looking, because we are startled and stare up at the amazing surroundings. The coins suddenly vibrate in our hands while a stockade of glass displays is presenting many scenery changes, brought forth with our personal information.

The breathtaking facility has supposedly been here for thousands of years and is the size of a square furlong (220 yards). We both read about the framework of the facility, with words that float in the shape of a slow revolving cylinder.

Trying to compose ourselves because of excitement and

amusements we share amongst this happening. After settling down, we separate to different areas of interest within the facility. I am quite intrigued as to what I learned about the structure. The facility is seven stories beneath the Earth and quietly resides as a self functioning environment. The floor is one large area of what appears to be one sleek continuous shiny onyx stone. The ceiling is about four stories high, with a vibrant blue artificial sky, with a cast of soft sunlight evenly throughout the facility.

John and I wander from our areas of interest in a delirious state, very thrilled and unable to speak because of the wonders that encompass us. The walls are made of a glass texture and seem to have a purpose of delivering information by words and scenes.

There are many outcroppings of the walls that jut out for a function. These three narrow rectangular walls are designed to extend out and come forth towards the center of the facility. They are sliced into equidistant sections; an assured marvel of engineering.

We learn that one sectional corridor is for extensive time travel and another is the "Knowledge Study Center." The last section is what John and I are dreading, which is the "Doppelganger" (duplication device) area, and is our last task to be done when we are ready. The final task will be completed, by simply inserting one of our coins into a circular slot. I am not sure if we will forfeit the use of that particular coin, once deposited. At that time, all the imprinted information that we receive today and thereafter will be used to design our duplicate. Mind you, John will choose his own time, till when he is comfortable and I will decide on my individual time, to when I am ready.

I read again, something I know but trying to reinforce my thoughts. To duplicate one's self in every regard, is for the purpose of filling a void in the time and to avoid any chance of creating time riffs in the fabric of space and time. Very interesting, I have notice the words "the fabric of space and time," are quite often used together. Later on, I must inquirer about this.

Currently, the mission for John and I are to live our lives as normal and wait for the appropriate and comfortable time, to "exchange" our lives with our individual counterpart (selves). I am not sure, but I think my transfer (swap) will come seemingly, when my first public appearance for political office is to take place?

For myself, this should be very soon and I will have to sacrifice my daily life and become an outskirt or bystander to it. But I am young and resilient and have been on my own for some time now. This understanding will be from a vantage point of just observation and is quite alright, considering this small sacrifice will save so many. For John, he is younger and will have many more years to spend with his family. His counterpart won't materialize until that needed time. Hold on, I don't want you to think I am giving up Anne, because I'm not!

Still in "wonder" of this advanced building, we stroll to the Doppelganger corridor. I elect to go first and walk into a glass horseshoe enclosure with instructions of simply to stand and wait for one breath. A blurry gelled light passed over my being from head to toe and within one second a click noise sounded, indicating I was finished with my biological reading. So I simply stepped out. It was painless and quick, like nothing happened. John says, "All right Abraham, that wasn't so bad." John follows after me and is quickly complete.

This scan is for precautionary measures, just in case something happens to one of us. God willing nothing will happen. After an initial amount of studies and training are accomplished by John and I, then afterwards, our counterparts can finish the rest of the preparation to their accomplished goals. In greater regards to the process, we can update our scan at anytime and important to do so right before our daily lives are surrendered.

Now that we are scanned into the Watchers' system, the counterparts will be created when the appropriate time does occur. In the future, our new counterparts will be informed and trained further, only if necessary. If additional tasks are needed, it would take place at the Knowledge Study Center, according to their purpose at hand. They will have full knowledge of our complete lives but only up until today or any scans updated thereafter. Furthermore, in accordance to the Watchers, they will both become fully versed to become the Presidents of the United States.

We, on another note are now walking towards the Knowledge Study area and are about to learn the full understanding and purpose to what is the task.

The room is rectangular but there seems to be a pyramid shape field of energy amongst the center of the room. There, a chair lies in the heart of an energy field right below the apex of this small pyramid. I walk gingerly towards the chair and see my personal bio information within a glass panel. I sit reclined slightly, settled into numerous shiny slots within the chair. The slots travel between my head and spine. Suddenly, surrounding my whole body, a rapid light of blue hues and speckled white light flash with one burst. "Whoa, I feel refreshed. No, but yet I feel the same but enlightened. The Watchers have given me an assorted amount of knowledge tailored just for me.

John rushes over to receive his personalized information. They call this process, 'an upload.' The Watchers explained that part of the machine converts photonic particles (magnetic light) to knowledge and is the practice called, "Adapted Philosophy." Supposedly, there is a special "stone' at the heart of the machine. I think they use the stone in order to make a compatible organic transfer of knowledge?

The machine materializes information and targets an area of the brain that is appropriate for absorption and only uses a tiny percent of an individual's brain capacity. This was good news for me because I need all the space I can get.

This is truly amazing. This facility was once used as storage for space faring vehicles long ago and I am not sure by whom though. Incredibly, in one of those rooms is now a time travel area that has a selection local to choose from entire wardrobe collections. The clothes are according to the time period you wish to travel. Basically, you select the clothing for that time period by touching a glass with a displayed collection of clothes. The different varieties of fashion can be customized to my size and shape.

A re-materializer machine accesses various elements related to clothing and constructs what items of clothing you select. This process is called, the "magneto organizer." John calls it, the "neat-o organizer." Somehow, it transfers elements and molecules towards making a replica of your selection. I assume that part of this technology is used by the Doppelganger machine. Today was a good day on behalf of learning, for both of us. I feel ready and prepared to travel to any-time period, but of course there is no need to travel, until I am relocated once my counterpart is created.

It is fascinating that the Watchers have deciphered the universal understanding on how the reality in which we live in is made, block by block. The knowledge explains how there are identifying subatomic particles (TID's) that are connected by frequencies or inter-dimensional invisible strings that tells or programs an atom or element, to what it is supposed to be.

The Watchers possess the technology to alter these signals in order to shift matter itself. Before they are able to perform an alteration, they need to release the original atom from their bond of existence. They do this by unweaving the subatomic particles that are woven to the inter-dimensional spatial fabric, by the means of an apparatus called the "Variable Isostatic Synthesis."

I look as if I've gotten lost in my excitement with this new knowledge, as I apologize to myself in my daybook, laughing. I am so excited to share this information but I hope not to be boring. But I will further my findings on this subject in the future and wish to lend any helpful awareness with the understanding of time and space.

After learning an immense amount of relevant information I stroll to a different section in the study center. John seems to be busy on the other side of the facility. I see optional lesson programs displayed. The different advertisements are for one of self defense. I am going to enjoy this one. During this lesson I selected a physical upgrade in order to perform the complete program. Not sure if I should of done that? On to the next; let us see further down the list: Air Pilot, 'No,' Automobile Driving, Motorcycle Tutorage, 'No, no,' all are of the future which I will not need. Oh wait, 'All about Guns' and 'Wilderness Survival,' yes! Within seconds of my selections I am all the same but with a slightly higher skill set.

John and I complete our desired learning uploads and discuss our next meeting. We decide to connect with each other every six months to update our lives and to bring forth any ideas in pursuit of the mission. We will both continue our studies that we previously were undertaking. For one thing, I was studying law and will continue to do so. John was very interested in psychology and government.

We leave the facility with confidence and quite frankly, we had the opposite feelings before this meeting. The Watchers have made it clear about this important task for both us. Once the mission is in full motion, we are going to select carefully, a future Vice President in my time that is trust worthy to use one of the coins and be a part of our union. To limit risks, the selection for the future vice president will also duplicate himself, in order to support John in the near future and in the many years to come. The fewer people that know about the mission, the less risk we will have.

This special individual will have to possess certain characteristics which will not obscure any of the timelines (before and after). Reason being, is because this person cannot leave his current life and must obey every duty that is commissioned. The Watchers reveal that there are only one or two people that fit the acceptable profile in my current era.

The person that we select will have to devote their entire life to the cause. This will take effect in the future, in order to fully prepare this individual to assist the counterparts in their efforts to acquire the presidency.

This new person doesn't necessarily have to become vice president, just as long as each counterpart is successful to become president. That will be the ultimate priority of this newly selected person. There is a strong possibility though, that the two counterpart presidents will have the same, true person as vice president.

Before I leave the political front, there is something I would like to accomplish. Presently, there is bit of time before I have to leave. I want to attempt one more stab towards a run for political office and then I can hand off my aspirations to my counterpart. There is an election to the Illinois House of Representatives on August 4th of this year. This will be an all out effort on my part to win and would be before I have to set forth. My responsibility is great in the means of reassuring the route of the presidencies goes unscathed. My life soon will be changed but God willing, always moving forward and growing with Anne.

CHAPTER FOUR

A RUN FOR OFFICE

It is in the latter part of the day, close to four o'clock. I head home to get ready to see Anne. I am in a good mood because I am looking forward to our usual Tuesday afternoon stroll. Eager for the evening, I become a bit silly, thinking, what is "o'clock," is it Irish? Maybe it is supposed to be, "Sunup, Top of the morning-to-yah, Mr. Eight Already O'clock. Holding back a laugh, I become swiped with delight, being youthful in my thoughts. Wait, o'clock is just short for, "Of the clock." Laughing, I don't know why but I am writing this down in my daybook.

I plan to take her out across the way to the Trading Post. In the back part of the Post, there is an outdoor eatery area that she would love. It looks out over acres of a vegetable farm and is connected to a cattle ranch trade section. It will be great to watch the sunset.

I make my way over to the Rutledge Inn to meet Anne. Greeted by her father, I present myself and ask him if he would like to join us, because of some good news to share. He says, "It is quite alright young sir, but do tell me the news when you get back." As he walks away he turns back around and asks, "Oh, can you tell Mr. Stevenson that I will be putting in my order by the end of the week." He turns again and strides away towards the back of the tavern and says, "Thank you Abraham." I quickly reply, "Will do, duly noted Mr. Rutledge."

Therein, I hear the sounds of ruffles against the stairs,

it must be Anne. I do not know what is more delightful, the anticipation of being with Anne or insofar to actually be in her presence. I would weight them as equal and declare both of them equally significant.

At the bottom of the steps I await with a smitten face of delight. I bend slightly as Anne arrives and before she can reach the last step, I bow and reach out my hand while she places hers atop of mine and I say, "Greetings good lady." I look down at her delicate hand, embraced therewith a white laced glove and ruffles that are spun around her wrist. She replies with a witty greeting all of her own, "Good afternoon my Abraham." I smile and chuckle quietly.

She sits down while I go to the tavern's bar to fetch a glass of bubbly water for Anne. As I wait for her drink I look over at her and start to realize something endearing. Thinking, wherever she might sit or perhaps touch, seems to become better. For example, when we were at the general store in town, that has yards of material for clothes, Anne touches the fabric in consideration for purchase and yet does not buy. Soon after, the other ladies that are in the store are drawn immediately to the same fabric, which she had just studied. Also, if she is sitting in a chair where there are two identical ones, it seems that when I sit in the one chair she was just in, it feels more comfortable and affectionately agreeable. This sounds a bit off, but there is some energy that is adorably good with Anne, I can assure you that.

Together we walk down Main Street on a cool but tolerable night. The Sun's view is in an admirable descent yet enough to keep a warm flow on this spring evening. A gust of dust spins its way in front of us as we finally reach the Trading Post Eatery. So I quickly open the flaps to my jacket to block any sand that might reach Anne. Excitement brews into laughter from the burst of wind while we stutter step into the front door.

Anne and I pass through the trading area and see wood crates gathered on the floor, stacked to the left of the room. Next, we notice the writings and a sign labeled for rules, times and operation. There are a few goods for sale against the front counter and some on the tables.

I pick up a carved wooden horse and say to her, "Anne, did you not know there is going to be carriages in the future that do not need horses to take you on a journey?" She looks at me with great attention and says in a puzzled way, "And how will they move?" While I put back the small wooden horse atop the counter I carefully reply, "It would move by itself, with the assistance of a machine device that spins parts underneath, in order to make the carriage wheels roll. It is similar to a Potter's Wheel and thereby one has to steer and control the direction of the carriage, just like certain farm equipment." She says with a proud smirk, "So Mr. Abraham Lincoln seems to be quite the inventor, hmm." I smile and motion politely with my arm to indicate that are table is ready and say, "After you."

While en-route to the table I see a cooking pan that is similar to the one used at the Rutledge Inn and reminded me of a funny moment that Anne and I had just a week ago. She was trying to make a point about the political system within New Salem and drew out a heated issue, but because she could not point with her index finger, hence the heavy cooking pan in her delicate hand, she used the metal pan to point at her father and me. I readily said, for her concern and in order to ease her approach, by pointing and saying, "You listen hear Annie Pannie!" This was uncharacteristic of me which did make the moment even funnier. Realizing, how she was flashing the cooking pan around in an aggressive fashion, piled on logs of laughter between the three of us. From this day forward, in order to present an endearing quality to be cute with Anne, I call her Annie Pannie, if and when the occasion arrives. There is one other name I refer to Anne, with a familiar by-name connection; it is Annie M., because of her middle initial to her full name.

I claim not to speak too openly at times. I pause to commit in order to openly say "I love you." The resistance is apparent because of the loss of my mother and many others that I had loved dearly. For this part of my life, to be entrusted to love was the point of no return.

This privy hint of mind, gives me a hesitance towards this expression, because of the possibility of being shattered and unable to recover. My actions though supersede any doubt beyond the result which is "love," thereby a work in progress. But understand, when I do use the word "love" (without being provoked), on those rare occasions, you can trust the sincerity to where I rest it.

Well engaged in conversation with Anne on this outdoor dine to dusk evening, I bring forward the news about my attempt to run for a political office once again. She tells me to be decisive and to follow my passion. This laid rest to another wonderful night with Anne. Grateful for her support I became focused and able to discern between my work life and politics.

With dedication to a hard trail out on the campaign, I came away with a victory, hereto a representative of the Whig party and was elected on August 4th to a seat, with the State Legislature for the Illinois General Assembly. Now, for the first time I would be commissioned from Washington DC, representing the Sangamon County area in its entirety.

I continued my work as the New Salem postmaster but lessened the hours devoted to surveying. This would be a temporary detraction to the work load as a surveyor until I was ready to relinquish my political standing and State Legislature position to my counterpart. Hereafter, I would again join the expansion that currently exists within the work trade of land engineering, but probably away from New Salem.

Even though I feel the Watchers are oceans apart from me and John Kennedy as well; if needed, I am certain their assistance would be prompt. As to my loyalty and dedication to them, support would be equally on demand.

My accomplishments were mounting during the first year of political office and life was growing in all aspects, to be quite satisfied. My new found experience would be considered necessary and be of assistance to my future counterpart. All knowing, that an update to the Doppelganger soon will have to come and my relinquishment of this portion of my life deemed foreseeable. I will serve to the end of my 1836 term, insomuch to begin the exchange before letting go.

The law books I seem to be collecting look to be building a block heap on Mr. Taft's desk. After I grasp the content from within these books, I will keep them readily available, for reference if needed. I am eventually going to become an attorney or should I say, "My other self," thus laughing to myself.

I return back from Washington on Saturday, July 25th to drop my belongings in my room, thinking of the whereabouts of my quill pen. While I search and shuffle the order of my room I hear a knock at the door connected to the store. It is Mr. Taft and with a frown of concern, admits to a sickness that is involving my Anne.

I immediately leave my home through the doors of the store that lead to the street. Flushed, I turn to a quick pace towards the Supply Barn, a storage building for food supplies. More than just a storage supply house because it is the biggest dwelling in the main part of town and connected to the L shaped part of the structure, is an upper floor area selected for treatment of the sick. There are tracks and rows of beds for helping people who are in need of medical attention. The building is owned by the father of my teacher and friend, William Graham, who we called "old man Graham," because nobody called him by his given name, which I am not sure of myself.

I approach the building uncomfortably and hustle to the stairs that will direct me to the treatment vicinity part of the building. Clumsily, I stumble on the first step and brace my hand on the following step and lift off to continue my stride upwards and climb to the top of the steps.

I enter into the room, where the sixth window reflects Anne's position. I greet an unknown lady with a quick but weak salute and pass by two other *not* well people. I lower my tempo to be calm, while Anne lays wrapped straggled amidst some white sheets beneath the last window in the room.

The creaks beneath the wooden floor seem to announce my presence with each step I take. My being becomes instantly drained, as my curiosity builds. Anne sees my approach and with her arms extended, she signals me with excitement. When I am near she says in a syrupy voice, "I don't feel well." I melt with a view to embrace. So while I bend slightly to give her a gentle hug, she says sadly, "I have pain all around my stomach and I feel weak." I ask subtly, while I settle her back onto a yarn pillow, "Has the lady given you anything to make you feel better?" She replies carrying a crackling whimper, "Yes, Miss Ruth Corbett is in search of medical recipes to help with my pain." I respond, "Please Anne rest while I ask her some questions. She nods yes with an adorable face amid her tears of disappointment. As I move away from her I see her frail hands clenching the top of the sheet, while she pulls the linen tighter under her chin.

To see Anne cry at anytime, for whoever is the onlooker becomes a panic stricken event. Her top eyelids become flattened across half of her eyes, unleashing a deluge of tears and her forehead crunches while her top lip disappears. But when the eye lids lift back up, revealing her beautiful blue saddened eyes, an immediate alarm jump starts the observer to find the quickest solution. I have walked into walls and stumbled over furniture in a need to find resolve for Anne, to when she snivels or be it a cry.

Treatment of the sick in this time era is not at all up to par. The following day, Anne seems to have received strength after my visit and so, Mr. Rutledge and I bring her home to rest with instructions. When we arrive at the Inn, I help Anne up to her room. I will never forget what she says, "You really do not know if it's your home until you leave it." I then smiled and kissed her forehead and placed her tenderly in her bed. I had made mention of my return after I finished the rounds at the post office.

Her condition over the next two weeks seemed not to improve but also didn't appear to be worsening. But I assure you; this incident put the scare of awareness in me, that life itself is too short. During these two weeks I had thought a lot about not waiting till the end of my State Legislature term next year and turn over my political life to my counterpart earlier. I need to tend to Anne rather than to squeeze a few last gratifying moments for myself. The inevitability of the switch is to come, so it might as well be now!

I take one of my coins, from a book that was once my father's. It lies hidden beneath a pile of law books and is called, "The Age of Reason," by Thomas Paine. Because of this book I was able to situate the extreme experience with the Watchers and place it into perspective, so it was easier to identify with. All the readings I have absorbed, assists me in my everyday living, this book included, and as well as the decision to take this next step towards transformation. I cannot say this enough, "Reading is the key, to already solved problems."

With a vigorous march I make my way to the Sangamon River cave, telling myself, that I will continue to take care of my postmaster position till I find a replacement and possibly take my surveying profession away from New Salem along with Anne.

Anne and I have waited a long and respectable time for John Macnamar to return, furthering his withdrawal of any letters to Anne. Anne did send a letter to John Macnamar to explain her intentions of breaking off her commitment to him but as she mentioned in that letter, she would like to be honorable and to do so in person.

En route to the Watchers' facility, thinking, when the physical transfer takes place I will have my counterpart live between Washington and Springfield because of his elected official duties and I will live, where our lives do not intersect.

To make sure we will not be distinguished as the same person, my counterpart, of who is to become president, will wear a beard without a mustache and I will be with a mustache or cleaned shaved. This, in order to not be identified as each other …

Soon after, I carefully enter the cave and make way to the duplication device (Doppelganger) area to update my scan, but before I do so, I finish the learned study programs the Watchers needed me to upload, before the final transfer. Within seconds I have a full extent of law and other psychological knowledge within my mind. I shake my head in disbelief on many levels, along with a cheerless quiet laughter as I approach the Doppelganger with my one coin for my final scan.

❋❋❋❋

It is Tuesday afternoon, August 25th clear blue skies, not a cloud to be seen. I walk towards Anne's room and hear a commotion between her brother and sisters. Mr. Rutledge says, "Anne is suddenly running a very high fever and a rash is now evident from around her neck. We think she should be taken back to the "treatment area" at Graham's Supply Barn." Mr. Rutledge's right arm is trembling. He continues, "Nothing seems to be working here and maybe Ruth Corbett who is highly regarded, can administer something and quick!"

I announce to Anne's brother, "Go and get a carriage ready in front and I will carry her downstairs to it." Mr. Rutledge says that he will bring her belongings and states to the others, to stay here.

We rush into the carriage as I hold a wet cloth to her head. Her body lays wilt across my lap. A single tear silently rolls from her right eye as she is unable to talk. Her precious body bounces relaxed to the trot of the horse, hauling the cart.

We arrive a short distance from the Supply Barn and suddenly halted because of ongoing work. I act quickly because of the hurdle in front of us. Without hesitation I lift up Anne softly, coddled with my right arm bent and with my left hand I support her head and carry her firmly across my chest. Her legs dangle below the wrapped linen as I hurry. With a brisk walk I weave in and out of obstacles to finally reach the bottom of the steps, thereby, near the entrance of the treatment location. I leap two steps in time while Anne is sifting through our ascent to the building.

I timed the open door to pass through; while at the same moment a gentleman holds the door as he exits the building. Without delay, Ruth Corbett directs me to the same previous location, from when Anne was last here. I approach near to the sixth window, feeling half shuttered and see a reflection of her now awaited relieve.

Anne's father, Mr. Rutledge comes into the room, while I settle her pale unwell body down without any sudden movement. Above the sheets of the bed, she drifts backwards within her bowed pillow to leave go of her valor, while her legs and heels sweep against the sheets. The sound of this stings my spirit. My opaque eyes crease close as my breath waits for my sight to reassemble the room. My heart aches to witness my Anne in such distraught.

Ruth comes over with supplies then delivers a concern and says to both myself and Mr. Rutledge, "I am so sorry, it is not safe for both of you to be close or next to Anne, she has Typhoid and her fever is growing. Miss Corbett soaks a sheet in cool water and covers her entire body in order to bring her temperature down.

As we stand a slight distance away from the bed, we both stare at Anne in a state of disbelief. Miss Corbett grabs a dry cloth and begins to let it bathe within the water basin. She then opens the window slightly, not to stir the air but for a hint of freshness.

I step forward and grab the wet cloth from the basin and say, "Please, it is late, I will stay here by her side, there is no place I would rather be. Please, you can relieve me tomorrow, it is quite alright." Followed by my statement I attempt a stern smile but the sadness behind the smile amounted to just a grin. All the while I place the cool cloth atop of Anne's forehead and gently brush the cloth into her hair. Both, Mr. Rutledge and Ruth leave at dusk along with a young gentleman whose injuries were attended for earlier.

I am now alone with Anne in this large room, along with many empty beds, still and quiet, when suddenly the room becomes oh so much smaller. I look so hard I can no longer hear; is what I see real? Something that is so pure and right should not perish and is a conflict between youth and purpose. I pound my chest. My heart hinders my ability to talk.

I see a glimmer from the moon that invites its way to her window. Two candles burn bright at either end of her bed. The one closest to the window flickers with every breath she provides. I bow to rest me head beneath her shoulder, to hide my tears from her. Her arm comes from under the sheet as she attempts to put her hand on the back of my neck, I bend closer.

I dare to look up and see her burdened eyes barley open, while a peek of dim light is reflected back from the candle flame. I reach back around to hold and share my hand with hers, which is rested at the back of my neck. Her hand falls slowly and weakens, so I hold and support her arm, in front with me by her side.

Fear shouts deep into my soul! No! I see her tiny chin shake, so I grab her perfect hand and hold it so dearly and place her fingers to my lips and cry, "Oh dear God, mother help us, angelic mother help me, please ask God to cometh thy graces? If You can dear Lord, create, to take a miracle out of nowhere!

Her eyes open as she turns to lift her head so slight, to hint for me to look towards the window. So I place the palm of my hand kindly to support the back of her head. As I look up at the window I see our *full lit moon* staring down upon us, perfectly posed suchlike a mystical portrait. Anne's selflessness, while in her fragile condition, expresses to remind me of our pledge of that exceptional moonlit night, the night we dedicated our devotion to each other, our "union of loyalty and love." While I think back to this joyous occasion I smile through tears of hope as I still stare up at the moon and feel the presence of God all around us. While in consideration, this could be the miracle I prayed for, so I look back at Anne to share my smile with her, to discover, "She is with God," in rest, in peace.

My body, mind and spirit become paralyzed, following a single absorbed frightened emotion. To let go of my love is impossible, yet to be grateful for every second in time I had with her, gives me the strength to breathe.

The luminance of the moon hovers over her body like an angel spirit ready to go to heaven. Her calm face shines to a peaceful wonder. I have to leave go of my hand that bears support of her head. With a clash of restraint and agony I eventually yield to rest her head within the limits of this pillow. I reach over to relax my hand to her hair and lightly kiss her forehead to say good-bye, "Forever, I will love you Anne."

Dedication
In my future findings I came across this lovely song:
Lyrics for Annie's Song

Come let me love you
Let me give my life to you
Let me drown in your laughter
Let me die in your arms

Let me lay down beside you
Let me always be with you
Come let me love you,
Come love me again

Written by my friend John Denver

I step back in shock and realize she is really gone. My mind filled with woes and is adrift while the moonlit night is obligated to be replaced by the awakening glare from the all attending Sun. My breath becomes erratic and my heart pains to beat. I fear the goodness and the pieces of my heart will forever be buried with Anne. For any recovery will strain my ability to ever love again.

I am weary to what happens in the near moment. Blurred, I think Miss Ruth Corbett attempted to console me. I wonder aimlessly out of the treatment facility into an area besides the backend of a building. I collapse in of a corner under an overhang next to a woodpile. This work spot seems to employ the usage of splitting wood in order to supply the local stores with energy for heat and cooking. The axe leans dormant in the corner and the grounds are layered with grime.

Trapped in my despair, my body limps over the stacked logs that are not split. I dig deep in my mind to handle myself and become deeper crazed with no reason or answer. My breaths are shallow while I gaze in sorrow upon the large axe. Right alongside the woodpile, the axe remains still, in order to taunt me.

In the center of this work area, there is a big log lying flat on the ground, with a smaller log atop of it and was purposely left here at the end of yesterday's workday. This is a method I use as well. It indicates your presence of returning soon to continue your work. I stare with concern at the victimless log that rests still and waiting to be split. Is there anything I can do? I feel suffocated by these trapped and hopeless feelings.

With a flurry of vision I look back to the axe, then back to the log and getup with a fury of rebel. I lunge towards the axe, grab it, then swiftly spin it and slide it in my hands while at an eventual height above my head. With all in one motion I sweep the air as the axe sizzles. I cry out a roar filled with grief. Exploding and shooting out on either side, the log is chopped in two, along with breaking in half the larger log beneath. Each piece of the larger log sluggishly falls in slow motion to the soil.

The axe lies lodged into the dirt while my knees tap to the ground. A single tear lands in the dust, while I look over at a can of ashes that just fell on its side, as a result of a piece of wood that flew after I split the wood. The ringing from the can lingers in my mind and then all that remains is silence.

Suddenly, there is a whistle from a bird, which has just landed on a horse out in front of the buildings. It almost seemed like a calling. Suddenly, my interest peaks. It reminds me of a young reddish brown horse I purchased, named Robin, from Old-Man Graham's Supply Barn. I call him Bob, a better suited name for the young lad. I have the horse corralled in front of the "Everything Store," alongside two other maidens. I need to go; I have to do something, time?

Overwhelmed, I make my way through the town, ignoring everything and everyone. I get home to my room and retrieve a coin from within the Thomas Paine book. I turn to look at the book and say, "You were right Thomas Paine, hmm how did you know?" I shake my head and put the book back down. The one remaining coin is still secretly hidden inside the room.

In a rush, I scatter the other books over the top of the Thomas Paine book from my cluttered desk. Ready to leave with a small leather pouch attached and strung to my shoulder. Overly cautious, I reverse my course quickly and run back to stack the books neatly from my cluttered desk. Thinking, if someone were to come in, they might arrange my books in order to keep them tidy and possibly find the remaining coin.

There is Bob with his driving harness attached. Under his saddle is a blanket that I stare at during my approach. The blanket was made by Anne and gifted to me the day I purchased Robin (Bob). Strange, when I was face to face with Bob today, he greeted me with a familiar understanding. I patted him twice and unfasten the reins to a quick mount.

My transport was to a gallop with a bounding gate and thereafter, Bob gifted my destination in a short time. I arrive to the cave along the Sangamon River in a perfect spot for Bob to graze and drink while he is held fastened in my absence. I brace the palm of my hand on the cantle of the saddle and spin my body to dismount the horse in one complete motion. Bob jerks back a bit when my heels smack the ground, so I settle him securely and give a departing thank you. No worries about Bob the horse, because it will only seem like a few minutes for him, to when I get back from my natural timeline.

In fact, in order to reemerge in your proper timeline, you have to reverse the time from which you left, exactly. This is so, because "time" does not have a conscience and overlapping time will cause entanglement amongst your future or past selves, depending to where your travels are destined and if you are not synched, then you will have a subtraction of energy that is shared with your other self, from within a different time period and therefore, becomes further entangled.

I stumble and step into the cave with my emotions

building. Knelt on one knee I arrive into the facility, lost in all my causes. I walk gingerly over to the study and historic time section, to touch the glass screens. I punch in the word Annie and some type of lyrics for a song appears.

I surrender and lean for support against the wall. I bow my head down towards the floor with my eyes shut and try to untie my heart and pray. I cannot ask what I need because every time I do, my throat seizes. Tears mount while my hand slides and screeches in descent against the glass. I slowly collapse to the ground, legs folded. Fluids drip from my mouth and eyes, while a pang of pressure from within my head forces me to grumble and moan. I start to talk and mumble to Anne and tell her how much I miss her.

Suddenly, a soft white light fills the entire room. In a flash, the white light is gone, while my attention seeks for reason. There is an overall silence accept for a resounding pitch noise coming from the glass screens.

From this point, my state of mind is of hope, to which I would love to insert into the middle of my name. I come to stand and read a list of reactions given by the Watchers. I clean my eyes with my sleeve and see a list of articles, of what I call, "Articles of Faith." It is not only a list, but a sort of map with instructions for me, coupled with declarations and understandings.

I hurry to read the words clustered upon the screen. Is this possible and how? I can do this and devote such great effort! The declarations are finite and direct, stating if all is followed, "You are not permitted to reside in the current time period because of time infractions to the continuum and added side effects of current day outcomes."

I can rescue Anne without harm to anybody, but the action must be transacted within a 48 hour window! To have and understand, that her and I will permanently live in the future. I am to visit the past but only in the capacity to be alone and on occasion, with precaution in order to perform my original overseer position.

The Watchers give details on how time can be altered from a recent occurrence, if the action is completed within forty eight hours. Mainly, the separation of time after a person's demise lingers and still has its biological imprint that can be re-fused back together up until the 48th hour.

The Watchers call it the "Lazarus Effect" and is needed time to time to benefit a particular timeline. It seems that the time traveler (me), who attempts to change a happening in time, has to be careful (unimpeded) not to occupy the same space with your own self for more than a few minutes. According to the Watchers, the time traveler will then start to lose his energy to coexist.

The act to coexist is necessary and a definite risk that must take place, because in order for the "time change" to work in this capacity (Lazarus Effect), then both *selves* must be on the same wavelength, in a type of agreement or contract and thereafter, activated with a handshake or any other related contact. This will engage the time slip into the new desired need. Therefore, correcting time for a more favorable outcome. This rule of engagement gives me only a short amount of time to convince my old self to save Anne.

Glad for a chance, I have my "article list" of items to accomplish for the ultimate task at hand. I make my way to the wardrobe simulator, in need of clothes pertaining to October, 1984. There, I will find a medication called, "Amoxicillin." By following the article list, these pills or tablets will cure Anne, but only if I administer them to her within those couple of days before the worst happens.

Hmm, I am trying to figure out what to wear, from the assorted wardrobe selection screen. There is a black tee-shirt, interesting, a tee-shirt? Dungarees blue, ah sneakers? Thinking they are probably used to do quiet things. I need a jacket? This is strange, a red leather jacket with metal teeth for pockets? Okay my selection is complete. I am set, ready and excited to engage the simulator. Next, I produce my full attire ensemble within a minute. The process is complete and so I will get clothed. Fully dressed, I look at a reflection of myself with a slight hesitation, herewith my appearance and I am in question. Okay?

CHAPTER FIVE

MISSION LIST

Banking that time is on my side and re-energized with hope, I focus on the opportunity at hand. I have with me, my gateway coin and three $5 gold pieces, which should be more than enough for my monetary affairs.

I immediately approach the Gateway dressed in my 1984 clothes and I am about to select the travel period on the calendar. Not sure what area or location to select but all the cities will have what I need. Let's see, how about New York? Any city in New York is crowded and will be less difficult to find the medication.

I make my selection and press go, while nervously contemplating the future of what I am going to see. Instantly, I arrive in a cave alongside a river in Hudson Valley, New York. It is October, 1984 and it appears to be rural, hmm. Wait, as I turn around there seems to be an enormous amount of commotion in close proximity, apparently towards the horizon outlook.

I am reluctant to walk towards the noise, but I have to, so I make way with drive in my step. I have learned about cars and buses, but never saw them in their splendor. I become near to a black hardened road with slanted white lines and gulp. I am stunned by the complexity of the area. The buildings are oh so fantastic. It is fascinating, that through this environmental congestion, there seems to be an organized web and function.

There is what is called a "bus stop" and that is where I

need to be. Nearby, I see a bus tied up on the road, picking up over a dozen or so people. The display name on the side of the bus says "Terminator" travel through time. While the bus steers away I see more writing that indicates the words, "Avoid extinction Arnold something or other?" If I didn't know any better I would choose or prefer to use this terminator bus to travel back through time, very luxurious.

After a few more steps, I figure that it is possibly a theatrical performance sign. Oh goodness, I hope it has nothing to do with the Watchers. I snicker the words, "No of course not," but the picture displayed did give me a fright, to say the least.

I am relieved when I see a bus that has a smaller display sign that reads, "To New York City." I am at the intersection of 30th Street and 10th Avenue. I look carefully through the congestion and imagine that these cars can hurt a man equally to a horse and carriage. So I mimic the crowd and take a stride quickly to the line of people entering the bus. I am excited as I step-up towards the "bus driver." Everyone is using a picture or paying money to a machine in order to board.

I see a very large rotund Negro at the helm of the bus. He is checking and giving the approval to receive a seat. The people are moving at such a fast pace. I say to him, "Hello good sir, I am admiring your uniform," while I reach into my pocket and produce a $5 gold piece. He laughs and quickly says, "Are you kidding me, we don't accept gold on buses." I ask, "So this is unacceptable for my fare?" He laughs even harder and says, "Listen man, I'm going to let you on for free this one time, because you look like Abe Lincoln and you're wearing a Michael Jackson leather jacket." He gets more excited and combines his laughter with talking, and furthers, "These are two people I love, so get moving and go ahead;

there is room on the back left. His thumb points to the rear of the bus, so I smile and say, "Thank you."

As the busman collects his last fare, he starts to drive away while I stand and reach for an upper metal support bar to keep my balance before I receive an unoccupied spot. Hmm, standing, I smell something like black soot when the busman shouts back and says, "Hey Abraham Michael Jackson, if you want to get cash for gold, there is a place at the first stop in Manhattan, okay? I lean closer to him and reply, "Is that still the same as New York City?" The people closest to me start laughing very hard and so is the busman. I feel out of place waiting for his reply and so he says, "Yes sir, Abe, Manhattan is still New York City and are one and the same."

His laughter eases while he shakes his head side to side, when all of a sudden an Oriental child takes a portrait of me with a tiny camera. I look back up and out the windows and notice the development of over the past 150 years throughout the area. Unexpectedly, I see a space open up within the confines of the bus and slip further to the rear. Some odd fellows are amused with me, while they stare and talk to each other.

I feel the sway of the bus, which makes me comfortable because of the similar rhythm of a horses trot. I take out a likeness portrait of Anne from the back pocket of my dungarees and feel her presence.

Amazed at the speed we are traveling through this shimmering future city. I notice a rough blond haired gentleman with ink tattoos covered throughout his body. He is next to his Negro friend who appears to be much younger, but all the while he is gawking at me, so I say to them, "Do you think we will be in New York City by sunset?" One of the chaps smirks and looks at his friend, then looks back to me and says, "Come on homeboy, it's only ten minutes away." His face becomes disfigured and then releases a chortle, "Hmm."

After a few minutes I exit off the back of the bus as the busman waves into his drivers mirror to say good-bye. I respond with a "Thanks again" and wave, while the men who talked to me, follow behind. Somewhat confused, I stand on the road corner, looking in what direction I should proceed with. The two chaps approach me and ask to follow them; they know where I can get cash for my coins. So I reply with caution and say, "Where about would that be?" Their arms motion for me to come towards them and one of them says, "Over here." They are taking me off the road between and towards two buildings. I stop heading-in and say, "Thank you kindly, but I believe I will search along the main road."

As I turn to leave. The young blond tattooed man steps in front of me to distract my path and aggressively shouts at me while he draws a metal object and says, "Give me the gold!" I think it is some sort of weapon clenched in his hand. I suspect a knife or future weapon. His Negro friend looks nervous but with hope in his eyes. I look down at the object in his hand and then look back at him and announce, "I say lad, that would be stealing and therefore, it would be altogether fitting for me to injure your carcass and worse yet, there is a possibility I might render you unconscious." His face turns red and attempts to strike me. I easily catch his right fist and bury it in the palm of my grip, applying pressure to his hand. He belches a howl and complains that I have retard superman strength or something of the sort. He screams out loud, "Let me go, let me go!" I quickly lift the lad up over my head, to dispose of him in a large metal garbage container with one bag beneath him, to help his spill. I close the lid of this receptacle and announce to him not to come out till sunset.

I turn around to the other young man and he says, "It was his idea." I said with great concern, "Young lad, being with this individual can lead you down a path to the point of no return! Now, take me to your mother!" He looks confused and replies with slurring the word, "What?" I then speak with a stern voice, "Now, Immediately!"

I pick up the metal weapon from the floor and the young man says, "Press the middle button it's just a switchblade comb for your hair, not a knife, I swear!" I look at the piece with inquisitive eyes and touch the button. Out snaps a black comb hidden within this tiny metal bar. The young man says, "See it's not a knife sir! Are you really Abe Lincoln?" I respond, "Yes, but worse for you, because I am the younger version of him!" So I noticed and say, "Your eyes are looking in this direction; I assume that is where your mother is? "Yes," he says sadly. I reply, "Let us go and forever change the direction of your life." Thinking to myself, "I am surprise the young man did not try to run away." This might be his way of reaching out for help I gather.

We arrive at the mother's place of work. She is a waitress at an eatery called "Diner." The young man tracks his mother and asks her to come with him. She says, "This better be important, I've got customers." She walks towards me, but does not acknowledge my presence, while I wait standing in the hallway of the eatery.

The young man tells his mother, "I was just watching Brian; I wasn't going to do anything!" The mother replies, "What are you talking about? Who is this man?" "It's young Abe Lincoln!" The young man replies. The mother says, "Quiet Eric is this some type of monkey business you are pulling, I am in the middle of work right now!"

Suddenly, the mother is taken back while she looks at me and says, "Lordy-Lord, what do we have here?" I introduce myself, "Hello ma'am, my name is Abraham Lincoln and…" She interrupts me and asks, "What were you doing, a Thriller video with Michael Jackson?" I don't know why you're here but you're comin off a little creepy, young Abraham; if you know what I mean. Mm-hmm, Eric, you sure do know how to pick-em!"

She smiles and laughs, then quickly says, "So what seems to be the problem? "Well ma'am, it seems that Eric would like to change his life and no longer associate with an acquaintance called Brian. Isn't that true Eric?" The mother becomes disturbed and says, "Oh gee, what did Brian do this time," the mother asks. I respond, "Brian wanted to steal one of my 1833 Half Eagle $5 dollar gold pieces," Eric's mother cups her hand over her mouth and says, "Oh my, oh my," as she shakes her head. I then proceed to tell her that I need to get going, but I begin to say, "I wish Eric's father was here." She blurts out, "Eric's father is not around. I'm a single mom this month, doing it all." At this point, she looks fiercely at Eric. I then suggest to Eric to choose a positive role model in his life, to help keep his focus positive. He mentions the name "Red Foxx," as his choice. I smiled and said okay. Before I departed I reinforced my lesson by inspiring a high emotion level for the two of them.

While in the process of leaving I say. "I wish you then "logs of luck" and oh, I have three of these coins and I only need one to pursue my quest. So if you would like to accept one, ma'am?" I extend my reach and place it onto her hand. "My studies have estimated the coin to be worth over one hundred thousand dollars, if this would be at all helpful to you and your son; of course being, that if Eric is going to take his new path towards a bright new future? She stays silently stunned and walks away starring at the coin, meandering down the hallway.

As I walk away, Eric races down the hallway to his mom and I hear them say, "Oh my God, do you think he is really Abe Lincoln?" I then hear screams of joy coming from within the eatery. I learn thereafter, the young man becomes a well known actor, using the name of his role model (Red Foxx), hereby calling himself, "Jamie Foxx."

Next, I am en route to trade one of my gold pieces in for cash. I enter a store called "Cash for Gold" and a gentleman tells me he only has twelve thousand dollars in his safe. I told him to just give me one thousand, so you have enough money for the rest of your day. I have more than enough to make the purchase that I need. He says, "But the coin is worth over a hundred thousand or more!" I respond, "That's quite alright; you were very helpful, live well and stay prosperous good sir." He says, while I walk out, "Hey, don't I know you?" His voice dissipates as I wave my right arm exiting the store, while my back turns towards him, saying, "Yes you do."

I quickly ask and find a store with prepared medicines; it is called Gower's Pharmacy store. Once entering the store I have a bit of a problem when asking for the Amoxicillin pills. The store-man mentions that I need a script or some sort of letter from a doctor.

While in the confusion of the conversation, a gentleman from behind me taps my shoulder and says to me, "Wow, you are the splitting image of Abraham Lincoln!" I said, "Yes, we are closely related, my grandfather worked and grew up not too far from the heart of Imlaystown, New Jersey" He then takes out a paper slip and asks me to what is the ailment. He hands the slip to the store-man to fill my request. To my surprise the costs were nominal. I have decided to be "as-like" a normal customer, not to create suspicion.

The store-man hands me back change from the one hundred dollar bill I had given him. While I look down at the receipt and the change, I notice a barrage of presidents on the cover of the paper money and coins. I see George Washington on a one dollar bill and a quarter as well and subsequently, Andrew Jackson on a twenty dollar bill. I suddenly freeze in place and look down at a five dollar bill, to see an older picture of myself. Shocked, I have a moment from within my thoughts.

Hereafter, I see the exact duplicate of the thinner penny coin, similar to my Gateway coin but much smaller. From this point, I have learned that my counterpart has had a significant effect and impact on the United States. Truth be told, I felt a bit of proud.

Hidden amongst the herds of people, I gather myself and head back to the cave in Hudson Valley, New York. I receive a distraction, when I see a theatre release of this "Terminator" time travel drama performance. I am curious to understand, where the mindset lies in this current time period, on this oh familiar subject. Wondering if this performance has anything to do with the Watchers or will it be helpful in my quest?

So I weave out of the crowd to an odd glass booth and ask a young lady about viewing the performance. She explains that the "movie" is already started and is ending soon. I replied, "That is quite alright, I am here for a short time, so I would be willing to pay for a small segment of the drama. She says, "Drama?" Her eyes looked up at me and started to flicker while she sucks in her mouth to make a sound. She then says, "That will be $4.36 and flaps over her hand while looking elsewhere. I proceed to give her one of my Lincoln bills and say, "You may keep the remaining balance." Her eyes then roll beneath her eyelids while her mouth continues to chew a sort of tobacco and begrudgingly, the young lady bouts out a, "Gee thanks," as she motions her arm for me to go through the adjacent doors.

Fascinated by the girl's personality I make way in-through the doors and suddenly blasted by music, sounds and noises. While reaching for the arm of a seat in this large dimmed room, I give up because I cannot seem to keep my eyes off of the huge moving portrait display. I am still frozen; standing in shock, while my heart is battling the excitement. It is a much bigger display, than the others I have seen inside the Watchers' facility. I hear a whisper, commanding me, "Sit down." I turn back from where the voice was and deliver a short, "I apologize," and then stumble into a seat.

My heart continues to race while I try to calm myself from the overwhelming action in the movie. I see a human machine skeleton emerge out of a burning large carrier vehicle, chasing a scared couple. The man is slightly injured as they run into a work mill of some sort. I immediately wanted this couple to succeed in their escape and so they did, but unfortunately the gentleman dies, as so does the killing machine (Terminator) or not. The never dying half surviving machine reassembles its motive and continues to pursue the young nervous lady.

I do not want to ruin the possibility of you seeing the drama, so I will not release the ending to you. But I did thoroughly enjoy how the actress terminates the murder machine, quite real! While leaving the movie theater, there were smiles upon everyone's face, including my own.

Back to reality as the doors open to the outside street. My eyes need to be adjusted to the sunny day. So I carefully walk just a few feet and felt a bit bored after all the excitement from within the theater, yearning to see more at another time. Could life really be that exciting? I should not have to tell you, how grateful you should be to live in this era, so I won't.

Onward back to the cave, I anticipate to arrive at the Watcher's facility to drop off my dressing attire and money that I acquired from this era. I am extremely satisfied that I possess the one most important item in my hand. A must cure for Anne to avoid anymore suffering. With time on my side, I will return to a perfect point between the required moments in order to help; and God willing, to save Anne.

C H A P T E R   S I X

ALTERING TIME

Back at the facility I dress back into my Sunday best and grab my lapel with a snap and a stretch. My demeanor has to be a positive one, for I am about to head out and go save Anne. I am now in the past from a couple of days earlier, looking at my reflection, thus gathering myself in order to be settled. Knowing, I have to be strategic not to run into myself but introduce myself without creating a shock to my past self, if that makes sense? I do remember where I was and at what time, so there should be no issues. I also have to figure out, how to avoid the Rutledge family members, once engaged inside the Rutledge Inn.

My emotions fill my spirit with anticipation. Trying so hard to stay optimistic but I do know there is no guarantee. I can't shake away the fear, so I slowly walk to the display knowledge area and hesitate with concern. Thoughts of doubt consume me, because if something goes wrong and I was unsuccessful to cure Anne, it would be my last chance. So I bend to one knee and feed my heart with prayer in order to receive graces from the Almighty. "Please, oh dear God, give me the strength and knowhow to make her whole again."

In this moment, there is a scene in my mind from the future that somehow flows through my spirit and furthers the truth to this moment; while I see myself knelt from a distance in prayer for Anne. Drawn to this ballad in the Watchers facility, I feel some sort of significance behind it; to not lose Anne ever again. Onward I go, inspired while I recite this tune in my head, over and over to distract my nervousness because I know; I cannot lapse in my efforts:

Though she's already flown so far beyond my reach

She's never out of sight

Now I know she'll never leave me

Even as she fades from view

She will still inspire me

Be a part of everything I do

I'll think of all that might have been

Waiting here for evermore

A gift from the future is in my hands. I now ponder when to act and select the time of the day, which would be best to be with Anne. I have but little choice, because the earliest time I can go would be within a small gap of opportunity. Knowing the schedule of my other self, the time to act would be the night before Anne becomes deeply ill. This will be at the Rutledge Inn and I must trust myself. However, I must figure away to lead the other family members away from Anne's room in order to be alone in a private setting.

The sooner I get to Anne, the greater chance of the medicine working. So I begin an immediate departure from within the cave, because I have decided when to arrive at the Rutledge Inn.

I forgot and realize that Bob the horse is not here for me

outside the cave. Reason being he is still secured and waiting for me, from where I left him; in the future (my current natural timeline).

Ironically, I was carrying my shoes when I was leaving the cave and still had on the one thing from my 1984 outfit. Yes, I am still wearing the very comfortable and flexible sneakers from 1984. They were classified under a future sport called basketball. Hopefully, I will be back here very soon. Let me hide my shoes within the cave for now.

I look out over the vast dry land ahead and take a deep breath with my fists ready and tight. I race off to town while my basketball sneakers are now tearing up the soil, on pace in a dash. I try to arrive steady at the Rutledge Inn, herewith to recapture my breath. All knowing that I am inside (the old me from the past), upstairs in Anne's room at this exact instant; I creek open the entrance door to look and see only Anne's sister at the top of the stairs. To think fast, I mumble masked words up towards the stairs to her sister as if someone is in the lobby of the Inn and in need of some assistance. The lobby is empty but there are a few couples near the bar, towards the back part of the Inn's tavern.

Anne's sister comes down the stairs with her attention focused on the lobby as I am hidden from her sight. I am in a leaned position off balanced behind the door of the coat closet, supporting my awkward stance with my arm. Peeking through the door I see her wander aimlessly asking aloud, "How can I help?" She continues to search towards the back of the Inn's tavern, away from the stairs.

I quickly use the opportunity to quietly climb the set of steps but as I approach the last step before the hallway, I pause to think about seeing myself and myself reacting to me. My mind is racing at the same pace as my heart. I must and will be convincing. I cannot think anymore about this, I must open the door and proceed, "Go!"

My previous fears all of a sudden went away, by the thought of getting caught. It is my time to act with full command and do what I do best. This thought is my cue and supplies the motivation for me to enter. I swing open the door and slowly close the door behind me without sound.

There I am, seeing myself sitting in a chair alongside Anne's bed. Anne is at rest and asleep but as the old me or should I say the younger me; he emerges from a hunched over pose and then suddenly straightens his posture with eyes wide open. He says, "Good God, have the Watchers sent you to me? You are my duplicate?" Before I speak I see Anne alive again, asleep. I have to put aside any emotions in order to carry out the given instructions. For I must then "see-through" to convince my other self or I will never see Anne again.

I kneel in front of myself and say, "I am not the duplicate but 'you' from approximately a couple of days from now. I do not have the luxury of time, nor can the others downstairs, beware of my presence." He tells me to, "Please, have a seat," while his arm motions towards a chair at the foot of the bed.

After moving the chair closer, I sit and begin to say, "In my hands is a precious gift, allowed by the Watchers, which I received in order to save Anne. I say this with accuracy and with all legitimacy. Please take my written instructions and administer this medicine as prescribed"

My eyes are glazed over with all sincerity and to a submissive plead, while I place the bottle of medication and the note, with the directions atop the table in ordinary sight.

I hide my hands that are shaking, thus making eye contact and continue to say, "If done, there is a very strong chance, Anne will be saved, but I say to you, without it, she will perish." He looks back at me with great concern and says, "I trust you and I am without doubt but how or what happens to you from this moment on?" I then turn to Anne and can't help myself but to become distracted for a second, while I glimpse a single beautiful breath from her. This one second gave me such great hope. I look back to him and respond, "Forgive my attention, but in accordance to the Watchers, there is a two day memory imprint from within time, that can be changed. They call it the, 'Memorial Indentations' and are limbo or indeterminate states that can be altered within a 48 hour occurrence, in the matter of life and death. Which you and I have fewer than that amount to save Anne..."

I look at him and raise my brows to signal and emphasize the importance, *of now*. I further my explanation as he is eager to listen, "It seems the rearrangement or time reshuffling is spurred and activated by the two of us just shaking each other's hands in a union to consent. Supposedly, there is a time metamorphous that takes place involving minuscule (small) quantities of variations from within the time continuum. The Watchers say it is the realm of creation for "mercy adjustments" to those who have the graces to do so.

We both confirm the instructions one last time and agreed to act with confidence and put aside any worries of what if. With Anne in focus, we stare at each other with self-assurance and hope. Our right-hands glide into a handshake with our left hands to follow over the top of our forearms and simultaneously, we grasp each other's wrist for a sturdy launch into the unknown.

Suddenly, vibrations are all around us! We hear someone coming up the stairs as we look towards the door. A light begins to swallow us with surround sounds of ascending tones. A vapor of shinning light reflects back inward to dissolve this moment. Seemingly, my spirit is being absorbed magnetically and drawn or pulled to a destination, while recent memories are manifesting in my thoughts.

Right before the sound stops, I see or feel a mirror image of myself, adjoined and blended into a sitting position, onto the chair, where my other self was just in and then immediately I am released or separated, thus to be passed through and or funneled to the unknown. The next instant, I am at the table on the back porch of the Rutledge Inn and Bob the horse is roped onto my usual tree and no longer at the cave? I turn left immediately, to look across at the bar calendar and notice I am back in the future at almost my present time. It looks as if I am here those few minutes ahead in time, corresponding to the exact time I spent with my other self.

I turn right; my God in heaven, it's Anne! She is right next to me, snuggled in a blanket, drinking tea and says in a funny Irish brogue, "Mr. Abraham, you havin a bit of a fright?" I smile from ear to ear in this awe inspiring moment and quickly hug her to hide my gratuitous gush of tears. I let out a quick and tight, "Yeah." I stay steady with the lingered embrace in order to collect myself and whisper, "How are you feeling today?"

I let loose of Anne and settle back into my chair, masking my emotions as she replies, "Much better, now that you have showered me with this 'kind' cup of tea." She then picks up the teacup with two hands and brings it near to her lips to sip. She then shrugs her shoulders and squeaks out a cute warm giggle.

Just a few days ago, there were two candles burning at both ends of her bed, to mark out and corner her despair and now there is one candle lit between us, in order to witness freedom in a whole new perspective. For that sorrow, is not only in the past but also another time and it is reassuring that I am the only one who experienced or remembered those events.

To appreciate life with reverence is a part of me, now and forever. Our lives together will rekindle but not without certain sacrifices. As explained, according to the Watchers, Anne and I will be unable to live in this era or our time period because of the negative effect on the timeline (continuum). Anne was not a part of the natural timeline sequence after her demised date. Thereby, her actions in this time period would have reactions that could cause a *paradox* of serious complications.

The recommended three days after the altered time period is at hand tomorrow. So I think, how do I tell her? Firstly, about the Watchers, oh goodness! Secondly, that she can no longer be near her family and visit them only on rare occasions. I hope the seeds I have planted in numerous conversations will help not to hamper her gentle heart.

I wait till the porch is clear of any company to pursue this far reaching tête-à-tête (face to face discussion). I begin to reach into my pocket and pullout the bottle of medication and say to her, "Dear Anne, the medication I have been administering to you is not from around here." She agrees to say, "Yes, I have noticed the bottle has an odd design and the label on the container reads October, 1984. How can this be?

I rise to stand, with a soft reach to invite Anne to follow me and so I answer her, "Well, it is a long story and best if we can ride together on the back of Bob to a nearby cave location of undiscovered science. This will better explain the strange things I have said in the past and will better clarify this wonder with a visual understanding, nonetheless. She carefully says, "Okay."

We ride off together and I know that each new passing day, will be a gift of something dear. When we arrive at the cave I carefully ease information slowly in a story telling fashion. I explain, "The ancient guardians, called the Watchers, oversee our Earth in its entirety, since the start of humanity." Her throat gulps and stares at me as if I am telling her a ghost story. After the explanation, we enter the cave, viewing the cavern in its normal and natural appearance. But when I take out my coin and show her my inscription on it,

I can see her eyes are "listening" intently. Anne searches for my hand to hold because she is nervously overwhelmed and takes the coin to study it. I explain to her, "All you have to do is breathe and let go." She then practices with a quick breath. I further explain, "What helped me when I first saw some of the amazing things, is I attempted to look at everything as entertainment or well I tried to." Finally, I receive a smile from her. I am hoping that she is reassured and settled by my steady confidence.

I walk over to the Gateway control area and wave the coin to expose the control panel and calendar. She gasps and becomes startled. Thinking quickly, I use this opportunity to make clear of our sacrifice and say, "In no way do I feel guilt or regret for any of my past actions, nor should you. All in all, we did not affect or hurt anyone. I have followed the moral guidelines set by the Watchers, for better or for worse. Anne, our love comes with challenges, on both our parts but being with you trumps any surrender or home address. She agrees whole heartedly and thanks me for loving her so much.

The day went smoother than I anticipated. After I showed her the cave I had then brought her into the facility, but before being transferred into the Gateway, she had clung to me tightly. It was a scary but fun moment for Anne. Once in the facility I gave her the majestic tour. She especially loved the wardrobe selection area; I have never seen her so excited! We felt like royalty in every regard.

Towards the end of the day I brought her over to the *Knowledge Study* quarters and said to her, "Anne, would you like to hear music from the future?" She hurries a yes, and tells me she'd love to. "I especially picked out an anthem to pledge our joy." Hoping she is pleased with the song. So I then look at the glass informational display, smile and touch play, then watch her stare aimlessly at the music performance on the screen:

Altering Time

If I could save time in a bottle

The first thing that I'd like to do

Is to save every day till eternity passes away
Just to spend them with you

But there never seems to be enough time

To do the things you want to do, once you find them...

I've looked around enough to know

That you're the one I want to go through time with.

Written by Jim Croce

She listens while gazing towards the display screen with tears in her eyes, and then says with a soft cry, "It's so beautiful," just as the song is complete. But before she can turn around I am on one knee to display a handsome box wide open, to show her my angelic mother's ring. Her hands nervously rise up above the ring not knowing what to do; she takes an excited surprised deep breath and never releases it.

I put forward this heartfelt proposal, "Dearest Anne, it would give me great honor to share a lifetime with you and forever where we may go. I will follow and lead us with the highest regard, to 'preserve the union' of our treasured love. Will you, Anne Mays Rutledge, marry me? Anne's tears of joy are punctuated by her resounding, "Yes, yes I love you and will marry you, Mr. Abraham Lincoln!" Laughter trails the excitement as we embrace with a passionate timeless kiss.

"The moment is the masterpiece, like a maiden that is soon to be a bride!"

Thereafter, there was a song that was befitting with regards to everything that had transpired in my life, up and until this point. From the Watchers' archives I inserted part of this current portion of my journal and was given a result that equaled my struggles and accomplishments to a personal level. A song that I hope holds true for me and others.

"The Wall"

"The Promised Land is waiting like a maiden that is soon to be a bride"

This is one of those moments where your efforts to slow down time or halt it altogether, would be presumptuous but the wish itself is part of the fantasy. How, I have learned that these moments are few in one's lifetime and should be cherished. Gratefully so, I hear the final words of the song.

Gold and diamonds cast a spell
It's not for me; I know it well
The riches that I seek are waiting on the other side
There's more than I can measure
In the treasures of the love that I can find
And though it's always been with me
I must tear down the wall and let it be

Written by musicians called, Kansas, Steve Walsh.

All truths be-told: It was altogether strange to put into plain words about our plans because of these odd events that transpired and in addition, to divulge certain details to Anne's family, thinking; perhaps, without saying too much.

Afterwards, in regards to Anne's family, it seems that we did not have to make a fuss about the details and kept the discussions grounded without the bizarre portion of the Watchers. This was a great relief and it also was very comforting that the family was only concerned with our happiness. What little we told them, they had sworn to secrecy.

In the midst of these events, the Rutledge family had a private engagement and departure festivity for Anne and me. Understanding, an explanation was provided to the Rutledge's family, that one day in the future there would be a President Abraham Lincoln with my background but would not be me. Not to accept my bizarre story, would have been very predictable, but if it were not for the two items I presented to them, this furthered their convincement. I showed them a five dollar bill with a date from the 1980's and the medicine bottle made of plastic, with a child protection cap atop. The bottle also had a date, being October, 1984. These items seemingly eased the "impossible" to being somewhat plausible or possible.

If when, anyone would ask about Anne, they were told that she went off to the New York, New Jersey location to live and she comes back for the Holidays from time to time. Some people thought, maybe she pursued John MacNamar or possibly someone else...Let me let you in on a little secret, "It was Me!"

I have heard great stories from the area of New York, New Jersey from my grandfather. There is a town called Imlaystown, in New Jersey. My grandfather used to work at a mill right on Imlaystown Road and lived a stone's throw away on Burlington Path Road in a solid stone house. The rolling hills were picturesque and filled with wild horses and adorned by many farms. Also, the area was well known for one of the biggest pig farms at the time and was owned by one of the founders of Imlaystown, my grandfather's closet friend, Old-man Lawrence (Edwin).

Since I have to move to the future, I was thinking about going to the late 1960's because I am fond of the music and impressed with the accomplishments for mankind during this time period. Ann and I are eager to settle down in the vicinity of Imlaystown because there is plenty of surveying work due to a few military bases throughout that neck of the woods.

We will take what little savings we have and some important articles of matter, that are dear to us. The money exchange of our small savings and some items, should convert to a handsome sum of worth, due to its antiquity value, along with the exchange rate of inflated gold and silver prices in the future. This will give us a secure start to purchase a modest home and who knows, maybe start a family of our own.

We are headed out to the cave and take all of our belongings on just one trip; carriage and all. A good friend of mine called Austin Gollaher, drops us off at the Sangamon River bank, right near the cave. We wait for him and our two horses (Old Buck and Robin) to lean out of sight before moving our belongings into the camouflaged cave. Strange, looking at Austin travel further into the distance, it feels like watching my old life fade away into the vast landscape. After feeling all philosophical, I turn to see a ruckus of shuffling and moving. Anne is funny while she is rushing to get everything quickly into the cave. Very entertaining I might add!

Austin Gollaher was a childhood friend of mine that I can trust. Way back, when we were younger, we were playing alongside the river near to our homes. I decided to cut across the river by borrowing the use of a fallen tree. It looked like it was there for some time. Austin quickly got to the other side and there he waited. He was more nimble than I and smaller.

Austin told me to wait and hold steady when I was struggling in my attempt to cross. The river was in an aggressive flow that day and I did not know how to swim at the time, in fact I still really don't know how to swim. I can whirl above water for about twenty feet or so, if ever needed.

Looking up at Austin I snarled at him and waved him off to ignore his caveats (warnings). I soon then slipped quickly on some green algae attached to the surface of the log and swiftly fell into a panic, followed by-being quickly submerged in the water. With great effort I was then bobbing while reappearing, gasping and grasping onto any sticks or brush. Austin screams 'hold on' and quickly snaps a tree branch from a dead fallen tree. He yells to me, "Grab this, hurry!"

I had taken in some water being unable to speak and was very faint. I felt the branch touch the side of my wrist and thus, twisted my hand around to swipe a grip that I would never let go! It is hard to explain but it felt like the rest of my body gave up, but my one hand seemed to have eyes in order to hold on.

Austin saved my life that day and I am forever grateful, hence the valid trust I have for him. For, in the future I had retrieved a substance to prolong his life. Austin had always said, "I wish I can live to a hundred years old." Well, he was a simple man who lived alone in the country and wouldn't have affected any timelines, so I felt it, to be okay and give my friend a little bit of enchantment. To be told, he ends up being the only member to survive long enough to tell the story of Anne and I.

Alone now, exiting the cave, it is April 27th, 1964 at a waterway lake area called Assunpink. It is a tributary that flows to the Delaware River and is a jump away to the Imlaystown area, where my grandfather once lived.

The area is still rural as far as its development for the time period, but Anne is still in awe when we appear into the shuffle of society, while cars and trucks are moving about, weaving through traffic lights. The noise is some getting used to in this era, but I gather it is a tradeoff to the conveniences that the noise supplies. I say to Anne, in a snide way amongst the noise, "This is the rural country section of this day and age!" She reacts surprised and lets out a, "Good heavens!"

We are both in proper attire for this timeline and since I am fully shaved, I should be somewhat unrecognizable. From time to time I will grow just a mustache, after-all it is the 1960's. Ironically, in this time period, the current styles warrant the fashion of many more things other than a mustache.

I have taken the liberty to gather us some proper identification for the time period and after all, it is who we are. We had decided to keep Anne's name the same, but use her family's last name to fill the questionable familiarity with my face and or my old name. As we both agreed, my new legal name shall be Al Rutledge, not Albert, just Al. We figured; let's take the initials of Abraham and Lincoln, which reads through as Al, A plus L. "This will be our little secret between each other." I just laughed as I put this in my journal, but not out loud, it was more of visceral snort. By the way, I added this tidbit later on into the final draft of my journal.

I told Anne, that another good thing about changing my name and going to Imlaystown, is not running into the descendants from the Booth family. My grandfather had told us stories about feuds that transpired between our families. I think they were quarrels about land rights or something to that extent. Not to worry, after all this time, I'm sure it is 'water under the bridge.'

The house we settled upon is on Main Street in Allentown, New Jersey. The home is warm and was built in the era, which we were somewhat familiar with. It is slightly after my time, but very similar indeed. It was built in the latter parts of the 1800's. Noted, the portion of the house we were accustomed to is the firm porch and portico, which we are so fond of. The windows are so tall, that even I could step out onto the porch without a problem.

Anne and I only dreamed of owning a home of this nature. The day we moved in, was a glorious day! Oh dear, I am going to need a car or truck vehicle soon, living in this area. I have all the conveniences within walking distance, so I guess for now I will try to do without or maybe use a horse.

Oh, did I mention that the house has a mansard (man-sod) roof and is just a furlong or two, away from a, "Reed-Sod Farm," where they grow grass. I just failed immeasurably at making a joke. I am sorry, sometimes my humor falls short, I was trying to create humor but I realize it is a bit of a stretch now. Let me try again: "Mansard and Sod," they sound alike. Okay, I guess not. Anne does not encourage me to display this type of humor from time to time.

CHAPTER SEVEN

TIME CATCHES UP

From time to time, I would rendezvous and meet with Jack (the younger Kennedy) to make sure things were the status quo. He supported my actions, when I explained the happening in regards to Anne and myself. He said, "If the Watchers permitted it and said it was all right, then what more do you need, it was for love, for Pete's sake." He thereafter, then patted the back of my shoulder for a positive closure on the subject.

A few years had passed and it seemed as though the meetings with John, were not as necessary, when compared to past. He appeared to be preoccupied with his life and he too, respected my privacy towards our lives. After all, we were from two different time periods and we have reassured each other, that all was going well.

We understood, at this point in time, that his counterpart/duplicate would probably emerge years later, as well as my own counterpart, who will eventually have a more impressive role in the political standings of Washington D.C...

Time has a way of catching up with you. Something strange must of have been inserted into the timeline at this exact point. Suddenly, there is a time rift that oddly appears and panics my heart, directly to my soul! I first notice a weird feeling in my being and then, slightly off changes around me.

Not knowing what it is, I head down to the Main Street library. I walk to the middle of the Allentown Library and start to browse the history section with suspicion.

Immediately, I see two books, displaying the assassination of John F. Kennedy. I reluctantly grab the book with my right hand, while my left hand covers my eyes and presses against my face. My heart sinks as I no longer can hold the book in my grasp. I drop it to the floor. The book lies face down, with the pages scuffled open to the floor. A card slides from within the book, indicating that it is a registration card and oddly enough it slides over to the bottom of the bookcase.

As I struggle to pick up the registration card, I am blinded by my emotions. I turn my head towards the wall, not to be seen in such a state. While gathering myself, a silver haired lady librarian, quietly comes over to me and says in a low voice, "I still get upset when I think about President Kennedy; I don't have enough courage to read but one word in that book. To me, it feels like it was just yesterday. It is okay that you are upset young man, time heals all wounds." She assists me from my knelt position and brushes my right shoulder with a smile. After I smile back to her, I quickly say, "Indeed, madam," as I finally retrieve the fallen book. She walks away thinking I am fine but my stomach continued to churn in a hollow abyss.

Pretending I was reading, I turned the pages without acknowledging a single word within this book. Dazed in thought, I merged anxiety with reason to contemplate any possibility. I rub the side of my chin with vigor and say to myself, "Why, Why?" Anger then trails from behind and motivates me to take action and return the book to its original location.

While I attempt to put the book back on the shelf, I suddenly stop. There, in the exact location of the "history section" is the presentation of many books, which appear to me as a blur in this moment, because my attention becomes consumed on a subject that is shocking; the lenses of my eyes lean to an image that provokes clear and present danger. "Oh dear God," I stand still and numb, while my grip tightens upon the cover of President Kennedy's assassination book and stare. I hold on to the book this time, cemented in my hand, by my side, while I stand witness to a set of books that penetrates into my soul.

The energies that follow seize my being. Am I still standing? Further to be a nightmare, I am situated and undisturbed as my glance becomes a fierce intent look that collides into a row of books about the assassination of President Abraham Lincoln... They lay accepted on a shelf and are many. They are presented in a soldier course display. My spirit surrenders and is hushed aside while I assess whether I am really alive...

I immediately, nervously, grab two books pertaining to myself along with the book about John and wobble to the closest chair. Each book is wedged within my fingers; I land and place them on the table next to me. I race through the history of both events and after all my fact checking, it seems that each of the assassinations have similarities. There must be a link? I am raged against this dark outcome and I am immediately off to find out what went wrong. Everything appeared to be correct in this time period as well as other moments in time. What happened?

I quickly set out to the cave's Study Center inside the Watchers' facility, but before leaving I retrieve one of my coins to give Anne. I tell her, "Just in case something goes wrong." I hand her one of the coins and tell her I should be back in a few days. She pleads with me, "Abraham, Abraham, be ever so careful." Anne then releases me from her tight grip over my hand.

I am frantic while I race to the Assunpink cave. This new cave creates difficulty navigating to its location, due to the fluctuations of the lake's water levels. I place my coin in position and proceed.

I finally get inside the Watchers' installation. With wet feet I pull up information that is plenty on this subject. There are displays after display of information that is pouring in, with scrap piles of news that seems to keep in motion and adding up. I am striving to find out what went wrong with these tangents in time.

Here, at the duplication area, there are overlapping uses. Apparently, from browsing the entry to this facility and the use of foregoing equipment, there appears to be a mishandling of what governs the duplicator. It appears to be Lincoln's Vice President Andrew Johnson? I am with intense distress as I read the insider history about how the counterparts chose and vetted their Vice Presidents. Everything relied on a pact (trust) that appears to have been broken.

Searching onward, I am dismayed to find that the operation of misuse was by one of "my" coins, but how? The historic records indicate that my counterpart (Lincoln), felt to have an assured victory again for the presidency of the United States by picking Andrew Johnson as his running mate. Since Johnson was the one chosen five years before the 1864 election, from the two possible (Watchers') candidates, it was decided, there was no need to insert him into the political front until 1864. It was agreed that Andrew Johnson was a noted Democrat and because President Lincoln was a Republican, he would be able to reach voters on another political front. Therefore, receiving votes to feed both sides for his campaign tally; this would include Democrats as well as Republicans.

At the current time the Republican Party was still emerging as a newly started political group and was the reason why Lincoln reached out to the Democrats (Vice President Andrew Johnson). The problem mounted once the presidency was in full motion. A duplicate of Andrew Johnson was decided in the past and both he and his duplicate "made an oath" to be trusted with partial knowledge of the Watchers. Then, Andrew Johnson's counterpart was inserted to become vice-president to secure support for John F. Kennedy's presidency.

In total, the risks of persons truly involved are limited to only three original people with knowledge of the mission, Myself, John and Andrew Johnson. The historic archives state that Andrew Johnson's counterpart would watch over Kennedy and use the name Lyndon B. Johnson.

Everything was in position and the amicable plan was in place, until a coincidence of timing occurred on two fronts. In the middle of President Kennedy's presidency, Lyndon Johnson did not like that Mr. Kennedy was going to release the names within the secret societies that were taking over parts of government and expose their organization out of *Bohemian Grove*. Reading on, it seems the two Johnsons were members of this secret society and their agenda was threatened.

This secret society would thirst for control of the people at all costs. It all started a longtime ago, with a group that broke off from the Mason's Tribunal. The members of the Masonic line, such as members, George Washington, James Monroe and many others, believed in a capitalistic society, where the right to freedom was paramount and where individual growth should be built upon in order to pursue happiness.

The leader or one of the leaders from the Masons decided to form a secret society group called the Knights of the Golden Circle. Some affiliates of the Knights of the Golden Circle would pose as members within the Masonic Institution and was a front to move forth on an agenda for their New World Order. Their goals are to take over and position their members in power by any means and control the people they govern. Their purpose was to create division amongst the people and profit on their conflicts.

101

To further and spread their ideology, they would try to own, infiltrate and control all media outlets, schools and government. By purposely damaging economies, they would encourage the common man to rely on their assistance. This would almost guarantee to keep the majority of people from becoming independent and enslave most, in order to solidify their stay in appointed power and or high office.

President Lincoln's Vice President Johnson did not like the Emancipation Proclamation or freedom for the slaves, because most Democrats were major sympathizers towards the south and fought to keep slavery intact. Andrew Johnson had taken upon himself to use these narratives of information from Kennedy and Lincoln to corrupt the gift of what the Watchers have bestowed upon all of us.

Andrew Johnson was calculating and waited until the timelines were safe and sealed, since the moment of the Watchers' purpose was fulfilled. The Southern States will no longer secede from the Union and Kennedy was there to avert the Cuban Missile Crisis.

After this momentous occasion passes, Johnson knows that the Watchers will not interfere, due to free will/choice and time rift exposure. With this given, Johnson feels free to do the unthinkable and starts his unwavering wicked pursuit, by making an additional counterpart of him-self. This would then be a total of three of the same person and was clearly prohibited by the Watchers because of the negative impact it would have on the existing self and the other counterparts.

In order to get around the risk that was foretold by the Watchers of creating a second counterpart, Johnson attempts to make a younger version of himself, in order to avoid the severe danger of tampering with his own sound mind and his counterparts. This would now be two additional versions of himself. It seems that Johnson's agenda is worth more than the risk posed onto himself. He is without regard for the other versions of himself. Johnson presents a clear act of villainy and is an egotistical louse.

It's hard to believe that with only a few hours alone in the Watchers' facility, while duplicating one's self, Johnson found the time to access certain data to gain passage secretly after he left. But what could it have been? It is diabolical and stands to reason that his devious plan was already in place on the day of duplication. Good God!

As I try to figure out how he obtained one of my coins, I have a thought of how great Anne and I are doing, as compared to this sudden parity of tragedies. Why are they such polar opposites? I question, is there something to this? I shake off the thought and begin again to search and search, till I find the historic foot print on Johnson's access and searches. I finally come across proof, resulting in multiple entries to the Watchers' facility.

I hold my head and ask myself in a whisper, but how? Suddenly, it looks as if, somehow, from a sealed future, he was able to gain access to the information in my journals or book and knew exactly where my coins were at the precise moment in time. By rationalizing numerous sequences I figure out the obvious; he stole one of the coins from on top of Mr. Taft's desk (within my room), squeezed between the pages of my Thomas Paine book.

My neck eases downward in a disappointed notion, while I exhale with the sound of the letter "P," spurting from my lips. Stagnant and poised, I have to make a decision. There is no time for disappointment. According to the logs, the assassinations took place simultaneously, at the moment I had felt eerie and displaced. It must have been some sort of time shift that took place and I expect that the bad actors that were involved, just hours ago, had felt the same unnatural surge of feelings.

When I had saved Anne, I had a certain window of time

in order to rescue her and correct the outcome to a positive result. It seems that the same universal time restriction applies here and now. Thirty Three hours left of the 48 hour window to plan and right this wrong. I have just one opportunity to overlap time and I have to travel accurately to pin point that perfect moment.

I hope Anne does not worry, even though I gave her an approximate amount of time of my absence. While still researching, I talk to myself and offer my dear apologies towards my good friend John, because I hunt first, the pursuit and whereabouts of Mr. Lincoln's assassin, before your counterpart's shooter. Even though they are weighted equally, I assure you I will be there!

I look swiftly through the logs and the details of the security within the Watchers' systems. Oh no, to my dismay, Johnson duplicated the two younger versions of himself for the task to become the would-be assassins. How was he able to do this with only the one coin? Listed here, hmm, he goes as far to call one of them John Booth, who would be the assassin to Lincoln and Lee Harvey Oswald as to Kennedy's killer. It is fascinating, that Johnson took an adversarial name from the Lincoln's family past, the Booth's (land-use issues). How appropriate for his nefarious plan! With a quick breath I release one huff in disgust and continue.

There are multiple entries to the New Salem cave this past week, but one is hours before the day of Lincoln's assassination. I match up the outcome from history with the log entries. It is a record signature of John Booth; in fact most of the entries are John Booth as of late. Holding that thought, there is no time to spare and now, down to 32 hours to foil both crimes. I rub my fists together and head over to the time travel gate with my coin ready in hand.

I arrive minutes before the arrival of Booth at my old cave alongside the Sangamon River to have a vantage point for when this younger version of Johnson (John Booth) arrives. I have never lost a fight and don't intend to lose that title anytime soon. I wait but with vigor. I do not intend to kill this man but I also will not bring him to justice. Reason being, he is not supposed to exist at all.

I suddenly hear scuffling outside the cave as per someone's approach. A shadow lingers right outside the cave opening. I hear a rock plunge into the river. Maybe he tossed a stone? I stand still in an unforeseen location. He enters the cave whistling and flipping my coin with his left thumb and catches it in his right hand.

While he walks further into the cave, the light becomes less generous. I recognize the face, even though he is a younger man in the shadows. As he flips the coin a second time, it spins up away in a soft motion. While his eyes are focused on catching the coin, I grab his right arm and spin him around with a grunt. I pound my fist downward toward his neck and shoulder. He starts to shout hey, hey! He falls to the ground facedown and crawls to the corner and says with disdain, "Oh it's you, good, I will kill you here and now, you saved me the effort." He turns around injured and reaches for his gun. I take one giant step and grab the arm with the gun and proceed to lift his whole body like a burlap bag filled with mail and smash his torso upward, in order to smack it to the ceiling of the cave, thus dropping him to the ground along with gun that skips away at a distance. He frantically rolls over breathing like an animal and lunges towards me with a large rock within his grasp.

I lose my footing as we both drop to the ground, as he tries desperately to hit me with the stone, my arms block most of his attempts but it seems relentless. I soon spot the coin he dropped on the ground; it only lies a few feet away from me. While he is assaulting me with blows I try to push and kick the coin onto the Gateway's (star-gate) floor. I move the coin a few inches at a time, until finally, it makes the field area.

In a high emotional state I focus in on the coin. It is heads up on the floor, with my face on the coin, starring back at me. This gives me a burst of energy, knowingly what is to happen to my counterpart.

Understandably, I have three seconds to get to the gate field area; while looking at the coin, I grab my attacker in a bear hug and spin both of us onto the field location. Both of our eyes become wide open, while we are transported into the Watchers facility. The stone was left behind in the cave, leaving my adversary with no weapons; unfortunate for him.

I act quickly while he is weakened and frail from the additional punishment I granted him. Barely standing, I wobble him over to a time transport sending area, right next to the duplication hall area; where it all began. He spreads his two arms out to prevent me from tossing him into the cylinder transport hub. Trapped inside, he screams, "No, no! But I have no coin; don't do this!"

His struggle becomes futile with the last open crack of the door about to shut. I quickly lift up my foot and with great admiration I say, "Please excuse one of my size 14 Hush Puppies' shoe." While my foot is about to wave goodbye to Booth, he gives one last-ditch effort in order to escape the time travel hub. To no avail, my foot makes solid contact and presses against his body in order to release a rapid kick, which lunges him back, smacked to the floor. He fell back like a rag doll but still got back up; "a resilient little feller to say the least."

But still the same, I finally close and lock the door and say, "Lawlessness doesn't pay." He shakes his head and screams at me, "Where are you sending me? I say, "I will spare your life, even though you would have not done the same for me. I am sending you back in time where you may be of no harm, to anyone. Did I mention it will be slightly in the past? I then mumble under my breath and say to my-self, "Just about 64 million years back."

I quickly finish my selections with one eyebrow raised. While the door is locked, with Booth trapped inside I elevate my voice to say, "My friend John Kennedy once said, "It'll be *cool* to visit the dinosaur monsters, somewhere in Montana." He hit the door with his fist and says, "Where's Montana?" I respond, "It is going to become a state within the United States of America in the future but unfortunately, it's going to be slightly after your time, well, not anymore it isn't. It is now going to be *way, way* after your time!" I press the time locator indicator while I look over to see his hands pressing up against the glass and his mouth ajar. Simultaneously, I recite to him, "I declare you somewhat terminated, creep!"

Right at this point he vanishes and then I wonder where he is. I pictured him, for a second, running in and out of the way of a herd of giant Brontosaurus'. All the while he is panicking; a large dinosaur lifts their leg up and smashes him into the mud with its enormous hoof. Indented into the ground all frantic and stuck in the mud, he looks up crying and sees the Brontosaurus that stepped on him. The giant reptile suddenly brings its long neck and head, all the way down to sniff him. The dinosaur ironically just happens to have a beard and the same face as the Lincoln penny. I do beg your pardon, because I do sometimes get silly after overcoming a bout of stress.

Relieved that now I am now half accomplished, but still, the secondhand is burning with less time to stop Kennedy's assassin. So onward and upward I research the location for Jack Kennedy's killer. If I am able, in preventing the deaths of both Presidents, the reset of the new favorable timeline will be a reality at the forty eighth hour.

Without hesitation, I scan through the historic documents

and read. I take out my daybook and jot down a location of 411 Elm Street in Dealey Plaza, Dallas Texas, at 12:30 pm on November 22, 1963.

The second younger version of Johnson, Lee Oswald, seems to have mysteriously received employment from the Texas School Book Depository. It was a type of warehouse, which was used to store and distribute school books within the state. This is the location, where Oswald perches on the sixth floor to shoot Kennedy.

The southeastern corner portion of the book depository building; there, is where I need to go! Thinking, I only get this one chance. The building has seven stories in total and according to the building's plan drawings I would be less noticed if I travel up to the top floor and make my way down through the staircases, to the sixth floor. This strategy is probably best to be undetected and wait patiently for his entry.

My envelope of time narrows and will become permanent, whether I am successful or not. I have less than 24 hours available to stop this shooting. With the advantage to select anytime, I still must be careful, not to position myself too early nor can I be too late. Understandably, even though I can select an exact time, this still does not stop the true continuum time from a permanent seal after the 48th hour.

The Trinity River in Dallas is where I would be received by one of the Watchers' many Gateway Caves. This nearby arrival location would leave me 4.4 miles from the Texas School Book Depository building.

I get prepared and slip on my (1963 attire) Pro Keds sneakers that I have recently acquired for a trek such as this. What an easier way of walking rather than the Balmoral shoes I used for long walks, way back when. They did look great but punished my feet.

I embark to the New Salem Cave, then onto the Trinity

Cave in Dallas. I arrived with time to spare and I see an animal asleep in the corner of the cave. Wait, it's a female dog. She hears me and so her head lifts up. I lean low and say, "Hi, salutations to you." She reminds me of my family's dog, Honey. She definitely is the same breed.

She looks very hungry and that reminds me I am famished too. Since I have some time, I think it would be prudent to gather some energy for the trip. A light meal will be good and at the same time I can help this innocent dog.

After a quick back and forth from the facility, my newly found friend and I seem quite satisfied. Right before my departure from the cave, I leave a basin of water nestled behind the sleeping area of the sweet dog.

As I exit the cave I notice the weather is dry, clear and sunny, accept that I am surrounded by moving water. I am not pleased, and having a thought-back to when I almost drowned a longtime ago. It is now years later and I am going to heed that warning Austin Gollaher gave me when crossing the Sangamon River, all so many years ago.

I have learned that if you use three points of contact (hands and feet) while on a ladder or tree climbing, your safe passage and return is assured. So I start slowly with one foot on a stone and two hands on a horizontal broken log. The water rustles beneath me while I feel tall and awkward, so I continue.

Midway, my right foot slips on a rock and my new Pro Keds sneaker dives toes first into the water. I thought my whole body was ready to follow but I found myself planted with one foot still and secure in the water. After I open up my eyes I exert a short laugh of relief and realize I am standing in barely two feet of moving water. Walking out of the water lopsided because I was determined *not* to get my other sneaker wet. One foot in front of another, rock, water, then rock, water, till I reached land.

Frustration sets in, while on dry land, that my wet right foot might hinder my abilities to act. I see a large stone to use as a bench but before I get there, I hear two children yelling from afar, saying the word, "Bozo, Bozo!" They are in the woods, so assume they are hunting with their parents, yet their voices seem to be aimed in my direction.

I stand to lean on a big stone, in order to take off my now discolored sneaker and lay it to roast in the Sun. I twist the waterlogged sock into bookends till the last drip. The now, wrung out sock is ready to be dried while I scout out my journey.

While waiting, I say a heartfelt prayer for strength and afterwards I suddenly remember I have a couple of "Now & Later" candies in my pocket; I am very fond of these candies and they do give me a little pep as well, similar to John's cola. While chewing the candy I gather my belongings and I am satisfied that my sock and sneaker are dry, so then on they go. I am ready and so I set out, at about five score from my last destination in the past.

Finally I reach the surrounding area of Dealey Plaza. I start to see many people gathering for the president's motorcade drive thru in order to prepare towards his next campaign. Kennedy wanted to announce to Texas, how their resources can help bring peace and harmony throughout the United States.

My head is lowered not to draw attention as I weave amongst the many. There are great numbers of auto vehicles which I am learning fast how to avoid and they are very large in size. I look up to see this infamous building and feel a ring in my right ear. Ahead of my schedule I arrive towards the back of the building. I see a pile of trash surrounded by a mesh fence, next to a rusty maintenance door. There is a slipknot of rope through a small hole, where there once was a lock. I easily enter the building and slide back the rope through the hole in the door.

I sway with a quiet rhythm around every corridor and begin my accent within the staircases. There is a cold feel within the enclosed stairway. It is very stagnant and there is an odd smell that I am not familiar with.

Before reaching the top (7th) floor level, I check the entire sixth floor where the sniper (Oswald) is to be. It appears to be all clear on my hunt into every room. I scurry back to the seventh floor, across to a vantage point where I can see, both the front entrance of the Book Depository and yet, from the same location I can hear any movement on the northeastern portion of the building, via the sixth floor.

Patiently I wait while a symphony of voices, mingle amongst the crowds gathering. My pocket watch is set to Central Time and is trusted to display 12:15 pm. Impatient and nervous, I am checking both stakeout points with vigor. Wait! I hear a loud squeak from a door. The footsteps I hear are approaching the first floor staircase with an eerie echo. My blood is raging in my body; I must stay calm to make the right decision.

With every floor he ascends I feel closer to resolve this fatal happening. The door to the sixth floor opens and then slams shut, metal to metal, causing me to snap into ready mode. 12:21 pm, it is nine minutes away from the three shots discharged.

I leave my post to go forth. Determined, my stride delivers a silent approach to the staircase. I enter the staircase in from the seventh floor and while in my decent I see the number 6 laminated to the door. I quietly reach for the handle and it's not turning, I try again. Oh dear God, it is locked and a panic drives inside of me. I start shaking and look at my pocket watch, it is 12:25 pm. "No," I say to myself, I cannot go across to other side of the building and search for another staircase, I do not have the time!

I am not to care if he hears me coming at this point, because I am on my way! Still trapped within the staircase, I think fast. At the corner of my eye I see a red glass box, holding an axe, hose and water knob beneath its display. Without hesitation I break the glass with a swift twist of my torso, trailed by my forearm shattering the glass. I am sure Oswald is stunned by the sound but cannot move from his post. I am a master with the axe and with four whacks the handle of the door is unrecognizable and I am on my way.

Running down the hallway, axe in hand, I open my pocket watch and see the time of 12:27 pm. Previously, on this floor I had left all the doors in the hallway resting against the side jamb, but not closed. This would determine which room, Oswald would be in. As I hurry, I see beyond any doubt, the one door that is closed and was not a short while ago. I do not attempt to open the doorknob, because it would alert him of my presence. Instead, I launch myself from the other side of the hallway and let out a yell of vengeance while I break and plummet the door's entrance with the might of my right shoulder. There are explosive metal sounds crashing, while I coddle the axe and guard it against my chest. The door's top hinge lifts off as the rest of the door, wedges itself and becomes lodged into the false wooden wall, stuck.

Oswald turns around quickly, with a rifle at his right side. He is shocked and surprised while he gawks at my collision against two five foot file cabinets. Holding my balance with a slight spin, his eyes erupt to a wide alert as he realizes it is me. Oswald, (who looks slightly different in person) then lifts the barrel of his gun in an attempt to discharge a bullet in my direction. His gun lifts to a few degrees away from me. His aggressive intention is for me to be the recipient of his metal-ball bullet. He is about to shoot and cocks the trigger, but my axe handle sharpens his gun barrel, while I slide and pull it down, jammed against the desk. The loud shot discharges into the top of the desk, piercing a hole through the wood.

Immediately satisfied, that this particular bullet will never seek a victim or a friend. Within a second and without further adieu I press the wooden axe handle against his neck. In slow motion, he drops the gun to the floor while he struggles to roar. The gun clangs to the floor, followed by a bounce of shuffling metal.

He is forced backwards, yet he is still in a stance. We reach the window area where he was going to shoot the president. I hold his head outside this window locked under the wooden handle of my axe. Silence fills the air for the next few seconds. He can hardly talk or breathe accept for a groan, while his legs continue to kick the air. I continue to bear down on the handle against his throat while I tell him to, "Please, can you choke a bit quieter because the window is half open and there are many people below!"

In this steadfast moment of physical abolition (ending), I glance from a distance, to see the motorcade with John Kennedy in an open auto vehicle, with some colleagues and his wife, waving to the people. This softens me to ease the force applied to his neck and with good reason; I cannot kill this villainess chap.

In the seconds that follow, there could not be one more second forth, because at 12:30 pm, seemingly time stopped and stood still, as I see and hear two rifle shots echoing in Dealey Plaza. I see Jack's body lean forward flowering the other people in the vehicle. He is shot twice; once from behind and immediately from a second location; he is hit from the side. This angle was perpendicular to the first shooter, indicating a third gunman. I become horrified.

I shake the handle of the axe and rattle his neck and say, "What happened? What happened!" He replies with a raspy voice, "We had planned for any outcome to make sure the mission was carried out." He coughs with one arm in support of his body leaning on a table. He continues his struggle to speak but says, "We thought you might have showed up, but I didn't think so. Well, you failed big guy." He then lifts his leg up and kicks me. Well, I am not obliged to say where, but I did receive another taste of the Now & Later candy I had earlier after I bite my breath and then choke. Notation: *With all due respect, this is the one time I am not trying to be humorous, but delivering what happened straight out of my daybook.*

This gave him the opportunity to get away and run out of the room. I was slow to get started but manage to pick up my pace to exit the building. I come out of the Book Depository Building and stop because of the higher elevation, in order to scout and seek his whereabouts. I see him in the crowd at a distance, walking at a fast pace, trying not to draw attention.

Crowds galore, I run through the jungle of commotion to feel two thousand stares loaded with sorrow as Satan had just cried, "Charge!" What a victory "against" mankind. I feel like crying while in my run. I have failed but going to continue to do my part and make sure he is brought to justice.

I gain further ground towards Oswald but I am too far to track him because he turns the corner. People are outside their vehicles, wondering what had just happened. In a desperate state I see a vehicle, to what I read is a Chevy. It appears to have the "engine on" with its door wide open. This welcomed invitation or sign to borrow this vehicle is my only chance to make sure that he is brought to justice. In this case, the needs of many, trump the needs of the few. I always say, "Your own resolution to succeed is more important than any one thing, in a matter of speaking.

I enter into this uninhabited vehicle and slipover to the steering wheel because of my fast access. By using the steering wheel I pull myself back to an appropriate position to drive.

There is a bit of a problem, even though I am undetected; I have never driven. Darn, I did not elect to learn the driving simulator in the Study-Hall at the Watchers' facility. It was an exercise that John thoroughly enjoyed, hmm.

With a second of thought, I lean back to my past observations and remember certain visual aspects of driving. I jiggle the handle a few times, knowing I must get to the "D." "Oh; pull in the handle." The vehicle starts to show movement.

I mumble something but I don't remember what I said. I think it was, "Come on, guy!." The motor vehicle begins its motion and like a horses rein I turn to go straight. I am now suddenly noticed by the owner of this large Chevy and hear, "Hey! Hey, that's my car!" The window is opened down and I reply, "Hay is for horses but I am dedicated to return your Chevy shortly good sir.

I proceed to drive up on the curb and on some grass. I am a novice at driving and thought the cheers were of support but then I discover it was the owner yelling and complaining further and other people heckling but without support.

The owner of the Chevy had a hesitation of surprise when he saw my face and after hearing my earlier response. He screamed, "That guy just stole my car!" His hand pointed in my direction and furthers, "It was Abe Lincoln.," while he shakes his head in disbelief. He then collectively says in a high pitched voice, "Abraham Lincoln just stole my car!" The people looked at him in disbelief and then backed away slowly and one of them said, "Someone just stole your Lincoln? I thought you were in a Chevy." Another gentleman states, "I heard him say President Lincoln stole his car," and so, the original man asks, "Who? Abraham Lincoln?" The excited man yells, "Yes! Yes! "The guy on the penny, man!" Then, following an upward tone, he repeats to say, because of the lack of understanding by the onlookers, "The guy on the five dollar bill?" His expression seemed to be frozen in a frustrated state, as he looked at his car drive away, his facial features dropped to a sad defeated face.

Finally, I gain control of the vehicle, to what added up to many "stop and goes'." While in my pursuit of Oswald I am driving on a road named Houston Street. After seven blocks passed, I slow my vehicle to witness Oswald step into a wooded park called, "Union Park." I see a sign that says, "No Auto Vehicles Beyond this Point." But through the brush I hear and see a black vehicle with two men inside talking to Oswald. Oswald then gets in the back seat of the vehicle, next to what I believe could be Andrew Johnson?

As they pull slowly away I follow them from afar, carefully. Knowing what I know, I assume the men in the car had given Oswald a hand-revolver gun. The black vehicle then exits the park and drives over a bridge above the Trinity River, to an area called Oak Cliff. While I keep a careful distance in my pursuit I notice an argument between them.

Now, we are all a few miles away from Dealey Plaza. They slow down and stop on the corner of 10th Street and Patton Avenue. I am struggling to see Oswald clearly but he definitely gets out of the black vehicle and walks to the sidewalk. The two men in the black vehicle pull across the street to watch Oswald from a distance, while they are in discussion.

Suddenly a police officer pulls alongside Oswald while he is halted in stride. From this moment I am not sure how it happens but I hear four gun shots and could barely see because I am at a distance from this shooting. I do see Oswald running and the black vehicle racing away. The police officer was shot and killed.

To this day he is amongst my daily prayers. The History of his life was ever so similar to mine, being he had several setbacks and worked two other jobs in order to support his family. He struggled as a farmer and rancher earlier in his life and so he decided to become a police officer eleven years ago. He persevered in the Dallas Police Department and was cited twice for honor and bravery. His name was J.D. Trippit and I wish his family strength and peace in life.

When I turn the corner to drive towards Oswald, I find myself on Madison Avenue. The black vehicle is too far away and I do not want to lose Oswald. Oswald is now walking calmly and is unaware of my pursuit. He makes a left-hand turn onto Jefferson Boulevard in a relaxed state. There are not many trees or landscaping on this road, so he can be easily tracked. In the old towns, our boulevards were used for carriageways'; curious to why they would call it a boulevard. I stop and leave my vehicle within a safe area in order to observe Oswald on foot.

He approaches a movie theater called the "Texas Theater." For some odd reason I see him reaching into a trash container outside the establishment. Then suddenly I become aware of a display advertisement atop the movie theater that says, "Veterans month, 'like-during' WWII, bring in an empty can, for the price of admission and support the veterans."

It was a double feature this day and to me, it was more like a double "future" because of the flying vehicles and other futuristic weaponry to behold. The two war movies were, "Cry of Battle," an epic from WWII and "War is Hell," depicted during the Korean War.

Oddly enough, Oswald can only find an empty glass bottle and tries to force the ticket girl to accept it for his price of admission. She refuses and then Oswald barks at her and leaves the bottle on the counter and walks through the theaters entrance.

I notice across the street, a familiar name on a vending cart, that John had once told me about. It was a hot dog cart.

I see they are selling cans of cola. I walk over and purchase five cans for one George Washington dollar. The gentleman who is tending the hot dog cart looked very familiar. In a rush, I ask him to open one of the cans. He uses a triangle metal tool located near his waist. For convenience, he has it dangling from a string and draws it quickly in order to open a cola can. He makes two triangle puncture holes on either side of my can. I assume this is for drinking from two different sides of the can.

I look up at him to make eye contact while I accept my "paper-bag" of cans and say, "Thank you," with an unfinished long-tone within my voice. I patiently wait to pry his name. He replies. "Oh you're welcome. The name is Warren Burroughs. Everybody around this neck of the woods calls me Butchy." I lift the bag up high with my left hand to say goodbye, while the open can is secure in my right hand. I say while in motion towards the movie theater, "Thanks again Butchy." I start to drink the cola while I cross the street, not noticing a car approaching. I hear a sudden horn sound and look over at a vehicle that came close to striking me. At this exact moment I had choked on my cola from this fright. I passed the car and saw the drivers hands raised high, along with a confused face. I was almost hit and I need to be more aware of these vehicles.

Still, in full concentration on the front exits of the movie theatre, not to veer. I detect the girl at the ticket booth counter is still flustered from the confrontation with Oswald. I approach her with my now, almost empty can and say, "One ticket please." She says, "Hey Mr., you almost got yourself killed out there, you gotta be more careful." I respond, "Yes, I am a bit rattled as of right now and are you aware that hay is for horses. She smirks at me and I mention, "I am clearly not familiar with this "neck of the woods." (A term I borrowed from Butchy the hot dog salesman.) The reason for my "hay is for horses" analogy is because the use of the word "hey" in this time period, lacks respect within its context.

I glance over at the entrance while talking to the young lady and say, "Can you excuse me for a second?" I walk gingerly over to the entrance of the theater to peek inside and see Oswald standing at a food cart to purchase something to eat.

He seems to be having a conversation with a man in a black suit. I step back outside and again approach the ticket booth and ask, "Young lady, can you do something for me? The man that barged into the theater without a movie ticket was involved in the shooting of the President at Dealey Plaza and..." The young lady nervously juts out, "What? Do you mean President Kennedy?" Yes, and I am sorry for being the bearer of this news, but can you please alert the authorities while I restrain him inside?" Her face turns beet red and she starts to flutter her hands in a panic, exclaiming, "Oh my God! Oh my God!"

"Young lady? Young lady!" I try to capture her attention and stare at her with a stern face, while she is still distraught. She is in a sad state and says, "Sorry, sorry," as she wipes her tears. "What is your name," I ask. She replies with a straggly voice, "Veronica." Veronica, there is no need to apologize but there is a grave importance at hand. For that is for right now, to alert your local authorities to come here. She snaps into a nervous work mode and says, "Yes, yes of course Mr., I'm gonna call the cops. I got the telephone right here." She grabs the telephone as I nod my head towards her, in confirmation. While I walk away she says, "Please be safe, be safe!"

I pull open the door and take a deep breath before I enter. There are only a few people scattered throughout the theater. The ceiling is high with balconies above. I notice Oswald in the last row eating something out of a container. I see the color red in all the chairs that surround the theater. In looking down I notice an empty container that reads *popcorn*. I assume this is what Oswald is eating and so it appears that he has no guilt to what just happened.

Unfortunately, the lights above me in the hallway are turned on and Oswald suddenly takes notice of me and bounces up from his seat and is heading towards a door. I quickly follow him by hurdling a small knee wall and continuing straight towards the back of the theater. He opens the door and hesitates. He then turns to see my position and then displays his gun to me while in my approach. He then shuts the door behind him. I assume he thought by showing me his weapon I would stop my pursuit, hmm. I proceed to grab a gold shiny door handle. The door squeaks open as I see him jumping down many stairs at a time. His feet thump and then rustle while he finally reaches the basement.

I peek through the stair rails and see that I have two more landings to get there. He opens a door that reads engine room. I stop at the third to last step and notice that he has closed the door with a revolver in his hand. Because of my tall height I see over the wall of the room and while I am unnoticed I am carefully and quietly observing him towards the rear corner the engine room.

He waits nervously in the room, shaking while his gun is pointed at the door. I slip to the right and there on the ground is a metal crate. I view that the ceiling is low in this room and open from above. I decide to take and toss the crate up and over to the middle portion of the engine room ceiling. Hearing a crash, I hurry to the door and see a lighting fixture fall from one end where it was fastened. With this, the light tubes burst into pieces and Oswald lifts his arm over his face to protect himself. I hear a quick grunt and see him trip backwards and fall head first into one of the two sister engines that are very sizable.

I act fast, Oswald seems to be unconscious. I take the

gun off the floor and break the trigger-cock so that the gun is useless. Next, I pickup two cords or some sort of twine gathered in a circle, lying on a green wooden table. I put the gun in my jacket pocket and the cords I drape over my shoulder like a rancher. Just like a sack of corn I lift Oswald up and over my right shoulder and walk up two stairs at a pace to the movie theater auditorium. I decide to bring him back to his old seat; which was in the last row towards the middle end of the theater. I was successful, not to be seen by anyone.

After sitting Oswald's body in the chair, his head seemingly is wobbling. A patron comes up the aisle and sees Oswald's state. So I make eye contact with this lady and make a gesture with my hand that he was drinking. Then I whisper the word, "Whiskey," while I repeat the theatrical gesture of drinking. The lady stiffens her lip and nods with disgust, in the understanding to what I was portraying about Oswald. So then she passes by in a routine manner, without worry.

The lights are dim as I look around. The movie's sound suddenly becomes loud due to a barrage of bullets and explosions upon the movie screen. I quickly tie Oswald's wrists to the arm handle of the theater's seat, while he is still unconscious. While I fasten him to the chair I create figure eights above his lap with the cord, from one chair arm to the other. With the second cord, I lock and wrap his chest to a metal pole behind him.

Before I depart, I lay the broken revolver on his lap pointed in his direction, hidden beneath the cord. So, if he does awaken, Oswald might think twice about escaping because of the possibility of the gun accidentally discharging. Also thinking, the police will need the gun for evidence, once confiscated.

I stand in a dark corner near a back door. This area gives

me an exit strategy, once the police have Oswald in their custody. When the police do arrive and capture him, I will slip out this door and gather myself onward.

Suddenly, I hear alert noises of many police vehicles, coming from the front of the theater. Oswald awakes and starts to tug on his constraints, but then suddenly stops, when he notices the gun on his lap, pointed in his direction. In fact, his chin swiftly presses against his chest to move away from the gun, but because he is tied tight, he halted his attempt to jostle loose.

The authorities took him into custody while no struggle took place, but Oswald was insisting that his name was Alek J. Hidell; very strange indeed. To be plain, this time I did test the backdoor exit to make thoroughly sure it would open, when and then, I needed to acquire an escape route.

The abomination of these two men, both Booth and Oswald is unsettling by any stretch of the imagination. The appropriate phrase would be "bittersweet" for these outcomes, because from this point I am extremely disappointed about the assassination of John Kennedy's counterpart and the failure in stopping the killing of the Dallas police officer.

But within the ever important forty-eight hour time window, I was able to prevent and seal the following: one out of the two assassinations was stopped and to be rid of Booth and Oswald. While Oswald's fate is determined by history, it is somewhat off to the reference of him being a "patsy." Even though, he did not pull the trigger, he was an accomplice within the conspiracy ring against Kennedy. Also, the scheme was eerily similar to the Lincoln plot.

In my day, they used the word pigeon rather than the word patsy. The reason why I am intrigued by this "patsy' reference is because during my youth, my father's adjoining land was owned by a Calabrese Italian immigrant. He was the first Italian to settle in our surrounding area and his son's name was Patsy. Later on in my childhood I found out that his real name was Pasquale and growing up, he was the closest friend I would have, not to mention the great food his family would feed me.

Not convinced that time was changed, I make my way back to the Watchers' facility to investigate the results of what I had accomplished in the last 48 hours. There is something in my blood that feels that certain time occurrences cannot be changed because of the thickness of the time-thread. Suchlike the assassination of John F. Kennedy; it has countless layers and ripples woven through time and is possibly a profound imprint, cemented in time.

I arrive back to my trusted hometown, through the Assunpink Gateway and transfer to the knowledge facility. Weary, I check through the historical records and yet nothing seems to have changed significantly and oh dear God, including the assassination of my counterpart (Lincoln). I see red and pound my fist against the display screen! "But how?" Confused and dismayed, my blood flows faster while I search and retrace the records, but to no avail. I finally give in and hesitate to a thought of changing my approach. I immediately look over the data entries into the facilities, not accepting that my counterpart was still assassinated and seek out this outlandish occurrence.

It is true; information pertaining to the threads of time. The equation is quite difficult to understand but simple in its findings, being, the thicker the thread in time, the higher the difficulty to change time or almost no chance at all. My findings are here, but I still feel part of the blame in some sorrowful capacity.

The more bizarre twists of these occurrences are the results stating that, Booth had made a duplicate of him-self, unbeknownst to me and is how President Lincoln was killed, in spite of my efforts. Once again, history will take care of this Booth, in more ways than one; as I made sure the other Booth will bring no harm to anybody, ever again.

To forgive myself was difficult to say the least but it would be further selfish of me to subtract my life and to affect Anne in that way. I knew when I delved into the Watchers' labyrinth; there would be certain negative anomalies of such. Onward and upward, I know that God's hand always points ahead and so, let the days of the past worry for the day itself.

CHAPTER EIGHT

BACK TO THE NORM

I am back to the time I am supposed to be. Settled, in my favorite chair and it just happens to be February 14th. Today, I have a box of heart shaped chocolates for Anne on Valentine's Day. A thought I gather? But nothing compared to a letter I received from her when we were first acquainted. Till this day, it makes me feel whole and devoted, when I have this remembrance. In short, it explained how "Original Love" was so very special and that most of all, she had this with me! I know this is not a common occurrence with regards to relationships, so I do my very best to grab on to life with Anne and appreciate every moment.

I set aside the box of chocolates and stretch back in my chair while sitting. The chair is weaved from bamboo towards the back of the chair and the arms are made of walnut with soft leather padding, adorned with fastened brass tempered rivets. It is worn out, I mean, broken in. The chair has assisted me to arrange and rewrite the years of gathered material from my daybook and journal. In fact, all the furniture that surrounds me in this one room, especially my roll top desk, gave me the inspiration to carry on.

This room is unique amongst the many and mainly consists of a few furnishings from my old quarters that I brought from behind Mr. Taft's store. In addition, I have one round ornate table for my writing lamp, courtesy of the Rutledge Inn and Mr. Rutledge of course. I always appreciated the workmanship that was well intended towards this unique table. There are two types of woods in a geometric pattern within the top of the table; walnut and cherry.

But nothing is more comforting to hear, but the squeak of my old chair. It reminds me of a childhood memory, when my father used to write letters from his old creaky chair. Amusingly, it had two wooden spindles missing from its back. It was usual to see gray powder accumulate at the back seat of the chair because it was so close to the fireplace. Well, it is a fond memory indeed.

A few months have gone by and seemingly, today is the day I put the finishing touches on my final (book) writings of my past "unordinary" travels. My journal and daybook have been worn through and through.

My old friend, the original John Kennedy is living his life, in a new state called California. John was excited to tell me about an entertaining toy called "Lincoln Logs," that his family played with for years. "There is a line of irony in my life, represented or associated with logs and now people driving a Lincoln car, very amusing."

John is a good lad but from time to time he took advantage of having the identical look, amid the President of the United States and would be adored by my many ladies. One of those ladies was the very famous Marilyn Monroe. No relation to James Monroe, the fifth President. It is unfortunate that the rumor of this affair lingers in our history and I am sure to some extent it had affected the family members of the Kennedys. When all the while, it was my good old friend Jack; the original John that is, who was a bit promiscuous?

My concern about my writings is to make sure it is time released for John's one hundredth birthday, all things considered (May 29th, 2017). This leads me to my next notion. Wait, I hear some noise and chatter outside as I dip my pen in the inkwell. I am about to write the title of my book. Trying hard to concentrate I use a term with a vernacular from the 1960's and yell, "Hold on!"

After the careful script is applied for this title I place the pen down. I push away the chair from my roll top desk with the back of my legs. The chair wheels squeak a bit and roll on the wooden floor to a halt. I then stand to close the shutter door to my desk while I quickly glance towards the window, thinking in a haze of satisfaction.

With the book lying on an angle, in the front edge of the desk I say to myself, "It is finally finished." I pick up the book to hold it dearly, then I smile and flutter the pages with my thumb and take a deep breath. I rest it back in place on the surface of the desk and close the cover. Then in a hesitant emotional flair, I focus my laden eyes of joy towards the title of the book. It reads, "The Parity of Lives Abraham and John."

My hand slowly slides away from a soft embrace of the book's cover as my thoughts of relief, turns to a stare, which sifts through the moment within the company of gratitude. I hear a horn from outside my house and so I exclaim, "Coming!" I gather myself to retrieve a new or different attire.

Getting changed quickly, I put on a worn pair of Levi's dungaree shorts. The shorts were altered and cut by using Anne's triangular teethed shaped scissor, I might say. I was stubborn not to discard this full pair of dungarees, even though the knee areas had severe tears upon them. But with a quick compromise, Anne and I were able to resolve this tug of a decision, by letting her cut them into shorts. I'm glad I did and now they are frayed and ready for summer.

I hustle through the hallway looking for my keys. Finally, I spot them on top of my lime green refrigerator in the kitchen. Oh, how could I forget? In plain sight I grab a checkered thermos filled with orange flavored Tang, I hope. I then quickly wipe up some moisture with a Handi-Wipe, on my

Formica kitchen table top. The wetness was left behind, from under the thermos but was no match for a Handi-Wipe; at least that's what it says in the TV commercial.

On my way out the door I hear a calling bark from my yellow mongrel dog. In this current era he would be called a mutt, but suchlike his namesake, Fido, Latin for faithful, he is always a breath of fresh air.

There he is, tail wagging with excitement. Standing on the porch, I twist the key to secure the house door and then turn around to see my lovely family. They are excited and patiently waiting for me.

Because I have just finished my book, I sigh and then with an extra hop in my stride I stroll down the front stairs. I fashion a quick duck walk towards my daughter Clara to make her laugh. Oh boy, to see her smile. She is my 6 year old princess and alongside her is my son Albert, who is 7. My darling Anne and I were told that our two children were Irish twins because they were born less than 12 months apart. In my era, the reference pertaining to Irish twins was used as a negative when talking about a family. None taken though on our part, but it is funny how an insult in the past turns to a euphemism or friendly repartee (fun-like) in the future.

And there is Anne, patiently waiting with that all knowing smile. I approach my 1973 Chevy Station Wagon. It is a beauty and supports wood-like panels, which are decorated on both sides of the car. It has an astonishing 327 horses and reminds me of an old horse I called, "Old Buck." He did the work of two horses. So calling my Chevy, "Old Buck," seemed to be in order.

Anne is already in the passenger seat of the car. I tell my son to get in the saddle young sir. He proceeds to tell Fido, "come-on boy," while he stands outside the rear door. Albert lets go of the leash as Fido jumps on and into the back of the Station Wagon.

Secured and ready to venture down south to Florida, where there is a new park that is supposed to be glorious. It is called; well let me see if I get this right. It is called, "Disney World not Disneyland." I always seem to confuse the two but Anne has made it clear, to which one we are traveling to. On numerous accounts, she has corrected me during past discussions on this matter. So in the future; now, that it is the place (Disney World) we are vacationing to, I don't think there will be anymore misunderstandings (laughing to myself). We have been meaning to go on this trip for a few years now. In all consideration, this is our last trip before we move to a final destination, in order to make a new home, as well as a new and different time period.

After being well thought-out, Anne and I feel that the year 2017 has much significance for all of our benefits. This era seems to be at a threshold of medical competence that Anne and I are in favor of. When we considered our past medical issues in our earlier era, it became the determining factor that helps motivate us to live in 2017.

This time period is the furthest we would like to go in the future because going any further would be an uncomforting notion, because our lifestyle would not be what we are used to. Anne and I during the years have traveled to many locations before settling down. The one thing that we have learned in knowing the future and the past, is happiness is traveling through time together; not in decades at a time but in the precious seconds we spend with each other. What works for us, oddly enough is a recipe of balance, growth and complacency, punctuated by gratuitous appreciation. This continues to keep us smiling.

Since now, we have decided to no longer use any temporal technology of the Watchers. I will take my two remaining coins, one last time to the future and thereafter, secure them where no one can find them and I need not mention the location, hmm, to anyone!

Whatever the future holds from that point on, we are at will to accept it, for good or for bad. Through our travels, Anne and I have gotten up in age a bit (before our children), we decided to settle down and for life to take its line.

We have determined to move only a few miles away from our current location in the same town and as mentioned, just a few years further into the future (2017). It is only a bucket of furlongs away from the schools that Albert and Clara can attend.

In essence, we would make a left on a route called five thirty nine, (also called High Street) off of Main Street and travel a couple of miles and all alone on the left hand side of the road, there is a farm house that we had bought a few years in the past. We both contemplated this, as soon as we made a decision to relocate and purchase. We had to figure on what year this house would be for sale and then travel to that year to complete the purchase. We have been admiring this house for about 50 years and now we have it as our home.

The farm house is a center hall colonial; built again, in our time era. But as opposed to our previous property, this property has many acres of land, where Anne and I can maintain some horses and livestock, of which and what we are used to. We are looking forward to spending much time here. There are clusters of new homes across the way, which are terrific and impressive, but nevertheless, not for us. Being able to drive (I have gotten quite good at it, by the way or should I say "Gangway!"), gives us the luxury to function. In addition, being near to the Allentown schools, which are a stone's throw away, leaves us with a secure feel and happy to further our children's education.

The move to this time period, gives me a good sense of timing to release my book. This moment in time (2017) is just a few years away, whereas time travel will be acceptable through quantum computing (subatomic frequencies, lapped over plasmatronic fields), which is extremely interesting but not my cup of tea. Even though I had many intellectual uploads from the Watchers, I still had to copy down what I just wrote, but I am getting the "hang of it," as they say.

One thing I could not understand is how fast mankind has advanced in just a hundred or so years. I discovered within my travels, a consistency of coincidences. By researching this anomaly, I can tell you this, "We, the human species are on a fast track program, speared by the Watchers." Their highest priority is to make the human race, of one species as owners and controllers of the planet Earth. In addition, the Watchers want to release the human race from the bonds of the Factions (the gods). In order to do this, mankind has to become a space faring society.

I would like to share with you, what I wrote down, when I first learned of this. I said, "I didn't understand; what are we supposed to do in space, it is just space? God has provided everything here on Earth so that we can move forward and make happiness in a timeless bliss. Quite frankly, even though my understanding of things has changed dramatically, it still does not compromise my belief in the Almighty, nor should it for you.

To further, this "Fast Track Program" by the Watchers is apparently arranged so that the human race can protect themselves from other Factions who are already space faring societies. Evidently, some of these factions are fighting amongst each other in order to control the human race through genetics, in order to make us more like them or their individual heredity (genes). I hope the one's that look like us are winning. I just laughed but then again, maybe I am laughing because I don't think we can do anything about it? So I would clarify this expression of amusement as anxiety combined with laughter. I was unaware of the severity of their involvement until I was knee deep into my venture.

Another interesting aspect of all this; is how the Watchers are advancing the Human Race. They seemingly select an individual, which they feel is suited to receive sacred ancient knowledge, with the use of influential frequencies that are targeted to a particular person's biological signal. Again, this is not my cup of tea.

Oh goodness, I am one of those individuals! I begin laughing out loud and then I stop, to think in a serious way; I really am one of their selected. The question is, "Was it on my own accord, did I have free choice? From what I have observed from the Watchers' are actions that supply a variety of choices.

After digging the rabbit hole very deep on this subject, I will reserve your rights, not to reveal this information because this truth, if told, can alter your beliefs; possibly in a good way or bad. If you are interested in this current forbidden knowledge, you know where to find me!

I would have to say, "Yes" to the question, if asked, "Would you do it all over again if I were fully and completely versed of the eventual outcomes.

When publishing my book, I selected parameters within the Watchers' knowledge systems. The results were a specific span of time for the release towards the publishing and a choice from three possible authors in this selected time period. The selections of an author were considered on the basis, of their previous publishings and were in relation to my chronicles. But, I do have to make sure, that somewhere on the cover, the book title reads, "The Parity of Lives Abraham and John," as to be. My intentions are not to contact the author directly, but to have a means of communication with a liaison, in order not to create a frenzy of questions or alarm.

The book will be in the genre of, "historical science fiction," for now...

That is quite acceptable to me because after checking the results on this matter of my tome or writings, I see that the book will be satisfactory to me upon where it was intended to go in its future. I hope that this historic vision and understanding will complete any unanswered questions that might have loitered in your mind.

I have learned that the thread of time can be twisted very tightly; some advice for you would be, to choose wisely when it is time to resist in your life because you can only survive so many of these changes. So fight the fights that are worth battling for, because those few conflicts can take a toll upon your being.

As I say, now that I am getting up in my age, "I have but one good fight left in me" and I am not about to squander it on an insignificant void or foe. This 'saying' keeps me in tune during my time here on Earth and lays credence to think about alternate approaches towards certain aspects of my life.

It was such an enjoyable vacation holiday with the family and we all are anticipating going back in our new era, to see the nuances and added changes to the theme park. Now, my family is in the process of wrapping certain articles and furniture from our old original house on Main Street, in Allentown, New Jersey. We stand to keep our old home and use it as a type of storage for our quick leap in time. We prepared our old house in such a manner, that it would bear the test of time, because of the many years between our moves. In the future they call this preparation, "winterizing." Also, I was given advice to remove the tires off of my station wagon and put the car on metal stilts. In addition, I have arranged for our good neighbor and veterinarian, who I know will definitely be there almost fifty years later, to watch and take care of our first home.

Even though for us, it will only be a few hours, the house itself will be quietly resting for a few decades. I am sentimental or maybe I just do not like to throw away anything but I will tell you that I thoroughly enjoy having this old house, that will soon be "around the corner," as they say.

After the move, I put my station wagon in storage in an outside mini barn on the old property. I also kept my writing room in the same motif or pattern of my time period, never to forget to where I come from and to whom I am. There were many sacrifices along the way and now I will make the best of what time I have here.

It seems that in my findings, the people from the past and towards the future have not changed much but the technology at their finger tips is quite different. In my travels, back and forth in time, I hold certain affinities for *country line dancing*. It reminds me when Anne and I were on our very long honeymoon stage. It was a wonderful point in time together to say the least.

Back in the 1800's, we had something similar to line dancing when we were dating. It was called "shaker dancing" and was similar to line dancing in its attempts to be coordinated but usually became out of sync because of the vigorous efforts to keep a steady march, followed by repeated twirling. It was customary to dance till exhaustion because of the religious belief, that if one labors enough, then you will be closer to God.

As far as dancing in the church I would just say, "Even though I love to dance and thoroughly enjoy the camaraderie, I feel that dancing and clapping is more of a "me" thing and not as selfless as the original design towards prayer. In other words, when I am referencing God I need peace and quiet in order to pray. But then again, using the parts of the body that are "not" in harmony within a community can harm their unity. So as a priest had once said to me, "Whereby, if the human body and its various parts are working in harmony, God sends spiritual gifts and benefits." You see, this is why it's important to dance. My family did thoroughly enjoy the unity of dancing at church. I'll admit I do miss that.

Using the current technology of this new era, I can practice dozens of line dances and of course with Anne's assistance. I have mastered the art of line dancing and I am content by its entertaining reassurance. I truly get a "kick" out of (no pun intended) the harmony and bringing together, groups of dancers at certain events. (Please mind my futuristic jargon.) Therefore, I have "headed up" line dancing classes in order to share my enjoyment towards this art.

You can find me in this current time period as a headliner for "county line dancing" events throughout the year. Please join me at a place, in a huge log-cabin called, "Laurita Winery." It is located in the humble town of New Egypt, New Jersey and just a ten minute car drive or twenty-five minutes by horse from where I now live.

Please don't worry about coming by if you have not mastered the dances. The fun is all about the learning process. Just learn the basic steps via your technology device and you can apply them to all the songs. You can be reassured, that I will be shouting out the dance steps and even if you do not know the dance, you can still keep up. This will keep you honest within any of the songs and to take the benefits from. Let me see if I can put the noble into your nobility to dance!

CHAPTER NINE

REFLECTION

Being gratuitous is the key ingredient in order to forever gain a chance towards happiness. Please forgive me if I had made this similar statement in the past. I have seen too many unhappy lives or individuals in my day, including my counterpart.

Do I seldom mirror my judgment or opinion? Indeed, every morning I prepare myself for the upcoming day by grooming my perception, thus I pray for, with concern of the people I have left behind as well as my loved ones. If when a thought of someone appears into my mind's eye, unannounced, I say a prayer and then wish them well, foe or friend. This healthy measure interrupts past obsessions about things you cannot control. It is something that has worked well for me, so I am sharing it with you.

I have sensed the sadness of time and simply conclude, to the mere fact that you cannot stop it. Whether traveling forward or backward, it is at a constant, and without time we cannot exist. The only thing you can do is "realize" when a blessed moment is upon you and seize that instant because you know it will pass. I look at myself now and see a weathered face but a body of a youthful man, thanks to the super strength the Watchers had given to me.

Before my last move from my first home, I had made my most recent inquiries within the Watchers' Facility. My curiosity needed to be filled because of the fear to wonder in a countless circle for the rest of my life. In doing so, I found some amazing truths, which sets a whole new standard to why mankind does what they do and so it is.

First and foremost, is the confusing but spectacular way that all truisms (truths) are finite in time and interpreted by the onlooker as either fact or lack of understanding, as to why a particular occurrence happens?

The Watchers possess, what I think is special technology or some sort of spirituality connection in order to bring out true organization in a world that is by far disorganized. After further research on this matter, it seems the Creator has the same efficient methods of organization within the jumbled universe but on a much larger scale.

When I went to search about what went wrong with my counterpart President Lincoln, I needed to understand, with much curiosity as to how the Watchers laminate the exact facts. Somehow, the Watchers document every occurrence and or moment in time, of everyone and everything that takes place; in, on or above the surface of the Earth. In fact, they have continuous connections to all worlds.

To explain to you how it works, would be a bit of an injustice because this information is above my timeline. Hmm, okay... I will attempt a mild interpretation of what I think I have learned. The Watchers have this ability to use a method to see and record all, then duplicate any moment in time, like you are watching one of your movies. They call this, *Remote Viewing.* This technology, seemingly taps into an invisible realm of light and sound and reassembles resonating subatomic particles, thus duplicated from residual energy signatures. This energy is comprised of two components. The first is the dimensional biological recording sphere called, "Akashic Hub of Records," which is a timeless void of all our lives, before we were here, during and after. This is a gateway that is channeling multiple biological spiritual frequencies individually to all things that are living. I figured this is impart of how humans receive energies to our spirits, which in turn, rejuvenates our being and also assists in the healing process of our bodies, when injured. You understand that some or should I say, most of these teachings I have copied into my daybook are from my inquiries at the Watchers' facility. Although, I have been gifted with many uploads of clever statistics.

To continue, the second proponent is a larger invisible spherical energy that encompasses everything, including the Akashic Hub of Records. It is like an invisible skin that surrounds the entire universe and records every measure in time of not only biological living things but every bit of matter and material in our current existence. In essence, it reads and regulates the distribution of everything, in addition to its recording capabilities. This is all done in an inter-dimensional realm and is invisible to the naked eye.

I know now, that I have to pray harder in order for my prayers to be heard. Oh, let us hope not, as I say with a smile. It is quite spectacular to say the least. It makes sense that if God went through all the trouble in order to make the universe, would he not then record it? That would be like not taking any pictures or draw a reference of your loved ones for an entire life.

***

A day in our current life: Speaking of pictures, I just came across some family pictures that I hold dear in my wallet and notice that my driver's license is quite expired. It appears to be forty five years invalid. Oh dear, I must alert Anne of this because she had referenced an interest in driving, other than some farm equipment that is about in our yard.

While walking through the house I hear scuffling up the stairs. I believe Anne is working diligently on one of our closets; in fact, she has attached part of the hallway to our bedroom and calls it a *walk-in-closet*.

Clara has taught Anne how to purchase an enormous amount of gifts through our newly found advanced devices and these boxes or products are in attendance almost every day, laid upon my front porch, between the swing and the front door. There is an overhang or roof that protects the porch and therefore, Clara and Anne do not at all feel hesitant to order things at will. When I tend to the subject about the gifts, the girls quickly correct me and mention that the gifts are necessities and thereafter giggle towards each other while smiling back at me. What can I say?

It is a positive routine for them because there is that short interlude or five to ten minutes of happiness it provides to each of them. Maybe I am missing the point, because there is a mother daughter bonding that occurs and is invaluable. We have become so familiar with one of the men who drops off numerous packages, that we nick-named him Fred-Ex. His real name is Fredrick Peters, but we do have fun, from time to time with these endearing traditions, when connecting with close acquaintances in a familiar or friendly manner.

Lastly, I approach the bottom of the staircase and grab the banister and notice that the main post is a bit unsecure or needs to be tightened. While calling for Anne from the bottom of the stairs I quickly wedge a scrap of wood between the rails against the post for a temporary fix until I have further time. The piles of garbage besides me are the remnants from the construction repairs that Albert and I completed on the closet upstairs. The only problem is I do not have a current up-to-date driver's license and I am not too sure if they will let me dump these scraps at the Cream Ridge Township recycle facility.

Nevertheless, I do need a new license matching my new home address. Anne comes forth towards the top of the staircase and replies, "Hi, are you hungry? I will be done shortly and will then come down and fix you a surprise with something to eat. A new dish I have learned." While looking up the stairs at her, I smile and say, "Yes, sure, that sounds good, but would it be okay if we can eat on the back porch? The weather is pleasant as of now." While fussing with her apron and patting some dust away, Anne says, "Yes, that's a good idea because I can finally use the new dolly-cart that I bought." I become confused and respond, "Dolly-cart?" Yes, I had it delivered a few days ago; it's one of the few items I had delivered this week." I mumble under my breath with a snarl, quietly saying, "A few items, hmm?" Saying to myself, "Okay I gather that, seven is a few." Anne hesitates, wondering if I said something, but begins to explain, "Hmm, a dolly-cart is similar to the 'Dumbwaiter...' So I interrupt her as she releases her breath along with a stare and I wittingly say, "Why do you say that about the waiter at the Happy Apple Inn Restaurant? I understand he was a little shy but hey, maybe that's why my burger came out well-done when I ordered it medium-rare?

Her frustration turns to a bellow of laughter and says, "Oh please!" While she continues to laugh, Anne waves me off and slowly returns to her work but quickly explains that the cart is on wheels that carries the full meal through the house, especially to the porch. She then further realizes and states, "I had gotten the idea from the Happy Apple Inn Restaurant, but you already figured that out, Mr. Smarty pants."

While enjoying our meal on the back porch I am appreciating the hanging plants that surround the overhang area above our porch. I take a sip of tea from a cup that is part of a set and was one of the few possessions we brought from the 1800's. It was a dear gift from her siblings from when we were just married. I look at the gold trim edging atop the tea cup and say to Anne, "The flowering that takes place amongst the hanging plants do bloom often and they don't seem to follow the performance of other flowers, in part to be limited to one or two blossoms m a season. But how and what are they called？ Anne simply states, "They are called hibiscus. One is called

Live Red and the other one is Rosa. There are over a dozen of different varieties. The lady mentioned that they are a hybrid design of plant and has been perfected to have a residual bloom all through the season."

After finishing our meal I stand up and deliver a yawn and a stretch. Whoa, I almost hit my head on one of the hanging porch plants as I begin to load the dishes upon Anne's new dolly-cart. I say to Anne with no uncertainty, "I will cleanup because we have to get to the Department of Motor Vehicles (DMV) before they close. Plus, I want to drive the dolly into the kitchen while you are getting ready, even though I have an expired driver's license." Anne turns back around while walking away and says with concern, "Careful!" She heard my risky attempt with hurdling the one step from the porch into house with a full load of tableware. So after a very short and slight stumble I say, "I'm good," rustling while casting a smile in her direction. Anne walks away and says with her back turned, "Mr. Lincoln having a hard time being a waiter, hmm." I definitely heard a few chuckles of laughter down the hall from Anne.

With an hour to spare Anne and I arrive at the Quaker Bridge Mall motor vehicles in Mercer County, New Jersey, which is only a couple of miles away from Princeton University. Actually it is a bit further away than that, but the understanding in New Jersey is, a couple of miles is really 10 minutes or 10 miles. I have been trying to coordinate my schedule in order to visit and tour the "Princeton Plasma Physics Laboratory, which is the first or third Friday of the month at 10:00 AM. It has an array of fusion technology and an exciting underground facility. I wish to compare this complex with the Watchers' facility, therefore, another reason to acquire a new driver's license, because it is the required identification needed in order to tour this fascinating plasma laboratory.

The front of the DMV building has a design frontage made all out of glass and in my approach; I am a bit worried because of various amounts of long lines to wait on. After entering the DMV building, it appears from the thick of things, it is very unlikely to see any Quakers from Pennsylvania in the Quaker Bridge Department of Motor Vehicles. Pity though, because in my era, my descendants were deep rooted as Colonial Puritans and Quakers, even though I was brought up Baptist. Overall, it seems as though Quakers are not in abundance in this time period, but I am sure many of them have transformed into a peaceful faith. As a young lad, I had learned about the abolishment of slavery and equal rights in support of women, for the first time from the people who were Quakers. Therefore, because of the Quaker heritage and principled moralities, thus further developed these strong convictions by my counterpart, President Lincoln, in regards to the matters of slavery and women rights. I am proud to say that the Republican Party that my counterpart (President Lincoln) began, finally fought 50 years later and passed, for the "women's right to vote!"

After further study, it seems Anne and I both have to wait on a line in order to be directed to another line. I proceed to move to the back of a line while Anne is shadowing me. Well, should I say, to what I thought was the back of the line. All of a sudden, a man comes towards me in an aggressive fashion and begins to yell at me. While he is looking up at me, the Hispanic man says to me, "You have just cut the line; I have been waiting in this line for a half an hour and now, you have just cut it!" His eyes refer to a longer line towards the back of the building. His accent was hard to decipher but with help of his quickened body language, he points three times to where I am supposed to be.

My facial expression is fastened to a distraught look. I am instantly grappled with a variety of different emotions and I am undecided how to respond, so I quickly glance at Anne to say nothing and proceed to the back of another line. The right line, I hope? So it seems there was a pass-through opening on this apparent line, which created a large break in the herd of people and thus camouflaged the end of the line. Well, you know what I say about people who make excuses, so maybe I should just offer this one up, to my inexperience.

During this stuffy detention, I notice that mostly all of the people enduring this "sit-tight" process are preoccupied with their handheld devices. At first I am scared and ask myself, "how can society let this happen? But then realize, I have a phone device as well and was just sharing a prediction of weather with Anne, hmm.

An hour passes and Anne and I reach the informational desk. The lady seemed to be mad at us before we could speak, so I said to her, "Good afternoon ma'am." Before I could say anything thing further, she was quick to reply and says, "I'm not that old!" I was confused and say to her, "My wife needs to take the written driver's test and I would be glad about renewing my driver's license.

The information lady with the very long eye lashes and blue hair, looks at me and begins to shake her head and says, "You should lose the mustache and grow a beard. Wow, you'd look just like Abe Lincoln then," as she looks at me with a lingered daze. She looks towards Anne and quickly says, "Oh and no offense." Anne says in response, "Not at all," while turning her attention to me, Anne continues to say, "Wouldn't it be altogether fitting to even know Abe Lincoln, no less to be married to him." Anne draws a big smile.

We both become startled, while the "information lady" suddenly slaps two forms on the table to fill out and thereafter, quickly separates the applications on her desk, and slides the forms that correspond, to each of us and says, "Sweetie you're going to go over there," as she points to a partitioned area.

She then refers me to a line where I coincidently stand behind my hostile Hispanic friend. Unfortunately for him, he did not have his six points of identification, as he was attempting to attain a new license, in which more proof is required.

My turn has arrived at the counter. Another entertaining lady takes my completed form and begins to stamp my paperwork. Soon after, her fingers slide and click on a keyboard in order to input my information, when I notice her long multi-colored fingernails. They possess tiny bits of jewelry attached to the top of each of them, along with a ring around her thumb.

As I look over to check on Anne, the lady stops typing and says, "Excuse me?" She rolls her eyes and further says, "Seriously?" I don't understand what she means, maybe because I am mind-struck by an earring that is pierced into the center of her tongue and become preoccupied, while asking myself the question, why?

It is nevertheless strange, that in this time period, why so many people have grasped the theatrical part of life during their everyday existence and play a roles/parts governed by the current society they live in. While an attempt is made for individuality, with a bit of creativity, it unfortunately falls flat because even though there are more than enough performers of this era, it seems as though, they are all playing the same role or part, with no end in sight. My conclusion to this matter is, "These new generations of children are seeking a high level of 'attention,' which was not given to them by their parents because it seems that the technology devices replaces a major portion of parenting, detracting a healthy sociable level of upbringing."

The lady whose name I assume is Ivanka Vittadini, because of the label on her blouse, continues to say with a surprised look, "You realize the license you gave me for your renewal is over forty years expired. Where've you-been? Frozen, because you don't look as old as this license says?" I have to think quickly, so I lean in towards her, sporting a smart smile and say, "Oh, thank you for the compliment madam." Her eyes open wide, so I figure this will not do and therefore, I continue to drum up wit and say, "Actually, I am a time traveler and referring to the awkward break in time on my license, well, it is just a small part of a work related drawbacks or hazardous duties if you will." She blurts out laughing and says, "Well, if you try this again in another forty some odd years from now, it ain't gonna work!

So here you go," as she hands me a receipt of my paperwork. She tells me to take a step to my left and stand behind the red tape on the floor. Then she says, "Oh and don't forget your change, because we want a happy face for your new license. Ready, now smile," as she takes my picture. Afterwards, I say to her, "Thank you so very much Ivanka." She hesitates and looks back at me and laughs again.

Anne proceeds to turn the corner after the completion of her written test, while she forwards me a silent happy hello from across the room. She then swiftly raises her hand while holding up a paper, then mouths the words, I *passed*. Today went very well and I am delighted to share, part of a day in our lives, but relationships do <u>not</u> move forward without effort from each of us and how a problem is handled, when it is confronted is the key to keep connected.

❅ ❅ ❅ ❅

The one negative, in an attempt to have a "true" relationship, is your level of trust towards your fellow man. It becomes harder to manage and becomes ill-fated the older you get. Unfortunately, you need to trust openly in any relationship in order for it, to be successful.

In my experience, from what a man is feeling, I used to believe, "is twice as much towards what he is saying?" On

145

this note I stand to be corrected. The truths that I find in my efforts, lean in a direction that is unfiltered, in order to understand the horrors that bled through to my counterpart, President Lincoln. They are tenfold, not twice, "To what another man feels and does not show." I must confront these facts for closure, so to breathe fresh air, not in vain. I do this for myself and for the sacrifice that came upon my counterpart, President Lincoln.

Conspiracy is a word that defines two or more people planning to do harm and if said in conjunction or alongside with the word "theory," you would then have the phrase, *conspiracy theory*. Well then; the notion or the search for the truth will probably be shrugged away with less concern by the ears that hear it. There should be a word that describes, somewhat of a more severe action and or result, other than the word "conspiracy," and mind you, without an adjective coupled to the word.

If there are no coincidences and everything is conjoined collectively, through entanglement, then the similarities between President Kennedy and President Lincoln, along with other odd anomalies are unprecedented at the highest possible level and or chance.

It is oh, so very strange and eerie that John Wilkes Booth (the younger version of Johnson) was accepted into the Booth's family. Supposedly, John Booth had an older brother Edwin Booth, who was an illegitimate son and also was an actor. Edwin and John Booth's father was a famous actor of his time; his name was Junius (Julius) Brutus Booth. How a parent would name their child after an assassin is wide of the mark in principle, to me that is.

Junius, the would-be father to both sons and his wife, also had eccentric parents. John Wilkes Booth's grandparents were the same natives from New Jersey that had land issues with my grandfather, Abraham Lincoln. He was a military captain during the American Revolution War and a great farmer. John Wilkes Booth's grandparents name their son Junius Brutus Booth after Julius Caesar's *assassin* (from 1800 years ago). The name of Julius Caesar's assassin or right hand man was "Junius Brutus" or "Marcos Junius Brutus."

Coincidentally, the three Booth actors had an obsession with William Shakespeare's, "The Tragedy of Julius Caesar," a drama. They all positioned and or swallow up themselves to perform this play numerous times on an unprecedented scale. They would go so far as to gamble between each other to play the lead role of Brutus, thirsting for the role of the assassin.

The Julius Caesar tragedy was another adjustment or correction in Earth's timeline by the Watchers (with over 5000 years of amendments, along with every adjustment being orchestrated just over a hundred years apart).

In connection to the Julius Caesar and Lincoln's assassination, they were both murdered by their *next in command* or from their right-hand man and even more profound, that Lincoln was killed by a man obsessed with the murder of Caesar.

In addition, after the results following the killings, each of the men, Brutus and Booth were rejected by the majority of power and or public opinion. Their plots all became foiled and fruitless.

In Brutus' case, he was unaware that Mark Antony would sway the populous opinion against him. Mark Antony turns the tides against Brutus with the use of wit and within the, "Friends, Romans, countrymen, lend me your ears," speech, Brutus loses all credibility. This speech saved the people, from what would have been an onslaught of tyranny, enacting power and control and because of this speech; it eventually helped halt slavery to be set forth in the direction of and for the people. In exactly 1800 years later, to the moment, Lincoln delivers the "Gettysburg Address," which is the foothold that turns the populous against slavery. Interestingly enough, after studying the Gettysburg Address, along with other indicators, I conclude that the Watchers had an influence in the structure of the ever-so-important speech.

The spooky time overlap, between Vice President Andrew Johnson's trust and the confidence in the Secretary of War, Edwin Stanton, seems to be also misjudged; suchlike Caesar to Brutus and his colleagues. To further the correlation to this link, there is Caesar's surprise at his brutal end, after Brutus stabs him. Caesar's last breath trickles out a Greek phrase, "Kai ou, tekvov;" meaning, "You too, child?"

The importance of the Julius Caesar assassination for the Watchers was not the assassination, because in connection to Lincoln and Kennedy as well as Caesar, all of their murders were not necessary for the Watchers to make their important adjustment in time or to prevent history from straying off path.

The Watchers inserted Mark Antony to reassure that Roman history would not change direction, because the Watchers' sole intention was to usher in Christianity in the upcoming centuries, when the Emperor Constantine will be the authority of Rome. Constantine was another intervention and adjustment by the Watchers.

In just a few hundred years, Rome will control the largest territory under one rule. Once Constantine makes Christianity the main religion of his rule, then the beliefs of Christianity will flourish throughout the world. Soon after, the Watchers would retreat and step back from any further intervention within this timeline.

The Watchers would then be able to assist and inject mankind with the much needed morality and principals once again. For thousands of years, the Watchers have supported and shared multiple religions across the Earth in accordance to geographical location. Seemingly, they believe in a single supreme being, who is the creator of all.

The last of the significant coincidences between Caesar and Lincoln, I would like to mention, comes forth with the, "Ides of March." The "Ides" refers to the middle of the month that corresponds to the Roman calendar. The Ides of March is the 15th day of March and became a day that coupled its way, to burn an association with regards to the assassination of Julius Caesar and the day of tax and debt collections for Rome. This became cemented onto the Ides of March.

For this was a turning point in (Roman) historic time and was the same historic pivoting result, which was connected to my counterpart. President Lincoln produced an about face on America's history and led us through a tough path, to a unified reward and towards a righteous path.

On the Ides of April, 1865, the plot to kill Lincoln and his colleagues was in full motion and just like the cowardly action of Brutus in the assassination of Julius Caesar, he murders him from behind. It would be the eccentric John Wilkes Booth, who had marveled and played, numerous times the portrayal of Brutus, is about to cross over his dramatized sensationalism to reality. He acts out in the same spiritless way and shoots Lincoln from behind and creates the soon to be fatal wound in the back of his head.

"Our American Cousin" was the theatrical play that Lincoln attended the night he was shot. Booth, having seen the play "Our American Cousin" at Ford's Theatre on many occasions, timed his plot in accordance to the play.

First he persuades Lincoln's body guards to move from their posts in order to consume alcohol with them in a nearby saloon. While the men indulged themselves, Booth slips away and makes his way up the stairs to Lincoln's theatre box. Before entering the room, Booth carves a hole in the adjacent wall and peeks through, in order to see Lincoln's position. He times and waits for the part of the play when laughter is going to emerge. For this was his own cue to take action and shoot the President at point-blank range, with his one shot Derringer pistol.

The following day, on April 15ᵗʰ, 7:22am, across the street from the Ford's Theatre in the Petersen House, President Lincoln departs this life. Presidents, Lincoln and Kennedy were the two longest periods of national mourning in the United States' history. It is ironic that just a few weeks earlier, John Wilkes Booth was sleeping in the same bed at the Petersen House that Lincoln passed away in. With regard to what happens to Booth, post assassination; as always, the historic karma will eventually take care of the fate, intended for this "Dead Ringer."

So now, the 15ᵗʰ of April is the deadline for U.S. tax debt, as was to the similarity, of over 1800 years ago for the Ides of March. As said before, after the assassination of Caesar, the 15ᵗʰ of March was the outstanding day for the people under Roman rule to settle all debts and taxes on this notorious date.

An astonishing note: After my counterpart's death, President Lincolns coffin was exhumed 17 times and a confirmation that I am uncomfortable with. Furthering my thoughts about this, I might be responsible for at least one. When I had received certain strengths from the Watchers, well, on more than one occasion I would entertain the patrons in the local saloons by picking up a 55 gallon oak barrel over my head and take a gulp or two of the reaming liquid. I am pretty sure the barrels were close to being empty, I think? I have feared that in the name of science, they would be interested in why an older man, would have the body of a youthful lad. Hence, their possible suspicions to find out, not sure?

There are many coincidences occurrences that develop out of these timelines. During the timeline corrections, the Watchers have revealed that the changes in time require much overlapping within the time thread occurrences, in order to adjust time. The more you change time, the more coincidences are going to occur.

So if your life has many coincidental happenings, your timeline has been possibly altered. This is done either to prevent you from being great, because your greatness can have a negative affect on the timeline or to protect you from harm, because you are an important factor to keep the timeline in a positive direction. Either way, the Watchers do not want your life to head forth in that direction, if again you experience these flukes in nature.

In my research I have noticed, the more you try to change the world, the more coincidences you will have. This is the cause and effect that distributes an over abundant, number of coincidences and pertaining to the Lincoln assassination, there are no shortages of these coincidences or twists of fate.

The accuracy within the history of my counterpart's death is not at all complete. According to the historical recordings of the Watchers' *remote viewing* technology equipment, Andrew Johnson, Vice President and Edwin Stanton, Secretary of War, led a plot to undermine and take control from what was President Lincoln's current administration.

History has John Booth in the lead role as the conspirator, when in fact you just have to deduce who would benefit the most and to who is left standing, after the crime of obsession. Andrew Johnson, the "would-be" President of the United States and Edwin Stanton, who would have been the Vice President, if it were not for the survival of Secretary of State, William Seward.

On the face of it, at the exact time Booth was assassinating President Lincoln, Lewis Powell, a Confederate soldier wounded at Gettysburg months earlier, forced entry through the front door of William Seward's (the Secretary of State's) home. Powell, the intruder had a recognizable face because his jaw was somewhat distorted from a mule bucking accident. He then made his way through the house and gained access into the bedroom of William Seward, after two short battles with members within the house.

Secretary Seward was already bedridden, from a carriage accident that occurred a few days earlier and was an easy target for Lewis Powell to take his life. Powell repetitively stabbed and slashed the Secretary of State, Seward and leaves him to die. Powell storms out of the house but not before battling with Seward's son and injuring him as well. Fortunately, everyone survived in this assassination attempt, putting a wedge in Johnson's overall plan.

Edwin Stanton unable to receive his position of vice president set the way for Johnson and Stanton to be in a constant state of conflict, during Johnson's Presidency. This is part of the reason for President Johnson's impeachment and the House of Representatives attempt to remove him from the office of president.

Amongst the high crimes and misdemeanors, was the chatter pointing to Johnson as the lead conspirator in the assassination of the president. Stanton released certain valid points as an insider, which convinced the majority of Republicans of Johnson's involvement, pertaining to Lincoln's death and without revealing his own involvement. This matter was unbeknownst to Johnson. Johnson was a Democrat with obvious intentions, as he was a sympathizer for the Southern Confederacy.

There is a long list of firsts within Lincoln's presidency and Johnson adds to this record by becoming very drunk on Lincoln's inaugural day 1865. This being the celebratory beginning of Lincoln's second term as the United States President, but it would be Johnson's first time as his vice president. Andrew Johnson would become president in just a couple of months. His few words pronounced properly at Lincoln's inaugural day, became offensive to the crowd. For instance, he blurted out this comment, "Religion is just a guide for you primitive people." His acceptance speech to be vice president was an ominous sign of things to come. Just over a month later, President Lincoln was murdered.

Some of the fascinations of "firsts" for my counterpart were: to become the first Republican to win the Presidency of the United States. Also, being the first president to be born outside the original 13 colonies. In addition, to hold a U.S. patent, to wear a beard, a self-image to appear on U.S. paper money while in office and to be the first and only president to appear on a penny and most unfortunate, to be the first president to befall to an assassination.

Additional reasons for the "first" U.S. President, Andrew Johnson to be impeached. During the "Reconstruction Era," Johnson had ignored the constitution and certain new laws that were in place. As time went on, there were other indications that leaned towards his guilt as the head of the conspiracy to kill Lincoln.

President Johnson soon pardoned certain people who were found guilty in the plot to kill and help take over the current administration. He also watched the people, who did his dirty work and made certain they would hang or be shot to death, as they would never be able to point blame towards him.

In order to plan steps ahead, Johnson had arranged, so it would appear as if, he was supposed to be assassinated as well. He did this by including and hiring a southern sympathizer George Atzerodt, who was a part of a previous conspiracy to kidnap President Lincoln and then later, (plan to be told) after the kidnapping, hold President Lincoln captive until they legally try to impeach Lincoln without his presence and absence within the office. This to me is a familiar tone for some reason, similar to a strong déjà vu or coincidence, personally.

April 14th was going to be an easy, well paid day for George Atzerodt. His simple duties were to go to the Kirkwood Hotel, were Vice President Johnson was lodging, sit at the bar and drink, till later in the night after all of the devious plans were carried out. In essence, he was to pretend that he was there to kill Vice President Johnson and reassure that his presence at the hotel was known, in order to be witnessed and thereafter, rendezvous to Maryland, and meet up, to receive his payment.

Another precaution Johnson took, was for John Wilkes Booth to show up at the Kirkwood Hotel, where Johnson was staying and drop a note purposely in the wrong mailbox, so that there would be a mix-up or fuss and therefore, a witness to the note's readings. Johnson has his secretary go to the lobby and pick up this letter and announce it to the clerk. The letter was intended to be for Vice President Johnson. He reads, "Do not wish to disturb you; are you at home?" "Signed, J. Wilkes Booth."

The arrival of the letter was to signal Johnson, that the plan is in place and everything is to go forward as designed. There are multiple levels on how easily this letter can be taken as Johnson being involved but no one wanted to imagine the towering level of treason attached to this atrocity.

Too many times in my experience I have found a pattern, well, excuse me to some of you. I am not sure I mean this as a euphemism or if this is true in the future, but if you ever want to know what nefarious or deceptive plan a Democrat is up to or has committed, it is most likely, what they are accusing you of.

It saddens me on how all political contradictions, slowdown the achievements of mankind and in addition, hurt each other just for power. The end result filters down to a common denominator, family. The results of these behaviors conclude, "A family that reaps but never gets the chance to sow..." President Lincoln had fought against these types of behavior and even though my counterpart's success was grand, he did and had experienced the equivalency of just as much sorrow and anguish within his personal being.

President Lincoln carried with him, my accumulated past, up until the point of our separation and now that I have studied the Watchers' temporal archives, I have a pure understanding of all that had happened with regards to my counterpart's true history. I am swayed to be somewhat unassuming at this point. I tried very hard to approach this history with a level head and without emotion, but to no avail, I was unsuccessful.

I know now that some of my past held certain bounds to my counterpart, some good some not so good. One of those characteristic elements that were an inward struggle was the knowledge of the true love that I shared with Anne. This stymied his ability to persist in this category.

In fact, when he would hear someone refer to him as Abe, he would kindly ask them to refer to him something other than. Abe or Abbie was an endearment and how Anne would exhibit affection for me; hence my counterpart's struggle with this issue.

To my understanding, my counterpart had the pressure of becoming president and chose a type of love that encouraged good companionship and was the bearer of logic towards the strides of something greater.

In 1842, Lincoln marries Mary Anne Todd. She was raised in the state of Kentucky and in some instances; she was referred to as "Molly," a nickname given because of Mary being a very popular name of this era. She would benefit from the precincts of her wealthy family and grow up to be very well educated.

She was drawn to politics and took after her father, who was in a constant circle of the political Washington D.C. privileged. Unlike myself and my counterpart, who were considered to come from humble beginnings. Extreme, a bit I thought, considering we had always paid our way, just not wealthy.

This issue became a wedge between her, my counterpart and her family. Mary Todd and Lincoln had broken off their engagement on more than one occasion, with some separations done secretly. My staunch view on this matter is my counterpart developed a comfort for a gal that was very educated and had a maternal physique, being warm hearted and reminded him of our wonderful mother. Nevertheless, they reunite and with a ten year difference in age between them, they decide to put together a short engagement and get married on November 4th 1842.

Mary mothered four children, all sons. Their first son was born in Springfield, Illinois, August 1st 1843. His name was Robert Todd Lincoln. He followed somewhat in his father's footsteps in becoming a lawyer, politician and businessman. He was an active Republican and served three US Presidents and unfortunately, he was the only son to make it to adulthood amongst Lincoln's four children.

Robert Todd Lincoln passed on July 26th 1926 and from his children, became one of the last descendents and relative of the Lincoln's family line. His name was Robert Todd Lincoln Beckwith, who died on December 24th 1985. In my opinion, we are all descendents of the Lincoln family!

Their second son, Edward Baker Lincoln was born on March 10th 1846 and was named after Lincoln's friend Edward Dickinson Baker. Tragedy finds the Lincoln family when little Eddie died of Typhoid fever a month shy of his fourth birthday. He was a tender loving child, and before he passed, he insisted on nursing a helpless kitten back to health, who he loved dearly.

William Wallace Lincoln was the third son, who was named after Mary's brother-in-law, Dr. William Wallace. He was called Willie in his youth and it was an endearing way for the family to bond with him during his childhood. But once again, the Lincoln family is struck by the horrors of Typhoid fever right before Willie becomes a teenager. William Wallace Lincoln was born December 21st 1850 and died in Washington, D.C. on February 20th 1862. His body was later disinterred (removed from the grave) from a cemetery in Washington D.C. after President Lincoln's death and brought to Oak Ridge Cemetery in Springfield, Illinois. There would be the final resting place for President Lincoln and his son Willie, on May 4th, 1865.

On April 21st 1865, Lincoln's funeral train will carry President Lincoln and his son Willie through to a hundred and eighty cities and seven states, until their final resting place in Springfield, Illinois. During this 1600 mile journey, Lincoln's coffin was taken off the train in different cities and placed in a decorated horse-drawn carriage and then settled into view in order for the public to pay their respects and pass by his body.

After her husband's death, Mary Todd Lincoln was pressured to move out of the White House, immediately following Lincoln's death. She had to fight and rely on public opinion in order to embarrass Andrew Johnson into letting her stay, because he was now the President of the United States and was very eager to claim his new residence at the White House.

Mary Todd receives approximately two weeks to leave the White House, in what she claimed to be her eviction to leave her home. Now a widow, Mary Todd writes, "The miserable inebriated Johnson, had knowledge and awareness of my husband's death. Johnson had some hand in all of this!"

The last and fourth son to be born was Thomas Lincoln. Born April 4th 1853, he was very squiggly as a baby, so Lincoln gave him the "nickname" Tad, short for tadpole. Thomas Lincoln was originally named after his paternal grandfather (Abraham Lincoln's father), but the name "Tad" stuck from the very beginning of his birth. Tad died just after his 18th birthday, on July 15th 1871, from what they think was Tuberculosis or a severe cold.

After the death of her son Tad, Mary Todd Lincoln would suffer with major grief and depression, which permanently challenged her sanity. Tad's passing away followed the deaths of her other two sons and the loss of her husband, was too much to bear for Mary Todd.

Having understanding about a misfortune, doesn't necessarily ease your mind but resolves the notion to have further questioning that could "haunt" your intentions to reflect during one's life.

When the topic of my counterpart comes up between Anne and I we tend to pray and give thanks in connection of all the parties involved. For us, it is all of one hundred fifty years in the past but not in our hearts. It is deeply rooted within our daily lives, before and after these occurrences.

I blindly surrendered part of my life to the "cause" and in doing so I lifted up my faith, but yet somehow my sacrificed life with Anne turned out to be a gain and seems surreal on so many different levels.

Have I done enough to deserve such a good life as compared to others? A question that probably shouldn't be asked to one's self very often, because the answer could threaten and slash your ability to be grateful for what you really have. This in turn can defeat the "inspiration" within your spirit and alter a chance to "compose" the best you!

Similar to myself, my counterpart has made some inspirational phrases that I would like to share:

"Give me six hours to chop a tree down and I will spend the first four hours sharpening the axe blade."

"No man has a good enough memory to be a successful liar."

"If you want to test a man's character, give him power."

"Plainly put, the central idea of succession is the essence of anarchy."

"You say you will not fight for Negroes, yet some of them are willing and fighting for you!"

"The best way to predict your future is to create it."

"Every man's happiness is his own responsibility."

"In the end, it's not the years in your life that count. It's the life in your years."

"You can tell the greatness of a man by what makes him angry."

"My concern is not whether God is on our side; my greatest concern is to be on God's side."

"If slavery is not wrong, then nothing is wrong!"

"I do not think much of a man who is not wiser today than he was yesterday."

"He has the right to criticize, who has a heart to help."

"Those who deny freedom to others deserve it not for themselves."

"You cannot escape the responsibility of tomorrow by evading it today."

"You can fool all the people some of the time, and some of the people all the time, but you cannot fool all the people all of the time."

"You have to do your own growing no matter how tall your grandfather was."

"If you want to change the law, you have to enforce it first."
"If we desire to respect the law, we must first make the law respectable."

"If I were two faced, would I be wearing this one?"

"In this sad world of ours, sorrow comes to us all and often comes with bitter agony. The perfect relief is not possible except with *time*. Now, you cannot believe that you will ever feel better. This is not true, because you are sure to be happy again. Knowing this and truly believing it will make you less miserable now. My counterpart and I have had enough experiences in both our lives to make this statement."

Abraham Lincoln

To forgive Andrew Johnson is an odd question? I have learned that forgiveness is actually for the benefit of the victim or to who was offended. Virtually, it is best to stop feeling resentment or anger towards the person who has hurt you and most of all, take from the experience in order to learn and thereafter, grow from it.

In Johnson's case, I pity his existence, for his entire history had no peace and he lived in a world of untruthfulness. To me, that is hell on Earth. So my revenge was to let it be and so I say, "In all times, men should not utter what they would not be responsible for, here and through eternity."

When looking back into the past, doesn't interest you anymore and you are excited about the future; that the new day starts with no mistakes in it yet...Then you are doing something right. This virtue I try to live by and was a struggle that I have battled through all of my life.

Abraham Lincoln

CHAPTER TEN

A GIFT & A GLIMPSE

As I sit and contemplate how to present some significant thoughts and experiences I have collected over the past few days, I understand, that my delivery is of the utmost importance. The volume or degree in which you share your experiences with others, should be measured according to the audience you are with. If what needs to be said is not presented in an amicable manner, the message will not be received. Every day of life that we live is a gift and I hope the messages and the glimpse I share, will also be considered a gift because it comes from the heart.

Criticism at times is not taken lightly. In the past I have taken exception to some judgmental accusations that my critics have accused my counterpart of having a lack of association with a structured religious institution. I take that criticism personally because there is irony in the attacks from the media on President Lincoln. As a citizen of the United States of America, aren't we able to practice our religious beliefs as we see fit? Both myself and President Lincoln have never denied the Scriptures its validity nor have we disrespected any religious institution, particularly the Christian religion. I myself, am a descendant of a family who were devoted Baptists and attended weekly services. There are two excerpts from the Bible that I am particularly fond of, the Book of Exodus in the Old Testament and The Sermon on the Mount in the New Testament. Also, two standards that I have lived by and have intrigued me after reading the

Bible are: Living a proper and balanced lifestyle. This helps us to distinguish our *wants from our needs*. Secondly, living a generous lifestyle reminds us that God will provide all that we need and that we have plenty to share.

When one wears their "heart on their sleeve" it is because of the kind and trusting nature of one's soul. However, if one decides to do this, you will find yourself more vulnerable and at risk of being hurt. I have found that true happiness can only exist if there is a willingness to be vulnerable. Your chances of happiness diminish if you are too guarded because matters of the heart are the keys to open up joyfulness in your life. My counterpart shares these beliefs as well. His trust in his fellow man might have turned out to be a deadly mistake one evening and he should more readily employ common sense. He at times ignored the present dangers that lurk about him. There was an incident that could have taken his life because he was unguarded and alone. A bullet pierced his top hat during a routine trip from the White House to his cottage home while he was in Washington D.C.; a possible tragedy that could have been avoided.

*****

As I look out from the back porch of my home in Allentown, New Jersey I admire a legion of cornstalks standing at attention. The weather is unusually mild but nevertheless, it is a beautiful day. I see my family out in the field. Anne and our two children, Clara and Albert are playing and laughing inside the cornstalks on the edge of the backyard. Near the crops is a pond and it is quiet today because the watering pump is silently resting. There is no need to water the crops because of the mild temperatures and the persistent rain over the past few days. I anticipate that this day will be particularly uneventful; I had no idea of what is in store for me as the day progressed.

My rocking chair on the back porch was very similar to the one at the old Rutledge Inn and it is inviting me to rest upon it. Honey, our dog, dashes across the yard in order to join the children for some fun, as I stretch and yawn. She publicizes her approach with an eager "woof" while I walk towards my rocking chair. I notice that the Sun is gleaming unusually bright and I begin to question its intention. I slide the chair back in order to avoid the sunlight and finally sit down. Suddenly a cool breeze interrupts the tranquility of the atmosphere. I have experienced brief cold fronts before, but this unnatural coldness begins to fill the entire porch. I quickly feel unsettled and anxious. I wonder if this change in atmosphere is related to the Watchers somehow, because it happened so suddenly and without any warning. Unexpectedly, I hear voices or some kind of awkward recurring groans. It sounds like a young boy is saying, "Father" yet I cannot determine the direction from where it is coming from. I am nervous that Albert might need my assistance but I can still see him out in the fields, safe with his mother and sister.

I hear the voices again, loud and pure. I am frozen in between a sitting and standing position in the front of my rocking chair in anticipation of the next sound or voice. I shift my attention toward the street in order to determine where the sounds are coming from. I can see my breath and I feel a cold shiver run up my spine. It is becoming progressively colder. Now I am hearing a loud sobbing sound and it is definitely coming from within the house, but I don't understand, there is no one here but myself. I have to investigate this unnatural occurrence, so I let out a bellow of breath and budge from my stance. I reach over in order to squeak open the screen door on the back porch and tread smoothly through the hallway towards the front of the house. I stop at the bottom of the staircase next to the front door and see columns of sparkling white lights engulfing the entire staircase. My body tightens while I remain cautiously distant from this illuminated anomaly. I deduce that the groaning and peculiar sounds are coming from the second floor. I feel drawn to this *mysterious unknown*, as curiosity gets the best of me. I am assured that my family is safe and determined to find out what is going on.

Knowing that I have to go up the stairs, I place my foot carefully on the first step. The dazzling light on the staircase surrounds my foot while I hesitate to commit myself and slowly follow with the next step. The sparkling lights appear as though they are under intelligent control, it must have something to do with the Watchers. While passing gingerly and with caution through the light I have a sense that I am being tempted or baited to carry on. The banister is providing me with the assistance I need so that my legs do not fall out from underneath me because of fear. I turn midway up the stairs to look out the large stain glass window located above the front door and witness a scene of people, a large crowd dressed from a different era. This cannot be because this area is overly wooded and secluded with very few homes. My view is somewhat distorted but I can see that their dress is quite familiar; it is mid-19th century clothing. Yet, there they are, the hoop skirted women and the men, in fine suits with top hats. Wait, this declares that I am watching a scene from the mid 1800's and the place is no other than Washington D.C... The people do not look happy; some are crying and some are filled with fear. This is not good and contributes to these occurrences' that something is not right. I look beyond the crowd and take notice of the ghostly building across the street. It is a brick building with five arches that houses white doors. The sign hanging above the building reads, "Ford's Theater." Suddenly, I hear a cry and moans coming from beyond the closed-door upstairs. I somehow know that I am giving witness to an apparition and I have to put my own fears behind me and proceed up the staircase in order to find out the cause of this unnerving situation.

I cautiously take one step at a time, which utters squeaks that are louder than usual. Until I reached the second-floor landing, many thoughts had ambushed my mind. The haunting moans increase and I am now certain from where they are coming from; our bedroom. My being becomes more confident knowing that this eerie ghostly phenomenon is not a physical threat and is unfolding right beyond the bedroom door. I am determined now to enter the bedroom, so I slowly inch my way to the bedroom door while each step strips away my self-confidence and is replaced with fear. I remain anxious, while staring back at me is the closed white door of my bedroom, from which something lurks. I am resistant to open the door, so I nervously scout out the hallway from my still position. I hesitate once again and turn to the right in order to seek a distraction. I see an old mirror framed in gold that came with the house. I turn to approach the mirror and it appears that there are two reflections of me that come into view. I am taken back and become frightened as I study the images before me. I see an old weathered version of myself on the right side of the mirror and a more vibrant and heartier version on the left side of the reflection. I dare to move closer in order to examine the images more closely and I am startled when I see both images mimic my exact movements. I am shaken greatly by this experience.

Is this a supernatural occurrence trying to covey something to me from my counterpart? Maybe it is showing President Lincoln's life as compared to my own? Perhaps my counterpart is attempting to communicate with me from beyond the grave! Quickly, cornered in my mind is the thought of Mary Todd Lincoln and President Lincoln in their attempts to reach the *beyond*, by the use of séances, with the sole intention to receive spiritual communications. I anxiously begin to mumble a prayer under my breath in order to comfort myself amongst these unnatural surroundings.

The noise becomes quieter and then suddenly, the sparkling

lights from the staircase race by my feet and are absorbed under the bedroom door. A low hum noise remains, similar to the sound of buzzing insect's wings. The sound is familiar for I remember hearing it on the Watchers' vessel. My heart is once again unifying with my being and I feel comfort if the presence of the Watchers are here, but yet I cannot see them. I trust that whatever is beyond the door is benevolent in nature, thus gives me the courage to continue on. Released from the grip of the riveting images in the mirror I make an about face and approach my bedroom door. Without hesitation I reach out to make contact with the brass knob and with my right hand I begin to turn it. I gently set my left palm against the door at the level of my eyes and push it gently. I do this ever so carefully in order to anticipate and confront whatever is on the other side. Upon entering I whisper, "Lord, please guide me through this apparition in order to land on solid ground, if accordance with Your will." The unhinged sound during the opening of the door along with the woeful whispers comes to an abrupt halt. All of a sudden there is ultimate silence. I slowly enter and step forward towards the point of no return. Inside this soundless room I unexpectedly observe a gleaming light shining brightly, blinding me and coming through all the windows. Instantly, the light fills the room and captures me as I stand stationary, stubborn with faith. I begin to feel lighter and very relaxed.

The bed is now before me and vacant. I find myself weightless and hovering parallel directly above this bed. I am gently laid onto the bed and simultaneously I feel my soul lift out of my body. My spirit does not leave me but is rather tethered to my body somehow, I cannot explain.

My focus is hindered as the white light begins to exit the room. I can now see shadows of concerned people gathering and moving about the room but I cannot see who they are. Are they celestial beings or perhaps mystified ghosts lost in conversion or limbo? I look up to see the remaining small portion of the white light lingering and swirling in a slow circular motion upon the ceiling. Suddenly, a translucent opening in the ceiling allows me to see all the way to the heavens. I view the night sky and the twinkling stars. The outer rim of the swirl has a glittering outline similar to the brilliance of light I had witnessed on the staircase. Somehow, I fear that this lighted anomaly is patiently waiting for me. I am troubled because I cannot not hear or see properly and my spirit is uneasy. Despite my concerns, I am peaceful but my state of mind is quite different. I feel paralyzed and cannot move, yet my mind begins to understand the grade of consciousness that I am experiencing. I can now see with vagueness in my mind and I realize that I am lying diagonally confined to a narrow bed. With my feet pressed against a wooden rail-post, I recognize this is not heaven because I am too tall to fit within this single bed, a problem that I have had throughout my life with regards to sleeping accommodations.

With all of my might, I try one last time to move but I cannot. I lay beneath a multicolored quilt that secures my position. Beneath my body there is a plain brown blanket. I focus on the quilt and I realize that the work within the quilted blanket was intricate. Each square had been darned with a distinctive pattern. There is however, a cross-stitched grapevine that connects some of the squares, making the quilt look as if it had a greater purpose. Perhaps this demonstrated my preference and desire to be at the winery, a place of comfort and happiness in a different lifetime.

All of a sudden, the clarity of the apparition that I am experiencing unveils itself. A piercing sound screeches into my head, needling my senses, when all of a sudden I see myself waiting to die! Could this be? I speak aloud, "Oh Dear God!" The Watchers have switched my spirit with that of President Lincoln or have they? But yet, here I am in an hourglass of woe! My heart grieves heavily as I echo a plea,

"Oh but Anne and my beautiful children are oh, so in my reach. Can I be with them one last time? If this is not a dream, should I pray and embrace the time I have left?"

I quickly settle down because of this next experience I witness. It is a beautiful gift and rescues my spirit. It will remain with me always. The walls of the room are covered in wallpaper that was popular during that time period. The patterns begin to transfigure right before me, permitting me to witness an inter-dimensional miracle or apparition, while the shadows appear to be bothered and around me somehow, preoccupied. The stripes within the wallpaper become illuminated and transform into pathways for souls. These pathways are ones of valor and the spirits rising within them truly deserve this peaceful honor. Adorned on the wallpaper are mystical doves that begin to come alive and move about as they ascend between the striped pathways. The doves are of the purist white as they are guided and united along the illuminated pathways to their final resting place in heaven. The souls begin to show themselves in spirit form, between the wings of the doves, for who, in truth they were. They are in the hundreds and being deployed one behind the other, surrounding the walls of the entire room. I realize they are the casualties of the Civil War, soldiers and civilians from both the North and the South. They are the souls who had perished and sacrificed their lives for the beliefs they held dear.

I cannot stand to give them hope or send for the cavalry to assist them, so I pray that the angels guide and hold every soul close as they direct them straight to heaven. I feel that from, deep within my own soul, the desire to say, "I hope the Lamp of Liberty, which God has planted in all our hearts, will burn until mankind no longer has doubt, that all of us are created free and equal!" I calm myself down because I need to save my energy. I now understand that once all the scores of souls are elevated and depart from this room, then as will

I funnel in their footsteps. I proclaim that I am just one life, but be reassured, that if I die here and now, I will be the last casualty of this war of rebellion, the Civil War!

My eyelids are heavy and remain shut as my mind continues to allow me to perceive vision with haziness and with an acute awareness of my surroundings. It feels like a battle between body and soul, a contest of strength if you will. Suddenly, a single tear, makes itself known in the corner of my eye. The great and lonely sorrow consumes me as my face is now completely pale. I hope my spirit has enough faith in order to stretch and reach the divinity of God's hand, because I feel my spirit is prepared should I have to depart. What I have to offer the Lord is a life of kind deeds. If it is my time to leave this Earth, I am ready and deep rooted with kindness and love, for this gives me peace.

I increase my efforts for my ability to breathe and carefully meditate. There are faint sounds of chatter amongst the living shadows and I hear someone mention war. The word *haste* rushes into my fleeting mind. With regards to wars, I have learned that throughout history, almost all wars have been started, forced and caused by less than a handful of people.

I must settle down. I wait, for I know that the time will come for me to go and prepare myself for what I already know what is about to happen. The morning Sun must have risen for I feel the warmth of its rays on the back of my hands. If 7:22 a.m. is that stubborn immovable time in order to enter into a new beginning, then now I am prepared to meet with the open arms and a lifted heart to my Creator. These last moments will be dedicated to the value of time and what it had meant to me throughout my life. This, before I set forth into the unknown.

I now have a weak sense of hearing and sounds are becoming limited. I cannot capture all of the sounds well; however, I do hear bits of words about Ford's Theatre, Petersen, Stanton and Mary. It seems that Edwin Stanton, (the Secretary of War) is escorting Mary (Mary Todd Lincoln) out of the room because it is too much for her to bear. I do declare a very strange notion to identify with. I found it very odd and out of the ordinary dilemmas and I will seek to resolve it when and if I do reach heaven. Edwin Stanton always had safety concerns and drew caution on-the-side of President Lincoln, like a brother. Yet, to my dismay, towards his actions and acceptance, with regard to Johnson's influence and why partake in his dreadful plan? Good or bad, you must persevere and carry on, with knowing the truth. Without the accurate reality of or to live the truth, one cannot grow and be happy. You can be content but only to a degree, because if you subtract "expansion" from your life, it is impossible to obtain happiness and therefore, your pursuit towards this goal will be stationary or paused.

Yes, I am aware that John Wilkes Booth laid in this very same bed, just two weeks ago. My honor and nobility are no match for his negative energy that he left behind in this very spot. After all, I am "Honest Abe" and I do not tell lies! I laugh to myself and continue to feel weary, confused and delirious to the knowledge of all that is. If I can share another truth while in a silly mood, I would like to state, "The only thing I admired about the William Petersen's house was the twisted coil staircase design that welcomes their guests." As my daughter Clara would say, "Very cool indeed." Numbness settles into the lower half of my body. It feels like pins and needles. Yet, I feel so complete, from all that the Watchers had given me, because it seemed so real!

Should I completely surrender to the notion that I am President Lincoln? I hold desperately onto what was my own existence and I dream one last time in order to grasp the feelings of what I think was my life with Anne and myself. If I believe hard enough, then maybe the Watchers can use their wings of assurance so that I can journey back to Anne and my children. I will miss them dearly, please....

My final gift: So clear, does this song and vision run through my being. I dance about in a theatrical predicament, all on my own and compose in my mind this profound belief of moving pictures. Hallucinating or not, I gather my concluding strength after everything else dissolves and forgive me for not giving in. The song that spoke to me at the Watchers facility suddenly begins to resonate within my dreams. "Thee Remembrance," looking back, I say and sing:

"I was the one who had it all" Anne's first smile back to me, when we worked on the drapes.

"I was the master of my fate" John and I are in the Watchers Facility, training and jumping through time.

"I never needed anybody in my life" Surveying lines of chains, then working as a postmaster.

"I learned the truth too late" When Mr. Taft tells me, Anne has been struck with a sickness.
(Finding out both Presidents (Counterpart's) were assassinated, when I was in the library)

"I'll never shake away the pain" On my knees weeping at the Watchers' Facility.

"I close my eyes but she's still there" I see Anne's dress flowing and dancing the first day we met.

"I let her steal into my melancholy heart" Anne and I on a blanket eating and drinking on the lawn. (My counterpart starring and dreaming onto the White House lawn as this scene disappears)

"It's more than I can bear" My counterpart looks out, then turns away from the White House window.

"Now I know she'll never leave me" On horseback charged to the Watchers' Facility to save her.

"Even as she runs away" Her last moments by the bedside, at the Supply Barn treatment area.

"She will still torment me, calm me, hurt me, move me, come what may" Starring at my coin.

"Wasting in my lonely tower" Standing on top of the capital building and turn to dance with lady liberty, who turns into Anne.

"Waiting by an open door" I pray on the staircase towards Anne's bedroom door, after the cure was given, hoping it will work.

"I'll fool myself, she'll walk right in" "And be with me for evermore" Thoughts of my proposal.

"I rage against the trials of love" I'm in a court reading a document, the room turns to a wedding.

"I curse the fading of the light" Window distraction towards the moon as Anne passes. Fist clenched.

"Though she's already flown so far beyond my reach" I lay peaceful in the Petersen House bed.

"She's never out of sight" I see Anne in the backyard, tending to the crops and animals.

"Now I know she'll never leave me" "Even as she fades from view" Anne vanishes in the yard.

"She will still inspire me" "Be a part of everything I do" Reading the Gettysburg Address.

"Wasting in my lonely tower" My fingers tap on the arm of the chair, seated in the Lincoln Monument.

"Waiting by an open door" Atop of the Washington Monument I slide down to the front door.

"I'll fool myself she'll walk right in" I sit on our staircase beside the front door of our home.

"And as the long, long nights begin" While waiting, the house becomes darkened and aged.

"I'll think of all that might have been" I closed my book, The Parity of Lives, Abraham and John.

"Waiting here for evermore" As the white light fills the room I settle back into my body.

Just as I reconnect, once again, my spirit starts to hover above my body, while I watch the last *grain* of sand *land* in, at 7:22 AM. I see my body below as I am lifted evermore slowly through the house and see the shadows reveal the people who were gathered below.

With all that I lived, within those unconsciousness hours,

between, April 14th to the 15th seemed as though I spent a lifetime with Anne, compressed into a pocket of time for a gracious gift and a glimpse. It seems somehow in God's instinctive and resourceful world, the Watchers or by some means, has given me a great reward to experience these unique alternate outcomes.

But how could I have known about so many things? The shooting accident I had experienced in Ford's Theater, must have enabled my spirit's energy to connect with "God's realm" in some sort of science irregularity? Nevertheless, I am assured that someone else received this connection in order to be speaking right now. I hope I did not suppress my past purposely; I am sure it had much merit in all facets and please forgive my falling short, in my efforts to seek the reality that was my own trail. My fatal or mortal excuse is although, a noble one.

While my body gradually rises, I am suddenly tempted to look down from this high-point above Washington D.C... The buildings become ever so much smaller. In my surrender to go to heaven, I question the distance I am about to travel. I wish to be more certain because I always thought that heaven would manifest itself in an instant.

My body is limp while I continue to rise with my back to the city and my eyes towards the heavens. I start to question this route and then suddenly as my faith is weakened, I begin to slow down my ascent into the heavens. I look down while high above in the sky. I then twist my neck to the left, in order to see beneath my body and then to the right, with a strong concern. The upward momentum suddenly stops completely. Oh no, God! Was I supposed to forgive all the conspirators, who planned my death? I mutter this notion quickly. I then squeeze my eyes shut and panic, while waving my arms and legs in the air, attempting to swim backwards but without water.

Suddenly, my body begins to freefall and a loud buzz noise

increases all around me. I turn my body to face Washington D.C. while a whirlwind pushes fiercely against my face. A bucket of air is then guzzled into my mouth. I cannot breathe, followed by a shriek and continuous effort to holler in terror, which I provide willingly.

What just happened? Suddenly, a breath is swooped into my chest; my eyes rapidly spring open, while my hands grip with fear and hold onto the arms of my rocking chair. My whole body flinches as my feet slam against the deck porch, letting out a big bang. I then tone down my embarrassing scream to a quiet choke. Suddenly, I hear with a firm voice from within the backyard, coming from the front of the crops, "Are you okay, honey?" So I wave and say, yes to Anne with a smile. I exhale a loud breath of relief and hear from Anne, "We will be coming in shortly to prepare dinner." I respond with a strong voice, "That sounds swell," as I realize I just had the most unbelievable vivid dream, oh dear Lord.

I bend my head down while still sitting in the rocking chair and smile hard. While I keep this permanent grin, I shake my head from side to side and then look up and take a hay stalk of grass and clench it between my teeth. I rest back into my chair and begin to look back over at the children playing with Anne, while the rocking chair rocks.

Ending View: The view of the porch becomes further and further away and you are transported to one of my line dancing gatherings at the winery. There, you will hear me teaching and shouting out steps, like, "Heel-toe, Jazz-box, Kick-Ball-Change, Rock Recover, Grapevine, Weave and others. The dances to learn are the, CC Shuffle, Cowboy Boogie, Boot Scootin' Shuffle and others. Then yes, you can meet Anne, Clara and or little Albert can assist you with your dance steps. Don't worry I'll be around there all the way till April 5th 2037.

Thanks you so much for your support,
Best to you,
Abraham Lincoln

Alternate ending:

While my body gradually rises, I am suddenly tempted to look down from this high ascent above Washington D.C... The buildings become ever so much smaller. In my surrender to go to heaven, I question the distance I am about to travel. I wish to be more certain because I always thought that heaven would manifest itself in an instant.

My body is limp while I continue to rise with my back to the city and my eyes towards the heavens. I start to question this route and then suddenly as my faith is weakened, I begin to slow down my ascent into the heavens. I look down while high above in the sky. I then twist my neck to the left, in order to see beneath my body and then to the right. The upward momentum is stopped. Oh no, God! Was I supposed to forgive all the conspirators, who planned my death? I then squeeze my eyes shut and panic, while waving my arms and legs in the air, attempting to swim backwards but without water.

Suddenly, my body begins to freefall and a loud buzz noise increases all around me. I turn my body to face Washington D.C. while a whirlwind pushes fiercely against my face. A bucket of air is then guzzled into my mouth, followed by a shriek and continuous holler of terror, which I provide willingly.

Wait a second, I have been yelling for almost a minute. Maybe I am in heaven right now, because while in the midst of this fall I reach into my pocket and appearing out of nowhere is my trusted old pocket watch. It is likely an instant desire fulfilled. I open the watch to look at the second hand and realize that I have been in a freefall for an extended period of time. Should I take flight and soar through the air like a bird because Washington D.C. is becoming more into focus at a closer view.

Before I close the pocket watch I see a round lovely picture of Anne placed within the cover. That is my second desire answered. By the way, the picture was taken from the other Everything Store, where on occasion we would eat out.

Oh goodness, I click the watch shut and then desperately take form to fly like an eagle across the sea, while approaching near to the Potomac River. But before I smash myself directly into the city of Washington D.C., I notice that I am headed right into the Lincoln Monument, which I realized later on, was the inscription on the back of my penny that the Watchers had given to me. Now that I recognize I am he, the president, I would like to thank the people that were kind enough to build this enormous monument in my honor and oh, by the way, there is no charge to get in, it's free! It is a very surreal location with a relaxing picturesque landscape I might add. Oh goodness, I forgot I was falling. So I quickly begin to spread out my arms to fly.

Hmm, oh dear, I do not have the ability of flight, very much to my dismay. I have just seconds before the land collides to my fast approaching body. This is not good, so I can only do what I can do. Put my arm around my head and curl up into a fetal position, thus gathering up a volcano of sound, deep from the pits of my stomach and YELL!

Suddenly, a breath is swooped into chest; my eyes rapidly swing open, while my hands grip with fear to hold onto the arms of my rocking chair. My whole body flinches as my feet slam against the deck porch, letting out a bang. Then I hear with a firm voice from within the backyard, coming from the front of the crops, "Are you okay honey?" I wave and say, yes to Anne with a smile. I exhale a loud breath of relief and hear, "We will be coming in shortly to prepare dinner." I respond with a strong voice, "That sounds swell," as I realize I had just experienced a vivid dream, to my relief, oh dear Lord.

I bend my head down while still sitting in the rocking chair and smile hard. While I keep this permanent grin, I shake my head from side to side and then look up while I take a hay stalk of grass and clench it between my teeth. I rest back onto my chair and begin to look back over at the children playing with Anne.

Ending Scene: The view of the porch becomes further and further away and you are transported to one of my line dancing gatherings at the winery. There, you will hear me teaching and shouting out steps, like, "Heel-toe, Jazz-box, Kick-Ball-Change, Rock Recover, Grapevine, Weave and others. The dances to learn are the, CC Shuffle, Cowboy Boogie, Boot Scoot-in' Shuffle and others. Then yes, you can meet Anne, Clara and or little Albert can assist you with your dance steps. Don't worry I'll be around there all the way till April 5th 2037.

Thanks you so much for your support!
Best to you,
Al Thomas Rutledge or aka Abraham Thomas Lincoln

P.S. I made my Confirmation with Albert and now I have finally received a middle name, after my father Thomas Lincoln.

LINCOLN'S ADDITIONAL NOTES

To the answer of how & why?

As promised I have retrieved some information from the Watchers' facility and some from memory. My quest by providing this information is to settle an understanding of where we live and how we function. I truly believe if we base our lives in avoiding the truth, in order to not live in reality, then I fear a downfall will be waiting for you at every turn. Isn't true happiness when your life is in a forward motion, surrounded by people that love you "back?" That is why I share this information with you, although quite boring at times, nonetheless, part of the reason to be light hearted when speaking to you and a valid attempt to be entertaining, somewhat.

So have a toast with me, as an expression of honor and goodwill. I recommend one glass of red Barbera wine from California, Portalupi Winery. Actually, John had recommended it to me, not too long ago. It is in the vicinity to where he lives now. Hmm, maybe they were right about my drinking? Saying, it was the only thing I was not honest about; and I think that deserves an *lol*. Please excuse the upcoming lol's, because it is new for me and I am a bit excited about sharing this fantastical quantum material. Cheers!

I would like to start with the matter of "How" and begin here in order to get to the more important, "Why?" Well, to put into plain words, there is a mainstream term called "Dark

Matter" and is the full answer to the question of, "How." Well, there you have it, yah? Okay, let's move on, right? Excuse me, for my attempt to be British because I bumped into a chap in New York yesterday and his personality stuck with me, very entertaining I might add. For some reason I always feel as though the British are more polished then we are. I guess it is just what they call now, an inferiority complex.

Nevertheless, Dark Matter is the explanation to how everything works. An explanation in its simplest form is usually good to identify with. This is what I gathered from the Watchers facility: Dark Matter is so much more than gravitational effects. It is how the universe works, you included. Dark Matter is not detectable with the human eye but in the future they will develop spectacles "that can see what can't be seen." Actually, this was a phrase used in my co-authors last book, Jesus' Mentor. This technology will soon be discovered by means of understanding the "Auroras" or also referred to as the "northern lights." The solar winds' charged plasma particles reveal a different array of colored gases, such as Oxygen, hydrogen, nitrogen and more. The colors represent each of the gases that are ionized along and from the magnetosphere. This atmospheric phenomenon, combined with photonic frequency syntheses will eventually "see what can't be seen." Example: Wormholes, Spatial Fabric, TIDs, Radio-waves and more...

❂ ❂ ❂ ❂

Suchlike the Periodic Table, which has many elements, Dark Matter as well, consists of multitudes of different features and all are invisible. Each of these anomalies fills an important role in the building blocks of our world and ironically, none of their collective frequencies collide with one another unless they are purposely fused together by the Almighty. *(Dark Matter is called by some other intelligent species as the Holy*

Spirit, mainly people from the Pleiades star system, in the Taurus constellation.)

Just like the millions of ingredients that make up Dark Matter, your mobile devices, radio stations and other wireless devices, none of their frequencies or broadcasts collides with each other or for that matter; they are invisible to one another and to us.

People look out into the heavens and see a lot of dark space, with an occasional star here or there. But in actuality, the Dark Matter is not just in space, it is through and though in all features and the sum parts of your life. It flows through the Earth, including your body and is the platform or foundation of outer-space.

Let's start from the beginning of Creation. God created all, wait, I forgot that this is 2017. I do not want to offend certain people who have been influenced by the local media and TV shows. So I will use the term Creator so that I will be respectful to the politically correct crowd and I hope it is okay to capitalize the word Creator; well thank you good sir.

Picture, if you will a small pocket of space. It could be in front of you, below you, above out there or in you. It doesn't matter, just as long as you have a clear image of a block of space, dark or lighted. Within this pocket of space are many invisible things, millions upon millions of things and their "entire parts" do not run into each other and or see each other or are you able to see them.

In order for you to look at but just one strand of the many, you would have to know the signature or the exact resonating sound frequency, to the strand anomaly you wish to see. This is similar to selecting the "Hannity" talk radio show on your AM dial. By the way, I am just repeating a slogan I heard from my most preferred radio station. You must understand, I created the Republican Party and I can reassure you of one thing, God will forgive you if you do elect leaders from the

Democratic Party, well, unless it is my friend Jack Kennedy, he is the exception. Oh and I forgot to put the "laugh out loud" acronym towards the end of that statement, lol. I know I am getting a bit off subject, but the reason I used the word "statement" instead of "sentence" is because I am hoping for the co-author will make this book into an audio version. Also, I am trying to entice Bill O'Reilly to be the reader of my audio book. After all, he did have a successful run with *Killing Lincoln*; therefore I would be much obliged. I must note, he does donate the profits of that book to charity, if of course when you buy it on Bill O'Reilly.com. Did you know that Republicans donate 2 to 1 over Democrats in regards to charities, which of course, if you exclude the top ten richest people in the United States because they are all Democrats and that's the way they'd like to leave it! Oh goodness I am starting to sound a bit like Hannity, lol.

Getting onward. So by imagining just one anomaly or an invisible strand in a vacuous part of space, is the starting point in order to understand Dark Matter. In addition, the "lens" or technology in which you view this particular spectrum has to be forced into and adjusted to an antimatter realm or we could say an inter-dimensional location. This means, not of our 3D practical familiar dimensional world. Trying to say, what dimension is its location is merely a waste of time. There are just too many localities, maybe another day.

The plain and simple analogy can be explained by driving in your car and selecting a radio station on FM or AM radio. There are many choices to select from, just like the millions of cell phones throughout the world; all of them have their own frequency signature. What's more, is suchlike the radio, if you widen the band, there can be an endless amount more stations or receivers (endless). But today we are only going to select one station or frequency within Dark Matter. Magical or not, these radio frequencies could carry audio (voices or sound) and or lighted information. The information is similar to the genome or genetic individual signature that is inserted onto all of your cells at the conception towards the beginnings of your life. Well, such is the same for Dark Matter, like the multitude of the atoms (subatomic) and molecules attached and labeled (signature) to the Periodic Table Chart, the Dark Matter does the same within its characteristics and consists of an assorted array towards different varieties of inter-dimensional characters. Together, these characters all support the world in which we live in. So if we can, select a wormhole as our one invisible piece of the Dark Matter puzzle.

Are you still following? Hey, I can say "hey" when calling another person in 2017 and it is not offensive, also I may be insulted by my closest friend, just as long, he or she puts the acronym "Lol" towards the end of a statement or message, lol. I am in the learning stages with the current technologies and jargon, so please bear with me.

I am going to back up a bit to the beginning of Creation. I thought I already said that? According to the Watchers' Study Hall, there is a biological program in place in order for existence to be. I do not want to go beyond this program because then I would confuse the whole point. So let us stick to the program in its entirety and I will bring back the wormhole discussion.

Therefore, about Creator's bio program; seemingly, it is based in probability distribution and yes, there is no way to have a finite equation attached to it. That's the Creators whole point, lol. The meaning of the word "probability is the ratio of numerous outcomes, which once becomes exhausted through choice or chance and creates an equal set of results that a main event will occur.

We need to understand that the source of this program is traversing billions upon billions of bits of information in order to fill every outcome that is possible and therefore, it is a moot point to label such an action (or equation) or we can just conclude its good old God. Like a daisy wheel of change, impossible to monitor, but if one knows how the block chain works within the crypto world, then understand, it is a billion times harder to track and this is so, because of the ever moving and changing bio-code, encrypted within the Creator's matrix. This is coupled with the Creator's instructions to make sure that all the probabilities are met in the spectrum, to which the program has allotted. There is a main reason for the Creator to go through all this trouble, but you will have muddle through this quantum mumbo jumbo before that climatic answer is reached, smiling with my face. Can we start a new popular acronym possibly (SWMF smiling with my face), no, yes I am in agreement, not to, okay.

All of these many informational distributions happen while the millions of inter-dimensional anomalies (strands) occupy the same space and never intersect, layer upon layer, unless of course, the Creator wants to create an inter-dimensional compound strand. This is the same principal of when atoms are fused together magnetically in order to make a compound, suchlike "water," $H2O$; Hydrogen and Oxygen married together. One example of the Creator's inter-dimensional compounds (IDC's) and is the attachments of wormholes (vortices), which are woven directly into the Dynamic Fabric. Dynamic Fabric is another invisible anomaly, which is the platform that everything stems from. Both of these anomalies are of different design but provide a necessary function when together.

An easy explanation could be the analogy representing the functionality of the heart. The heart of the body is the Dynamic Fabric and the artery, which provides blood to the heart, is the wormhole. Two different designs but when compounded together, it creates a wonderful GPS system to navigate through the universe and both are invisible to themselves or on different wavelengths.

The Creator's program consists of all the information and parts (materials) that are the universe or universes. Such as the Periodic Table (a gathering of elements), Dark Matter also has different weights and measures for its own recipe or function. But like the human body, there are millions of things going on.

Let me break it down to just one inter-dimension (invisible) anomaly, out of the many and is one of the most important ones. This particular anomaly is similar to the "brain" which governs your body and mind. The "basis" (or one of millions of characteristics) of Dark Matter is the Dynamic Fabric as mentioned before and the brain behind it all. Please now ignore my earlier analogy of the heart, lol. Picture a large special soul that runs everything. This is the platform that supplies the dynamic realm or energy to the universe, the Creator's source.

Stating, mostly every component in our world is based upon spherical properties and is universal throughout the cosmos. Also mixed into every spherical atom and molecule that makes everything visible and invisible (including you) is the needed ability or must function of the Dynamic Fabric.

Isn't it amazing how a small tiny bug called a gnat, can function and live with practically an invisible nervous system to the naked eye. Okay, now times that by a million (shrink it) in regards to its size and make it that much, much smaller (infinitesimal). That is still not small enough to describe the subatomic particles that govern our *Third Dimensional* reality that we live in.

But for a moment, picture millions of tiny balls or spheres all put together in order to make a pebble or a small stone. Do not worry, I didn't forget about Dark Matter's Dynamic Fabric. There is a point to all this and no; I know you thought to yourself, "Oh Dark Matters, like my family member that just went off the deep end, lol. Oh my goodness, I lost you?

Getting back to the pebble in your hand, well, it is in your hand now; and you're looking at it, you know it is made of gold, aluminum and trapped within this rock are some gases called helium and oxygen. As you already know, the subatomic particles are spherical (mini-globes) are at work together in the pebble. The actual substances that are inside the atom are very little. Most of the inside portion of an atom or subatomic particle are mostly hollow and therefore, a lot of empty space. So imagine, they are already so small and practically impossible to see but yet, they are only using a tiny portion of their own spherical make up for functionality.

Please make believe you are hearing, quite elaborate sound effects as you are absorbing this information, so not to lose your "focus" because your life depends on it! So, the pebble in your hand has the properties of weight, matter and gases. (There also is a plasma process going on in the atom, but that, I will have to show you in person.) Within the small rock we will extract two of the atoms: The first will be the gold and the second will be the helium. Okay, in order to understand Dark Matter, we have to fill some voids of function to see to what can't be seen.

The gold atom is made up of many spherical (globelike) subatomic particles within its core and just like a tiny bugs nervous system, each of the particles have their own function. The particles amongst themselves simulate an ongoing theme that has been repurposed in many other aspects in all of existence. Plainly put, the particles react in the same manner as our solar system, just trillions of times smaller.

Here come the good parts. The subatomic particles within the pebble rock are moving and in essence, the rock is totally alive (as is our Earth). Bet you never knew that? Let me explain. The particles within all atoms are moving close to the speed of light and resonate (have a custom sound) with their own discerned signature. Even though speeds vary amongst all atoms, the particles within a gold atom run to a similar march (Almost reaching 186,000 miles per second of course depending upon its purity.)

While this mini solar system is underway, its purpose is so you can hold the rock in your hand. Wait, please, let me give a quick sample of our solar system, in order for you to visualize what is going on inside an atom. Or should've I said, the Creator's solar system? The Earth rotates, while traveling around the Sun. Our modified Moon is purposely tidal locked in facing only one way. It does this by rotating ever so slowly in order to be synced with Earth. This design is done so you cannot see what is on the other side, but this is off point. Again, the Sun travels (orbits) around a gargantuan black hole, we the Earth orbit around the Sun and our Moon orbits around the Earth, you get the picture. So, similar to a solar system; as-does the actions and performances that are inside of an atom. It is funny that the Moon, Earth and Sun are made of the spherical subatomic particles and they are in the shape of a sphere. There you have it, the building blocks of life, based on spheres.

I farm the chicken, I eat the eggs and then the shark eats me, no lol. It is altogether fitting that the subatomic particles make up atoms and then the millions of atoms are made into molecules and millions of molecules make a pebble and millions of pebbles make all the planets (pebbles, bam bam, time's a googolplex) (Planetesimals). Well anyway that is not my point. The question is "How does the pebble exist?"

The Creator's program has its own Periodic Table, consisting of different chemicals and matter (material), but even though it is similar to our Periodic Chart in its supply of elements, it is just a bit larger. You can yawn now, it's okay. This organized mix of elements are pooled into the program and distributed into a variable means to an end, a finite expansion of "soup," if you will, in its overall purpose to create the world. The limitations of the material is altered and adjusted, in order for the quantity of certain elements to extend as far as the overlapping program permits, which follows for the sole purpose of creating every probability.

In other words, the program will let you change and borrow an element for a specific purpose, just as long you are filling a void in a probable outcome. If not, the element will magnetically revert back to its original make up or will be recycled in order to realign the proper quantities and types of material that the Creator's program knows, that works. This is somewhat the opposite of "Occam's Razor," which is a competing hypothetical answer, which if chosen, has the fewest probable outcomes. The program is designed to "expand" for every possible outcome as mentioned.

In review of the program or should I say one addition to the program: The program distributes material and changes accordingly to promote every probability, but also, let me include the last major component and is the overlapping feature of the program, that is set unto every part of the program.

This is the attachment that the Watchers call, "Bifurcation." It is the process inserted into the overall program in order to propagate a constant forward moving world (improvements of efficiency). Bifurcation is the mathematical command within the program, in order to produce every probable outcome towards existence. It is instilled in almost every component with the universe and is based in fractals. Fractals are the disorganized tiny parts of Bifurcation that eventually become organized and create larger parts.

The importance of these works and parts of the program are necessary because, then the other components will not work. The definition of Bifurcation is, "the divisional growth from a single line or branch. Example: 1+1=2, 1+2=3, 2+3=5, or 1+3=4, 5+1=6, 5+2=7, 1+6=7 and as the process grows on, it will finish up at a different point every time, because of the random amounts of probable outcomes mixed. This is the selection growth process of Bifurcation and the reason why everything in our universe grows in a forward progression.

The Watchers have given the mathematical range to this expansion of improvements. It is 5/8ths to 11/16ths or 0.625 to 0.6875 out of an approximate 100%, if the negative opposing force is at 50% (you need the good with the bad in order to have free choice). This leaves a remaining balance of an approximate of $1/8^{th}$ to $3/16^{th}$ forward progressions, when weighing (offset) the positives against the negatives.

The growth Bifurcation process amongst living things is also referred to as inter-dimensional mitochondria and is the forward development of adding new cells in order to complete that livings things design. Thereafter, if for instance, once a tree is fully grown, it will go through the seasons with the Bifurcation process in full motion. In order for the growth of anything to take its course (you), the Bifurcation command via program becomes activated by the Dynamic Fabric's energy waving through, to cause the cells within a body to charge (or the sub-atomic particles to spin and orbit within the body's billions of cells). This is why the human being does not need to be charged, suchlike your cell phone. During the sleeping stage, the chemicals within your brain shift to a place where the Dynamic Fabric is at a constant and passes through you, in order to reenergize your being, hence a lifetime with free wireless service to give you, your giddy-ap, compliments of the Creator.

Bifurcation enables for the expansion and recycling of the universe at the exact Bifurcation rate. Bifurcation is the rate to which a planet resonates, the rhythm that your heart beats, history of the stock market, the healing of a wound, your time asleep, your breathing, work verses play or play verses work, it just doesn't get divided evenly. But the greatest function of Bifurcation portion of the program is its end result of its purpose. The Bifurcation process, when combined with the

191

Creator's identifying frequencies; moves forward the creation of all living things. This entails the creation of all new species and already existing life (plants, animals and you).

With the Bifurcation properties, the universe can be measured simply with the Watchers' Photonic Tachyon Emissions device and is simply a small globe that transmits outward emissions of lighted frequencies in every possible direction. These lighted waves pass through everything instantly and travels to the outer membrane of the Spherical universe for an instant reading of that moment in time. The universe would be flat if it were not for the Dynamic Fabrics funneling motion, but because the universe is "bifurcating" at the programs mathematical given, then the Field Membrane that encompasses our universe will forever expand at that rate. Until that one moment in time, when all the universes combined have fulfilled every probable outcome. At that point, it is judgment time for all the lives you lived in all the universes that you endured. Let's hope the average of you; over billions of years did well.

So, just like a computer, the programs major functions, consists of the Dark Matter that supplies the materials and energy, along with the command of the forward moving process called Bifurcation. Together they assist in the distribution of all inter-dimensional material; in preventing the duplication of any two things (no two snowflakes alike or two people or plants...etc).

Oh yes, how come the pebble is in your hand? A part of the pebble is gold and the gold you are looking at consists of millions of atoms and billions of subatomic particles. Within the subatomic particles are what the Watchers call, Slip Stitch Orbital Revolution or (SSOR). These families of particles are the working bees of an atom. They are half the reason why you see the pebble in your hand. These particles magnetically weave in and out of an atom and at practically light speed. The speed is so fast; it appears to be stationary to you and the pebble then is magnetically fused from within. It is part of the explanation to why you see the pebble.

Understand, while this family of particles is doing their job, they are traversing a weave (slip stitch) pattern in and out of the atom. When the particles leave the atom for that split second they are actually traveling out of our 3D reality (out of the membrane) and into a timeless portion of Dark Matter! This abyss type area is where the particle grabs on to the inter-dimensional (invisible) Dynamic Fabric and is woven tightly, thus it creates a friction, which in turn, forms a magnetic field that cannot be pulled apart (with conventional technology or you can melt it).

According to the atomic weight of the element (gold) is the amount of time that the instant orbital cycle is distributed or passes in-through our reality. For instance, since gold is a heavy element, its subatomic particles leave our reality for a short period of time as compared to a helium subatomic particle which weaves out of this reality for a much longer period of time.

The amazing thing is how over a 24 hour period, just how many millions of woven (360 degree) orbital super fast cycles there is in just one tiny possible invisible atom. This is why gold is so heavy and why helium is so light and practically invisible to us. The longer the particle rotates and cycles (orbits) within our reality, the heavier an element is going to appear on the Periodic Chart.

Shoo, as I take a breath; the other part of the reason why you can see the pebble in your hand is because of what I am about to suggest: Towards the center of every atom is the Neutron, which is the identification or brain (neuron) of an atom and works in unison to all components of a single atom. It determines the amount of electrons and all that other (isotopic) types of interior designs.

Picture, if you will, an antenna placed inside of Neutron for communication use. The purposes of the Neutron are many, but the most important aspect of the Neutron is the Creator's ability to change the identification of an atom if and when the program needs to make instant adjustments, hence the word neutron, which is derivative of neutral. Neutral means, "not decided until its characteristics are pronounced" and you are probably familiar with the middle of your stick shift of your car in order to choose drive or reverse. This purpose of the "neutron" within the atom is to identify and realign reality in order to fulfill all probabilities and along with Bifurcation goal, in order not to be repetitious (no two snowflakes alike).

The Watchers reason for the name describing this part of the atom's component (Neutron) is because of the function, that is ever so important to an atom and as said, it is actually "Neutral" in its design, because it is not fully engaged or permanently attached to any particular atom and is always ready to take on the form or type of atom bestowed by the program or someone with the godlike abilities to transform an atom and replace it with another brand or type (alchemists).

If this ability or technology is at your disposal, like in the ancient texts, you can shape-shift your body or design a machine to emulate or simulate a Transformer Robot, (Optimus Prime). In Greek, Optimus Prime combined means, to choose the best probable outcome that suggests equality or freedom. For all intent and practical purposes, it is somewhat parallel or coincidental to the Creator's program correlating to the Neutron.

Mankind has from time to time, either through technology or natural occurrences, altered this program, but the bio-matrix (Creator's program) has an auto-adjustment built in, that is ever changing and in an endless loop in its quest to keep things on track (God's Will).

The Watchers call this identifying process TID, which stands for Tachyon Identifier Datum or simply put, Transponder Identification. TID is the source of the program, directing "strings" of wireless frequencies to all the trillions upon trillions of Neutrons that are within the entire atom world.

It is basically a frequency, suchlike the radio waves of your car radio, which traverses or uses transponders at a faster rate than the speed of light (Tachyon) and therefore, invisible within an inter-dimensional realm (one of the billions of parts of Dark Matter). There is a theory in physics called "String Theory" and hopefully after full consideration, this added information from the Watchers will help prove the incomplete part of the hypothesis.

These frequencies emanate from the origin of the Creator's program and while all of the gathered materials that make up our universe are here, they all exist in our reality because of the TID or identifying process, in order to declare what is Oxygen and what Aluminum is or who you are! So in essence, through the identifying TID process, you are directly connected to God because all of the cells that make up your body are following the exact same connective principal, which governs who you are, representing the one and only, you, hmm.

Now that we are done with the true chromatography manifestations of subatomic features in existence, we can now address Dark Matter's most important feature, the Dynamic Fabric. It is the one of many components of Dark Matter, but does wonders for not keeping you young. The Dynamic Fabric is in the (invisible) shape of a sphere or globe, which in turn, manifests itself in order to take on the shape of the universe and this principal matches almost everything else that stems from creation. It is another imperative part of the Creator's program, such like Linux or Java Script in the computer world. There has to be somewhere or something constructed in order to stick or post your pictures to. The Watchers call the Dynamic Fabric, "The ultimate foundation underpinning our worlds."

The invisible Spherical Spatial Fabric is woven into a pattern, consisting of lines that intersect one another and create triangles within triangles and cubes within cubes (tesseracts). Essentially, it is a 3D skeleton (holographic in nature) that is tightly woven together with an endless amount of geometric designs, all in an awe inspiring repetitive pattern. This pattern is comprised of an endless sea of tesseracts, which are funneled through the entire universe at the precise speed of light and therefore, light itself is brought out to our world and again, is the product of the Dynamic Fabric, due to its inter-dimensional energy that flows within.

The two biggest functions of the Dynamic Fabric are to create magnetism through energy, in order to create time and light and the ultimate foundation (such as Java Script and PHP language), for adhering and posting "EVERYTHING" to our third dimensional world and reality. Hey, please don't be discouraged we're getting to the best part.

While the Globular (sphere) Dynamic Fabric resonates while interacting through other spatial anomalies, the Dynamic Fabric of tesseracts is being funneled into and out-from the Creator's power source or running program. The fabric instantly becomes recycled and or modified in a millionth of a second in corresponding to almost everything else that resonates within the universe and then traverses back but with a slight addition to its volume, because of the Bifurcation command within the program. The increase is adjusted to the speed and size of the Dynamic Fabric. Hereby, the universe is at an approximate rate of inflation, which is the average of $1/8^{th} = 0.125$ and or $0.1875 = 3/16$ths per second.

Nevertheless, the friction caused by the funneling of the fabric offsets its expansion somewhat. This is because the fabric operates in reverse as well as forward at the central point of the source. This gives the appearance that universe is expanding at a more rapid pace than it actually is. Therefore, the rate of inflation is subtracted by the reverse resistance, which results in a slight forward progression. I don't remember what the answer was to this equation, when I was searching at the Watchers' facility. I would guess that the answer should be the subtraction or reverse of the Bifurcation total, less than a hundred percent. No worries, you get the point, oh no, you are asleep.

Quick sample then: Visualize, trillions of bicycle chains, moving in one direction and the same one unique link in the chain winding back at the speed of light, towards the beginning of the source in a 3D perspective (holographic in nature). Hmm, so, for the reason why the Dynamic Fabric is moving and funneling in a residual spherical pattern and at the speed of light, is because it is simultaneously being charged with the power source or energy plugged in by the Creator (life).

If you can run fast enough, to catch up with the speed of the Dynamic Fabric, then essentially, you will not grow old because you have just cheated time (no proton decay, no aging). The harsh reality in regards to the creation of the Dynamic Fabric is so it can pass through everyone and everything at the speed of light. Unfortunately, if you do catch up to the fabric, you have in effect stopped and halted your whole nervous system and your heart would stop beating.

The reason why the fabric and its energies are synonymous with "time and light" is because it is a vital component to keep us moving. Explanation: While the fabric passes through everything, it gives life-energy and including the pebble as well. The inter-dimensional energy that the Dynamic Fabric provides makes all the subatomic particles spin and rotate, near to the speed of light. Not only does it give the energy to every living or non living thing, but it also provides the abilities for the big spheres we call planets or moons to spin and orbit (locked and permanently attached in with their own black hole).

In regards to planets or stars: The inter-dimensional friction causes a variable release within the static of the Dynamic Fabric, therefore, creating an assortment of different size connective and magnetized holes within the fabric that are spinning while funneling in their own moving station (similar to a water spinning into a drain). They are called black holes. Black holes are similar to wormholes except for the magnetic principals that are compounded by a planet or star. Thus, being magnetically fed by the Dynamic Fabric and kept alive in their plugged in movable (orbital) position.

Stating: The bigger the black hole, the bigger the planet that is created because of the intensity of the black holes natural given magnetism. The process and collection of raw material is also configured by the distance of that new plant's Sun. Another note: Towards the center of every Galaxy (Milky Way Galaxy) is a massive black hole, which the stars and planets orbit around. The fabric is funneled to and from this point and would bear the strongest energetic flow in our Milky Way Galaxy.

If you can combine a visual perspective, you would see different colossal black holes in support of a planet, moon or Sun, but also, you would see various amounts of rogue black holes or wormholes as well (alone). To observe wormholes and the black holes, if seen out into space, would look similar to the neuron memory system within the human brain, thus commingled with the Dynamic Fabric, racing through, in order to energize the world.

In addition, our planet also has its own GPS neuroactive system within the Earth. The connective black holes are scattered naturally all throughout the planet and could be enhanced by placing a megalithic structure in a predetermined (Ley-lines) location. The two largest black holes on Earth are located at the Bermuda Triangle and directly on the opposite side of the Earth, at the Devils Triangle, below Japan. White

Energy is funneled through these two locations and is absorbed into the colossal Pedestal Black Hole that attaches and pivots the Earth in outer space, in order for our planet to revolve and orbit the Sun.

Although the Dynamic Fabric passes through everything, there is a change in the state of energy, which flows through a black hole or wormhole. This phenomenon is called White Energy and enables a field of anti-matter energy in order for an inter-dimensional bridge connectivity to take place, between two points in our reality. This in-between bridge area or wormhole seizes the White Energy properties, as soon as the energy from the Dynamic Fabric passes through these vortices. The Watchers navigate through these connective planes, which do move but are in a set traceable pattern. UPS Universe Positional Systems is the name of their navigation technology, which is shared amongst the Factions.

Unfortunately, there is the sadness of time. When the fabric passes through us or that pebble, the energy from the fabric, even though it supplies life to all our cells, but it also creates proton decay, which is hand and hand with time.

So we are all caught between a rock and hard space, I mean place. On one hand, you need the energy to beat your heart but on the other hand, you don't want to get old. How do we prevent this or not? The pebble seems to decay a lot slower than we do (a million years slower). We rust away way too fast but we do need the fabric to pass through us. So let's stop the proton decay. In order to do this, we need subatomic computer technology and then we can live for 27, 000 years like the Watchers. I cannot lay claim to this technology because it is not mine. Remember now, I am "Honest Abe" and I do not steal!

I am an advocate to advance this fast track program, so there is less suffering and trials of incident. I borrowed some information from the Watchers, with of course; their permission and I will try my best to convey this knowledge to the best of my ability in order to help.

Since I have been on the subject of the notion of "How" and "Why," I think it would be altogether fitting to build onto an equation that I came across many times within the Watchers' facility. The equation represents, more or less the "How" of what we are talking about. The reason for the equation was to advance the human race to a point. The $E=Mc2$ is the mathematical equivalence of logical expressions and signifies that the "c" meaning light squared is meant to explain an enormous number (186,000 x 186,000). This arbitrary number presents the notion and understanding to say, there is a lot of power cooped up inside of matter or an atom.

When an atom is split and split again, it could amount to a varied amount of emittance and instantaneously elevate great explosive power and not at a decisive rate or preset finite number. Therefore, if the inter-dimensional energies within the Dynamic Fabric provide birth to light, then how can light be equal to energy? It can be a proponent or supporter, such as a mother giving birth to a child and in some regards they are similar but the mother is not equal nor can the exact match be produced from the given.

You cannot match two separate relativity components within the matrix because each component cannot survive without the other and therefore are not equal. For that reason, the result would have to equal an action, not a sistered component, in order for the result to be equal or logically qualified to be its equivalency. Simply, E equals energy, M equals mass and C equals light and together, what are the equivalent actions they all produce? There are some who indicate that the light squared (c2) is the equivalent to motion and is assumed, because in essence we do need motion. Light is at a constant and is a given but motion is an action. Thereafter, we can easily say, EMc = Stir or Motion, but doesn't this fall upon the same analogy of a mother giving birth to a child. Are they truly equal? Another example is "Fire" or "Plasma." You can gather that EMcS = Fire, because fire produces energy by burning matter, while moving and has lighted properties, hmm. I am now scratching my head, yet not for the reason that I am confused but because I think there is a bug in my hair.

If we take the universe as a whole, we have to figure out, what main finite actions and affects, that all of these proponents within the universe, possesses and produces toward an equivalent purpose or to "equal a finite ever-changing result." It maybe a moving target? Wait a minute, I have it written down here, somewhere; oh yes, EMcS = R. The R stands for "Recycle" or "Reprocessed."

In order not to be rude, I should clarify whether you assume that sound resonance is a part of energy. It seems as though it should be, but since the Dynamic Fabric already supplies the energy and the vibratory (resonance) TID identifier frequencies gives the Dynamic Fabric and everything else in the world its own unique signature (identification), then we can conclude what? Well, then yes, it would be impolite not to mention the TID sound resonance frequencies, because of their higher rank-and-file. In other words, if the Dynamic Fabric does not receive the TID resonance frequencies, then we would have no Dynamic Fabric and the follows suite for all of existence.

So let us give the proper invite or include the TID identifier particle frequencies to be label as a "T" in the optional equation. We can actually approach this with two results, each of them with imminent logic. The first equation would be the apparent, T = EMcS and the second would include or conclude the result-action or purpose, that is the equivalency of the TID frequencies, Energy, Mass (Matter),

Light and Stir (Motion), which is everybody's soon to be favorite, "Recycling" or "Reprocessed."

That is all I have for you right now, hope this will help and so let me travel back to Dark Matter, because it really does matter.

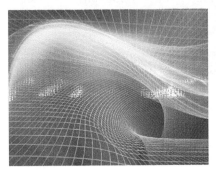 

In the vastness of Dark Matter is your spirits link to the "Almighty." This link traverses across Dark Matter to a biological hub (Akashic Records) that amongst all, is recording everything about you, and every breath you take.

In review, I had mentioned a few layers of invisible components of Dark Matter, but be reassured, when you look up into the heavens and block out a small piece of Dark Matter, there will be billions upon billions of TID string frequencies identifying everything in our universe in just that small block of space, along with portions of wormholes, black-holes, dynamic fabric and much more. When if, all can be seen simultaneously with your new interfacing spectacles, you will in-vision a colored lighted display that will be so glorious, you will not survive, well, maybe you will.

The Dark Matter in the universe is what you see at night when looking up to the heavens. While in the past you have noticed only the lighted stars. Now, if you will imagine and try to picture the blank space between the stars and planets.

Furthermore, you will know that Dark Matter is the most vibrant and illuminated space anywhere else in the universe.

We can go further, on how multi-universes are created from the same recipe, but because of choice, all the similar universes never turn out the same (no two snowflakes alike). The reason for that is the program will not allow the same choice by anyone or anything. That is why sometimes you try so hard to succeed at something but weird happenings take place in order to prevent your success. This is because you are selecting an already used idea that has been taken by you in another universe or someone else.

Within these multi-universes, your spiritual energy is used at different entry points in time. Because of choice, it is very rare that you will still be the same exact physical you in another universe. You will most likely be you but with a different body. This is why when you dream, there is a mystical connection between these selves. It is a strange occurrence when you are having a dream and there is no way you have been there or could have imagined it, to the tee. When you are having these dreams and you are in that strange place, please do not look into a mirror because you can lose your mind when you see it is not you and you are someone different.

Now that you're going to have insomnia, let us be grateful for the multi-universe. The raison d'être (important purpose) is the Creator has given you multiple lives and chances to be the best possible you. If for instance you had a bad life or a short life or maybe you were not a nice person, then in essence, you will have an average of all your lives combined together. Hopefully, this will give you an edge and God will reward you with Spiritual Nutritives that were acquired from being good. Remember, the Creator only counts the good stuff, yet if you are a very good person, then you will have more Spiritual Nutritives. Therefore, more choices to where you want to go or what you want to do (afterwards).

Well, you have a lot of time to decide, because the Watchers Study Hall mentions that all our spirits are sliced from an energetic realm from the beginning of time. So in happenstance, you my friend have been around for billions of years and will be around for billions more. It is like everlasting life. Since your spirit operates on its own inter-dimensional level, it is immediately transformed at death to a new beginning. Again, this new beginning will consists of choice, free choice, suchlike everything within the cosmos. This is why tragedy happens. If God stepped in to stop it, then there would be no free choice and all the worlds he created, for the purpose of, would be for nothing.

The whole purpose of the billions of universes and the billions of lives or the billions of planets is "Yes," to create every possible outcome to fulfill the programs destiny, but that takes billions of years and billions of universes and again "why" because that is part of the "how" and not the "why" answer. Reason being, after an enormous amount of time has passed and the program is filled completely, it will all stop and will your spirituality be up to par when that time comes.

The answer to "why" is up to you. How much does the Creator/God truly love you? Well, now that you understand, the Creator has given you billions of worlds and billions of days and chances to get it right, you should then understand and appreciate or marvel at the amazing work the Creator has constructed, just for you! The Creator made you in his image and likeness in order to give you, your own existence and free choices (this has nothing to do with your physical appearance), so you can be you, and along with the freedom to join to what is pure. If your spirit has enough Spiritual Nutritives at the end of times, there, I hope you will cross the finish line in order to be back home, with a new pure everlasting you.

Or go elsewhere; it's your choice

The Here and Now

"Mathematics cannot be invented, only discovered." This said by Nikola Tesla.

The inter-dimensional 432Hz sound frequency resonance that is combined with the Bifurcation sequence, in order to construct Dark Matter (Dynamic Fabric), which enables "Reality."

First we create the Tesseracts (cubes within cubes, with triangles within triangles), with the Bifurcation Command (Programmed for Growth and Expantion), then turn on the energy, along with the identifying frequencies while distributing all the material. This equals reality and to what mathematical key, configures all of this?

The number 9 seemingly is the glue (link) that adheres to all the constructive properties towards the inter-dimensional (Dark Matter) and our reality as well. The 9 is divisible by the 3. The three is the basis of how things are built.

Coincidence notes?:

432Hz = "A" in representation of a musical note. It adds up to 9=4+3+2.
Also travels with time: 10,080 minutes per week, 9=1+0+0+8+0. 1440 minutes per day, 9=1+4+4+0.

Geometry:

Each part of a triangle is 60 degrees, which is a total of 180 degrees, 9=1+8+0.
Each part of a square is 90 degrees, which is a total of 360 degrees, 9=3+6+0.
Each part of a circle is either 180 or 360 degrees, both equal 9.
A gross is 144 or 9=1+4+4 and there are so much more.

Continuation of Lincoln's notes:

Closing remarks, of more or less, to what I learned: There was a conspiracy theory that fell towards John and I but through science and time it has been proven to be true. So be it, a conspiracy theory is no longer theory once proven or more or less, if much more than half the people are convinced that it is the truth, then it is settled down as fact. The time of true disclosure to the world has been already in the process and the finale is coming soon, so let me speed up the process and take this, if you don't mind, for the better.

The human species have the given capabilities of using less than ten percent of their brain. It is ironic and very coincidental that our DNA also lacks the exact same amount in its arrangement. Is it designed this way on purpose, unfortunately?

The answer to that question is yes and I will attempt to explain with my best interpretation, of what is going on out there. This knowledge is from the information I had learned from the Watchers facility and understand I am only using that small percentage of mental output in order to be understood, but I will do my best. I can assure you that.

Before I begin, there is a bit of an issue with the history of our planet. I am not sure if I should skip this part, because some of you will not be interested. For the people who are not interested, are you truly happy? It is funny that the things in your life you are not happy about are the things you are not willing to face or draw from it, a true reality. But I understand because I still have a hard time grasping these particular pre-historic events or agendas myself.

The Watchers have been overseeing and protecting our Earth for hundreds of thousands of years. They showed me a map of our galaxy and pointed out the different locations, from where other intelligent species come from. There are twelve species (Factions) that lay claim or are involved with our Earth because of their many visitations in the remote past, before humans were here (two hundred million years worth).

The Watchers make sure although, they are at all times, at arm's-length and not to overstep our development process. The Watchers are not strict with their prime directive, just as long as the Factions do not intentionally harm us. The Watchers are a big proponent of free will, because of the Creator's similar design and concept.

There have been five stages of society life-trials in the past. The studies and observation have been done with intervention or without help, here on our Earth. The current stage can be characterized or understood from the "Book of Genesis or the Quran." These trials were conceived and implemented throughout the Earth's vast history. All the way from the dinosaur era, up until now, we are the fifth stage to be formed and we are called the human race or Homo sapiens-sapiens. The reason why we don't classify "Us" as a general statement of being Homo sapiens is because someone can assume that we are talking about primitive man. By saying Homo sapiens-sapiens, we are now indentified as all the same species (Human) and not the Neanderthals or other subsequent species, which by the way can be classified under Homo sapiens.

It is hard to grasp, to what went on here before we existed. It seems the Earth has been reset every time a stage has ended. For instance, the ice age was somehow brought on, by changing the Earth's axis and after that it was weather control in order to flood the Earth. Before the ice age, meteorites were purposely steered in order to target certain locations throughout the Earth and in some cases, were the use of atomic weapons, in order to erase any past history.

During the dinosaur age there were trees that reached the heavens and hundreds of them remain to this day and are all across the Earth as petrified stumps. Devils Tower (Bear Lodge Butte) in Wyoming is just one example. I would have loved to see how they got cut down and once they were used for their resources, the remaining stumps became, what we call now, "Mesa's," meaning table in Spanish.

The enormous tree trunk of Devil's Tower is one mile in its circumference and that is a lot of firewood it must have produced, but now, it is an enormous petrified stone and at this moment, a great beacon of energy along the (power grid) Ley-lines of the Earth.

The Watchers indicate that these hybrid giant trees were planted purposely along key points on the Earth in the remote past, in order to create an increase in magnetic energies throughout the Earth. In so far as to open (advanced) portals for space travel. Seemingly, they traveled back in time 200 million years to plant these larger-than-life trees.

Soon after, they would instantly travel once again, thousands of years in the future to harvest or chop down these giants. This method or process was called, "Time Yield Capsules." This was done in order to leave the remains of many stumps, strewn across the Earth, in an anticipation of a couple of a hundred million years passing, for them to become petrified stone. Once the process is complete, they would now have access to use the energies that come from these huge "Mesas" that are situated all over the Earth and used to assist their travels within the past, present and future time periods. Wow, nothing surprises me at this point.

I struggle to understand this reality, but seemingly, most of the intelligent species within the cosmos are not organically indigenous or truly from the planets they inhabit. Are you ready for this? We as a species are one of the majorities that have been seeded to a planet and not fully evolved from scratch, unlike (mostly) the other plants and animals around Earth, which were here and overall, not tampered with.

This is the obvious reason to why there is such an incompatible theme in human society. In addition, we are not in harmony like the majority of other species on our Earth and mind you, we are supposed to be intelligent.

Our DNA has a multitude of diseases built in and activated at anytime, young or old. This is done supposedly, to make us evolve faster. I would like to say, "What is the rush?" You and I have lost many close people because of this issue.

These results can be seen in just a quick moment, once researching DNA or just by observing and living on the Earth. If you couple that, with the fact that we use fewer than 10% of our brain capacity, then you will conclude these findings, as very contradictory to all other species and does not make scientific sense.

If we were a hundred percent indigenous to or planet, then are bodies would not need everyday maintenance. In regards to maintenance, there is the fact if you don't keep yourself clean by means of created technology (primitive or advanced) you will die at a young age and or a very short period of time, hmm.

We are helpless as babies and need the most attention amongst any species. I know there is someone out there that will dig up one finding amongst billions of species to advertise that my statement is wrong. I would just ask this individual, "It seems it so important for you to prove someone wrong, what political position are you running for?"

There is a question to why we need fur coats to survive because according to science we were completely covered in fur 10 plus thousands of years ago. Just a few more: brushing your teeth, circumcision, having an appendix removed, tonsils removed, and the cutting of hair in order not to get caught in the jungles when you were hunter gatherers, lol.

The most profound aspects to a non compatible society are the mere facts that we murder one another multiple times per day, throughout the globe and additionally, we destroy our environment on purpose. Listen, there are so much more, but I will spare you the details because if you are interested, you can find out more with little effort by the use of your modern search engines. Okay, getting back to what is truly connected to our lives. Remember that some parts of questioning things become enlightenment for you and you alone; unless you want to be herded; never mind then.

Have I previously mentioned the 12 Factions earlier? In order for the 12 governing Factions to be in agreement as far as the Earth and our solar system is concerned, they each received a portion, to possess and lay claim to their share of our solar system, along with one twelfth portion of a suitable location on the Earth. With each faction designated a geographical area to themselves, they begin to seed their own geographical area with the agreed upon human DNA and tweak a very small portion of their own DNA within the human DNA strands. That is the reason why the Asian cultures (people) have a vast difference in their appearance as compared to the European and or African descendants.

Once the individual human societies are seeded, they set out and teach the new societies in which they govern. At that point, the unaware people are given a god or gods from the heavens to teach them. When ready, each of the Factions, with this high priority and purpose, will promote and force by whatever means (Roman and world wars for examples), for all of the various locations to mix together and procreate. This will be the Factions attempt and hope to prove, that the historic conflicts that have plagued their worlds for hundreds of thousands of years, can now be driven together by the examples of Earth (The Planet of the Children) and forever keep neighboring peace within the heavens.

Hope I didn't lose you on this? They told me that most of the intelligible lives out there amongst the stars are hybrids (humans), suchlike, most of our pet dogs on our planet. We have done it to our dogs and they have done it to us and they are still tampering with us through our food system and other airborne antigens. I have said too much on this topic, so let's move onto the historic data.

Supposedly, these Factions have the ability to travel the Heavens at will and investigate many different solar systems in the past and future. So in essence, they are all time travelers and have been for a long time. Time travel is an everyday common practice amongst the Factions.

Since they know what type of past or future and evolutionary development that has occurred in all of these many solar systems, they decide and lay claim to a planet or moon that does not have a future for intelligible life. They leave no planet, moon or Sun unturned.

Their belief is to procreate intelligent life where there will be none. It is almost like they are partaking in a godlike role. Our solar system is one of those unfertile types, with no intelligent life in sight. So back through time, they have adjusted Homo sapiens and the human race and have wiped the slate clean about four other times. This time, it is more promising because of a joint effort on all their parts.

They have tried this type of Genesis project a few times in our solar system but were not united, therefore, causing conflict amongst each other. They have fought through the millennia in order to control the results of Earth as well. This is the reason why Earth's plans for the human species and their own past civilizations have been reset a few times. Because of these resets, there have been abandonments of these "once was," prominent civilizations. The Factions went as far as destroying or sinking beneath the waters, many cities and past structures, in order to erase enough history not to be in question by the humans. They would introduce myths and legends in order to, not have to broom sweep the entire Earth. As mentioned, other methods used by the Factions in order to "cleanse," are planet were, axis shifting, ice ages, meteor steering, weapons and relocation of an entire races to other inhabitable planets or moons.

If you wondering why upon all the ancient sites on Earth, there is not one blade of grass on any of these forgotten cities or wondrous locations, is because certain weaponries were used with chemicals (fusion weapons), during the "resets."

Unfortunately, 66,000 years ago, the Factions were not in agreement on the matter of Mars. The many civilizations on the planet were destroyed, along with the planet's moon and parts of the atmosphere; hence the word Mars, meaning, "of war." When full disclosure happens to the Earth's population, it won't be as much of a shock and we were made aware of...

There are humanoid type people still living amongst the holocaustic ruins on Mars and are in need of assistance because of the lack of food and technology. They are the survivors who live on an annihilated planet for thousands of years. The reason for Mars' Genesis project was not successful is because the Factions created hybrids that were of not the same species, suchlike the Earth were even though our genetics have a slight variation, the human race is still the same species. This is by far a better chance for the eventual goal for a unified planet. Mars was not the first planet in our solar system to become "terraformed." Terraforming is the process of intentionally transforming or modifying a planet or moon to support all types of life, mainly intelligent life.

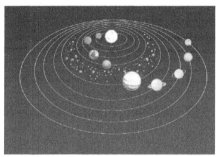 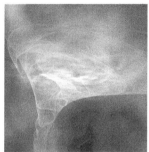

There was a planet between Jupiter and Mars, just like Frank Sinatra says. The planets name was Evander, meaning "good man or strong man." This planet was destroyed and left its moons behind, which still orbit around the empty black-hole that was a planet. This scattered rock area can be seen by all, till this very day and is called the "asteroid belt."

The reason why there was not an abundance of life in our solar system at an elected point in time (remote past), is because Jupiter, which is an enormous planet, grabbed hold of any moons from planets that were within the vicinity, closest to the Sun. So during the solar system's early development; unfortunately, neither, Mercury, Venus, Earth nor Mars were able to capture moons. Therefore, the Factions deemed these areas of interest to be acceptable for terraforming or being qualified for a Genesis Project.

In order to start one of these tremendous projects, the Factions construct one moon or moons nearby to the elected and soon to be developed planet. The designs and sizes of the moons may vary according to the project at hand. In most cases, during many of the moon's development process, the Faction will engineer outposts, in order to monitor and manage certain planets in various solar systems.

Since Mars, Earth and Evander were in an acceptable distance from the Sun (Goldilocks Zone), these terraforming projects moved forward. Mars was started before Earth because it was smaller and more manageable. Mars' moon was destroyed unfortunately and if we intend to go there to make a human base, it would be imperative that we construct a new moon in order for the planet to be habitable. Regrettably, Evander the planet was destroyed, so currently the Earth is in full attention from the Factions for thousands of years.

In order for Earth to flourish with life, the Factions had to travel back in time, to when the solar system was being formed and construct our satellite, the Moon. They did this by creating a spherical ribbed skeleton and thus transporting certain elements from the Earth, to the new moon, by means of wormholes or a process called Worm-vexing. Our Moon was created to be the exact size of our Sun, being at of course at its orbital distance to the Earth, This was done in order to create the most life possible, here on Earth and to behold the only moon in any solar system, to have a perfect lunar eclipse. Once we are able to reach the Moon, we can then observe the Factions' outposts and cities that were made for all the Factions that are involved.

There are almost two hundred planets and moons in our solar system and each of them are tagged, similar to an endangered species in which scientist track for their interest. The Factions hold their claims and trade the rights with other factions to these territories, but the most important part of the human development is the United States of America. It is a purposely developed nation with the sole goal to bring all the differences (physical and belief systems) of the world into one prosperous land.

This is why the Factions spoon-feed the United States citizens with the ability to invent. They target certain individuals with influencing frequencies tied to their biological signature so they can carry out extra advancements, in order to keep the human race on a fast track program. Mostly all inventions come out of the United States and will continue as long as the government sticks to the constitutions that have been given.

The co-author of this book has another book that explains this information in more details.

I bid you a farewell, "If I don't see you around."
I have to get going; I have a line dancing class to teach in about an hour.

God Bless you and your family!

Graffiti Section:

P.S. NASA has been funneling money since its inception to black opt programs. One in particular is called SDI, Strategic Defense Initiative and is the ongoing development of a secret military culvert operation that works with certain Factions in order to protect our planet. The Factions have been securing our planet since its beginning and now in the future, on April 5th 2037, they are going to release all responsibilities to us, the human race. Since the Star Wars program in the 1980's, initiated and was created by Ronald Regan, the human race has created space faring vehicles that are equal to the Factions and could hold thousands of people (Cruisers), suchlike cruise ships. There are a total of 12 of these vehicles currently and other types as well. They call this division, "Solar Warden and is the Earth's "Space Force."

Oh and the first heads on Easter Island are actual carvings made out of wood and became petrified stone, many years later. The giant tree they harvested was grown in the middle of the island and was a mile up in the sky. You can see the remains of the tree trunk to this very day.

Simply put, they would have contests amongst different tribes on the island, by traveling back in time millions of years, in order to create the carvings and thereafter, traverse back to their current time period to see whose sculptures would prevail. There were Hybrid Giants throughout the Earth and Easter Island was one of the many islands where the Giants were kept. The beings who created these giants, had technology that could turn a giant, tree or any living thing into stone or petrified rock, instantly. Medusa was a winged creature with hair that comprised of snakes in Greek history. All who would look upon her would turn to stone instantly. To this day there are stone mountains that appear to be these Hybrid Giants, which were created in the remote past.

Omitted from the Prolog:

Now, you will be given this action packed drama, on how this new time sequence came to be, thereby providing our "new historic reality." *(Actually, there is only ten percent of action in the story but I thought "action packed" sounded better.) This interlude of humor is a small sample of amusing snippets, surrounding the real and personal side of Abraham Lincoln*

"Dead Ringer" has the givens and cornerstones of previously proven successful books, films, plays and cartoon business models.
Best to you,
Robert Rasch

Evermore Songwriters: Howard Ashman / Alan Menken
Evermore Lyrics copyright ST Music LLC
Have I been truly blessed, given a gift and glimpse by the Watchers?
"Time in a Bottle"

Written by Jim Croce • Copyright © BMG Rights Management US, LLC
"Annie's Song" by John Denver
"The Wall" by Steve Walsh and Kansas

Please preserve the battle fields and join the Civil War Trust and its partners and preserve thousands of acres of battlefield land. Too many of the over 380 battles and battlefields have turned into commercial and residential development (housing and shopping plazas, etc...)

Dead Ringer's fan page would like to hear from you, on Twitter and Facebook!

Aside from my personal history, it seems, albeit there was considerable sacrifice; fortunately, the United States of America remains whole and prosperous. In addition, John Kennedy's success, avoided the worlds devastation. For that, we conclude and provide the correction of the two timelines, for the Watchers and for you, my good friend.

Enjoy and Appreciate-
Yours, very sincerely and respectfully,

A. Lincoln

A brief interlude:

So it seems we all think we are in the future, when in fact we are in the past.

An attempt, in order to grip that lingered moment; why it's too late because the seconds are too fast.

Then why do we feel like foreigners, from a land that never lasts.

Yet, so it seems everyone is up for the task.

Our spirit is known but unpronounced.

To the words of religion: In order to help bear our journey.

So why do we elect to have a guide, when we have eternity.

Lincoln's horses: Reddish Brown horse named Robin. Also horses owned, Belle, Tom, Old Buck.

The Ides is the middle of the month that corresponds to the Roman calendar of March and is the 15th day of March.

Francis Wolle a school teacher in 1852 paper bag.

Robert Rasch r8ash@aol.com **Let's get that radio show going again**! Aka "Mega Bob."

Silly comment: There is something about that holiday knick-knack that survives and is displayed or used throughout the year. Comment?

Lyrics for Anne's Song

Come let me love you
Let me give my life to you
Let me drown in your laughter
Let me die in your arms

Let me lay down beside you
Let me always be with you
Come let me love you,
Come love me again

Written by John Denver
Copyright © Alfred, Warner Chappell Music Inc, Warner/ Chappell Music, Inc

10 Project Proposal Queries

Prepared for: Group
Prepared by: Robert Rasch
August 14, 2018
Proposal number: 123-789

SUMMARY

Objective

To create partnerships, in order to produce any or all ventures.
LinkedIn profile name: Robert Rasch Author/Inventor/
Voiceover Actor

Goals

To assist with the production of any or all of the projects

Solution

Have a great team

Project Outline

Find the perfect fit,

- Genre
- Company
- Viability
- Communication
- Action

Robert Rasch

LIST of QUERIES

Historical Science Fiction: Tesla is in the works!

FEATURE FILM or BOOK QUERY LETTER

Title: "Elijah" Based on a Historic Science Fiction Novel by Robert Rasch

Logline: A Historic Biblical figure who's advanced race is in charge of expediting the human race, ironically, he becomes the architect of the New Testament and is the sole reason for Jesus' existence.

Author Robert Rasch: I've written a Historic Science Fiction called,"Elijah" "The secret prospective of the in-betweens" and would like to share a short summary.

LinkedIn profile name: Robert Rasch Author/Inventor/ Voiceover Actor.

"Elijah" is a unique story that combines the sci-fi complexities of "Star Trek" with the New and Old Testament's Biblical

Characters. The story is about a young boy named Elijah, who grows up to be the most influential person in the history of mankind. As he travels to different time periods, he sets up strategic technologies invented by him, to format what will become the New Testament. His father Aligious, was the architect of the Old Testament and instructs the young Elijah how the Earth's Moon/Satellite is a manufactured object. Thus, he explains how the Genesis project on Mars was destroyed in the remote past, thereby leading to the creation and seeding of planet Earth. After the *Quietus*, death of Aligious (father), Elijah finds himself overcome with depression. However, he remembers a promise he had made to his father and resolves to keep it; that being "To See What Can't Be Seen." With the help of the *convex spectacles*, Elijah travels to the barrier rift to connect with the "Almighty." With the assistance of a moldavite crystal he receives a response, not with the Almighty's voice but rather a checklist generated by the Almighty (Creative Energy). This check list was called the "Articles of Faith." Elijah asked this question, "What is the best probability that could be implemented in order to bring all the religions of the Earth together as one and save the most lives as possible. Elijah was worried because judgment day was coming soon." This day of reckoning will occur when mankind's technologies will become a great threat to the other Factions, forcing the end day, April 5th, 2037. In addition, Elijah uses the stone as a liaison to the "Creative Energy" and to spur the connective birth of Yeshua/ Jesus as means of salvation for the inhabitants of Earth. Thus, the stone crystal loses its orbit and in a fiery ball and lands in the city of Mecca, where it resides today in the Kaaba.

This story is based on historical facts and leaves the reader with many questions in wonder. All fictional inserts were included only if a coincidence applied. This story is the first of its kind and goes beyond the creative norm to introduce a whole new era or concept.

Best to you,
r8ash@aol.com

FEATURE FILM or BOOK QUERY LETTER

Title: "View Finder"

Logline: A tight group of Air Force Pilots stationed at a US Air Force Base in South Carolina, stumbles upon some hidden/cloaked holographic type of cameras that are networked across the upper atmosphere surrounding our Earth and appear to have been placed there from the "future" by the USA and or someone else.

Salutations,

Author Robert Rasch: I've written a Science Fiction Mystery Adventure called,

"View Finder" and would like to share it with you. If need be, I am available for Chuckles the Clown parties and I can juggle hamsters.

LinkedIn profile name: Robert Rasch Author/Realtor/Voiceover Actor

"View Finder" is written along the lines of films such as "Interstellar" and "Top Gun."

The story begins with a young man named "James," who works at a railroad yard. The railroad company travels and delivers supplies into and out of the air base called, "Shaw Air Force Base." With the dream of someday becoming an Air Force Pilot, James sets his sights on his goals, but with a cavalier manner (risk taker). His girlfriend encourages him to be professional, once he becomes a pilot, while they walk together through Fort Sumter, enjoying a historic tour that is based on the remnants of a famous battle during the Civil War.

Years later after graduating from the Air Force Academy, James and his colleague are on a routine training mission, when they both spot a glistening image of some sort appearing in the upper atmosphere, just out of reach to inspect. They don't discuss what they saw with their commanding officers. The following day,

subsequently, James veers off from his training exercise route and flies above the allowed atmospheric safe limits, to investigate the anomaly within close range to the exact coordinates from yesterday. Thereafter, in a secret operation; obsessed, James sways a few of his colleagues (an Apache Helicopter pilot) to join him to decipher the enigma. After a number of maneuvers, they figure out that the anomaly is a hidden/cloaked holographic temporal camera and is one, in a large network of other cloaked video/camera devices. The spherical network spans across the upper atmosphere surrounding our Earth, nonetheless, one of the cameras is having an issue with its cloaked functions. The inscriptions on the "View Finder" indicate coding. James and his colleagues join together in a witty camaraderie think tank and decipher the source-code, while discovering the signals are coming to and from the far-side (dark side) of the Moon. Hacking into the mainframe of the devices, James and his colleagues see that the temporal devices have been monitoring Earth from its inception. The men are awed and puzzled by the advanced engineering. Once the code is hacked, James and his colleagues begin to navigate through Earth's history, seeking and answering all the questions their heart desires (to see the birth of Jesus or find out if O.J. Simpson killed his wife, etc.) The designers of the "View Finder" are alerted and they are not human, and immediately their lives are in danger and turned upside down. Epilog: James and his colleagues, who are almost vanquished, eventually are saved by someone from the future.
I believe the development of these dynamic characters and the universal patriot theme in "View Finder" and will appeal to a wide array of audiences.

FEATURE FILM QUERY LETTER

Title: "Opulence" "Email Order Bride"
Logline: A guy who is struggling with his restaurant in Manhattan, who was supposed to be a computer engineer, finds

himself desperate and is talked into answering one of those bogus looking emails, offering money.

Author Robert Rasch: I've written a Rom-Com called "Opulence," "Email Order Bride" and would like to share it with you.

LinkedIn profile name: Robert Rasch Author/Inventor/ Marathon Runner

"Opulence" "Email Order Bride" is a unique story that combines the tension from films similar to "As Good As It Gets" and the complexities of "The Proposal." The story is about a 33 year old man that can't seem to get his restaurant in the black. Ryan reluctantly considers an email that was given to him by his friend Brian, which offers $30,000 to marry the daughter of a Russian business owner. The strict Russian father who owns a travel agency called "Opulence," believes his wife was killed by a Yeti (went missing) in upstate Russia, so he travels to his old vacation home to take revenge and hunt the Yeti (abominable snowman) any chance he gets. The young pretty daughter called Melissa, who's Russian father finally gives into her request (dream) to live in NYC to become a successful model/actress and most importantly, becoming a US citizen. Following the father's permission, Melissa gets her overweight sister to set up the private email (order bride). She wants very much to get away from her overweight sister and can't stand that her father is always in mourning/moping. The irony about the heavy sister's given Russian name is "Rotunda," coupled with the fact, that she is a member of a website called "ChubbyChicksChat.com." While on her "Chubby Chat" website, she sends the "email order bride" request to Ryan's strange funny friend Brian. Brian, who is secretly into rotund girls, has become close friends with Melissa's overweight sister via the website. The Russian father comes to America and purchases the condo adjacent to Ryan's and contracts Brian to knock down the wall between their two apartments, so it appears they are living together. Melissa doesn't have respect for Ryan because he took the initial payment of $15,000 from her father, causing a constant friction in their relationship. Yet, they find pleasantries with each other while sharing her grandmother's family recipe. After the 2 year requirement of being married and living a seesaw of separate lives, Ryan eventually falls in love with Melissa, thus travels to Russia to ask her father permission, "if he can stay married to his daughter." The father has no problem with that, especially after Ryan converts his quasi-successful rudimentary travel agency, into an internet travel site within just a couple of days. Ryan leaves Russia, but not before telling Melissa's father, he does not want the other 15k, in fact he would insist (as a loan) to pay him back for the original monies he received. This twist of irony and sequences has *not* occurred in other movies of films past, not really. The film would fill a unique gap within this genre and become one of the great classic romantic comedies. All the characters will contribute as an important part of the story and will be equally funny, such as "Seinfeld." This will appeal to everyone, including Vladimir Putin. Please let me know if this interests you?

Warm regards,

Robert Rasch

r8ash@aol.com

FEATURE FILM QUERY LETTER

Title: "Sleepers72"

Logline: A group of friends stumble upon an ancient scroll made of stone. Once partially deciphered, it reads, "Behold the Destiny of Who You Are" Instructions: Sleep-not 72hours-Alchemy (herb recipe)…

LinkedIn profile name: Robert Rasch Author/Inventor/ Pushover Voice Actor

"Sleepers72" is written along the lines of the 1990's-films called, "Flatliners" and "Highlander."

The story begins with the discovery of an ancient tablet by a group of young friends, with a puzzle of instructions. Once configured and followed, it gives the assumed path to greatness. Unfortunately, one of the six experimenters named Michael, who constantly leaned angry within his persona, didn't exactly spark his spirit, suchlike the others. Once a righteous person achieves the 72nd hour, of being awake and simultaneously is present at the cave, they are gifted with other worldly abilities unique to one's self. Unfortunately for the others, Michael did reach his greatest potential, "Wickedness." According to the other inscriptions, (found later, that Michael accidentally covered up earlier) once you kill the one that holds a special power (another Sleeper), the gifts and abilities magnetically fuses to the closest, "Sleeper." This thriller (action) elevates, to "An edge of your seat type film/script." The established intelligent and athletic vibrant characters supply a wide array of exciting stunts and nail-biting strategic planning, which steadily elevates an upward emotional charge, till the blockbuster ending.

Low cost film that will appeal to a very wide audience. The target market audience will be similar to that of the movie "Twilight." Please let me know if I can send you the script, and thanks for your time and consideration.

r8ash@aol.com

FEATURE FILM or TV SERIES QUERY LETTER

Title: "EBE (Animated Cartoon)"
Logline: An extraterrestrial young grey alien decides to rescue a 10 year old boy, who lives on a farm with his parents close to a secret underground city/facility.

Author Robert Rasch: Has written a science-fiction animated cartoon called, "EBE."

LinkedIn profile name: Robert Rasch Author/Comedian/ Innovator

Salutations,

"EBE" is written along the lines of films such as "Mars Needs Moms" and "Despicable Me." The story begins with a young friendly grey alien observing a ten year old boy who is in danger and then decides to rescue the child from being killed. The human child, Bernard is in shock, but gives his thanks to the Grey (EBE), as both of them converse in an awkward exchange. They become play buddies and help each other to understand their own species. EBE helps Bernard with his schoolwork and fine tunes his play skills, sometimes with cool hidden devices.

Later in the story, Bernard's dad becomes seriously sick and begs EBE to assist. Towards the end of the story, EBE and Bernard figure out a great idea to resolve a major world problem and use crop circles, in just the nick of time, as a wondrous form of communication to save the world.

During the cartoon, songs will be sung and there will be some witty line dancing by a bunch of grey aliens. In addition, the other songs will be: While racing in their separate kidlike advanced vehicles, a sad song when his father is sick and a catchy tune sung by EBE and his asexual parent.

I believe in combining a slight serious drama and a comedic approach in order to establish the characters, will send a joyful sense and understanding to get along and be friends no matter where you are from. The cartoon will also have, fun and adventure in a universal theme that will appeal to a very wide audience of children and parents. Please let me know if I can assist in anyway and thanks for your consideration.

Best to you,

Robert Rasch

r8ash@aol.com

TV SERIES Or MOVIE QUERY LETTER

Title: "The Victorian Girls"

Logline: A family from Boston travels to England to inspect a Victorian Home they just inherited from their estranged Uncle who went missing three years ago, almost to the day. Unknowing, the houses position is lying on a "Fairy Path" energy grid, which oddly enough activates and sends the entire family and their belongings, to be hurled back in time to the Victorian Era.

Author Robert Rasch: I've written a Comedy-Drama TV Series called "The Victorian Girls," and would like to introduce two written episodes. If need be, I am available to present my work for further development.

LinkedIn profile name: Robert Rasch Author/Actor/Guitarist

"The Victorian Girls" is written along the lines of shows such as "Back to the Future" and "Gilligan's Island." The TV series is about a current day US family that inherits their uncle's house in England and decides to spend a few days on vacation to discuss the future of the house. The single mother and her black tough friend Brenda, along with her 11-year-old son and his three older sisters are in disarray when they awaken on their first full day, finding they are not in the right time period, but in fact, in the mid to late 1800's. The whole family and part of their belongings are now stuck in the 1800's (cell phones and all), yet fortunate, since there is still a signal and connection because of some sort of vortices anomaly, while they still have communication between their own devices and in the current time period of 2019.

Immediately the mother panics and frantically forces everybody to go back to sleep, hoping they will wake up in 2019, but instead they find a strange man walking in front of them in his underwear, hence the British Uncle who had gone missing.

The family decides reluctantly to assimilate into the Victorian Era, along with Victorian morality, while diligently communicating with scientists in their time period in order to get back home.

The screen write begins establishing the characters at home in Boston, with their flaws and seemingly unhappy ways, because of what stemmed from the tragedy of their father's death/accident less than two years ago. Each character undertakes a series of learned paths while they live and experience the humble Victorian era. I believe this very entertaining storyline, creates dynamic comedic banter, example: portraying the mom's friend as a "black servant" to fit in with the era, but when they are all alone, there is a role reversal, Brenda has the whole family walking on eggshells (her character is similar to Florence from the Jefferson's). This will appeal to a very wide audience, while playing-down the current ideological controversies using satire, being; the black servant, strong woman and bringing back the Victorian Era. 5 year Season finale: The family is able to get back in time early enough to save her husband from the accident that killed him. Please let me know if I can send you the pilot.

Best to you,

Robert Rasch r8ash@aol.com

TV SERIES QUERY LETTER

Title: "EBE"

Logline: A young man trying to complete his last year of college for the last four years, finds a young tiny sophisticated grey alien washed along Santa Monica Beach and keeps him in his one bedroom apartment in secrecy.

Author Robert Rasch: I've written a TV Series called "Ebe"

LinkedIn profile name: Robert Rasch Author/Inventor/Digital Currency

Salutations,

"Ebe" is written along the lines of shows such as "Alf" or "I Dream of Jeannie" and the "Big Bang Theory." The series is about a brilliant childlike grey alien named Ebe, who talks with a sophisticated English accent and is approximately 20 some odd inches tall. With an arsenal of sarcastic wit and the uncanny ability to imitate (Movie Buff) any voice or sound, Ebe is quite the intrigue with his new roommate Carson and decides to give human life a try. It seems that his one "asexual parent" probably drowned in their USO Underwater Submersible Object (Ship). To begin the TV series, Carson looks up and sees a bubbly lighted disturbance on the surface of the ocean, then looks down at the shoreline and notices an object that washed ashore. Alone at dusk he approaches the oddity looking like and in the position of the Montauk Monster and says, "Oh wow, another Montauk Monster." Fade in; the little object answers back with a weak voice and utters, "Do I look like a dog with a bird's beak for a mouth? You ninny!" From there on in, they were best buddies for life. Ebe lived in the country of Peru, South America in the city of Andahuaylillas in the southern province of Quispicanchi. He claims to be Spanish and says he is not undocumented and does speak fluently, but he also is able to speak every other language as well. The nervous laughter builds within the many creative ways in order to hide Ebe and keep Carson's friends, family and girlfriend from finding out about his presence.

Similar to "I Dream of Jeannie," tricks were played on Dr Bellows and were hilarious, but in this case it will be the landlord, along with other distraught characters. I believe the connective storylines roll with the current "politically correct" mainstream focus, such as the asexual main character (transgender craze), along with accepting what's different from us (talking grey alien). Who knows, this might be a good desensitization for the future? Solid characters similar to the "Big Bang Theory" combined with the "situational" comedy will be a "huge" hit and appeal to a very wide array of audience. Please let me know if I can send you the pilot, and thanks for your time and consideration. r8ash@aol.com

ABOUT THE AUTHOR

Robert Rasch is the author of *Dead Ringer*, a traditional story with a modern twist. His writings will inspire many because of his unique approach to telling a story that has been told many times. This story provides a new perspective on the origin of everything. Rasch's ability to mix "coincidental-science" with the historical past will have you intrigued and questioning that perhaps there is more to it?

Other writings Rasch is working on and are in the making, include: *Opulence*, a romance comedy, and *View Finder*, a science fiction thriller. He is also the creator of several game applications and a freelance voiceover professional. He also holds several patents for his inventions and innovative ideas. The author is available for think-tank and scrum master tasks (Board Meetings). **R8ash@aol.com**